BLOOD OF THE SCRIBES

WILLIAM CALI

Copyright © 2019 by William Cali

All rights reserved.

No part of this book may be reproduced in any form or by any electronic or mechanical means, including information storage and retrieval systems, without written permission from the author, except for the use of brief quotations in a book review.

Cover by Michael Hirshon
http://hirshon.net/
Editing by J Wade Dial
jwadedial@gmail.com
Formatted by Drew Avera Formatting
https://drewavera.com/book-formatting/

This is a work of fiction. All of the characters, events, and organizations portrayed in this novel are either products of the author's imagination, or used fictitiously.

This book is dedicated to my mother.
I wish we had more time to get to know each other. I miss you every day.

BY WILLIAM CALI

Path of the Crusaders

Book One: Out of Nowhere
Book Two: Blood of the Scribes

PROLOGUE

The orb glowed, showering Yozer's chambers with dull light. Agme approached the artifact slowly, his hands twitching involuntarily.

For as long as he had served his great master, the object had collected dust in the corner of the keep. "The orb is a container," Yozer had explained. "It was made to store something of great importance. Pray you never see it filled."

But it is full now.

Agme had been pacing the room in a panic, awaiting news of Yozer's conquest. Days had passed, but he had been unable to summon his agents of the shadows, the crows, to gather information. *My conjuring powers have weakened. Something horrible must have happened.*

A pale white mist seeped in through the cracks of the door. It circled around the orb, passing through the murky glass, and clouding the contents of the sphere. Agme regarded the glowing orb with an evil smile.

"Master?"

There was a deep rumble and Draemar Castle seemed to quake around him. The noise was deafening; Agme braced his ears, trying to block out the horrid pain. As the rumbling subsided, a familiar voice greeted him.

"Who draws near?" Yozer's voice boomed from the sphere.

"Master! It is I, your faithful apprentice!" Agme studied the sphere. *Could this be the secret to immortality that Yozer had discussed?* "I knew it was you, Master. This essence, who else could it have been?"

"Agme. Yes." Yozer responded.

"To be reduced to such a state, Master. What has happened? You could not have possibly fallen in battle!" Agme cursed under his breath. *I warned him before he departed. I warned him that any person could die, even him.*

The orb was silent for some time, the mist darting from side to side. When Yozer's essence finally spoke, it was filled with choking hatred. "Pent! Pent! That damned brute. He has slain me. I must have been wrong... He was a Crusader after all. Damned Crusaders. Kill them all! Kill! Kill! Kill Pent!" Yozer began to chant the words, as if they were a mantra.

"Master," Agme stammered. "You may still draw breath. You spoke to me once of this orb. The contingency, you called it. Immortality, the secret to your resurrection!"

Yozer's chanting slowly died off. "Yes... I have taught you well, Agme. I shall return from the grave and wreak a horrible vengeance on this world. However, in this form, I have need of your assistance. As those shadow warriors you summon do your bidding, so shall you be my agent in the world. Certain elements are needed to fuel my return."

Agme frowned. He walked over to the nearest bookshelf and selected an ancient tome. Yozer's castle was full to the brim with knowledge. *It would be easy enough to just leave him to his own devices and claim all of this for my own. The secrets that I need are surely here. But...* "Master, you spoke of my crows. I had meant to send some to seek information on your whereabouts, but the summoning of them has become more taxing than ever. How can I serve you in this weakened state?"

"It is true," Yozer rumbled. "My power was vast in my old form, vast enough to augment one of far lesser talents."

Agme winced at the admission. He had long suspected that his growth in power was not entirely his own doing. "I see."

Yozer continued, "Even now, the effects of my powers should be fading away. The seals and runes I have placed in the world—that once prevented chaotic forces from unleashing their fury on mankind—will be lifted. Pent shall find a world much less safe than I'm sure he had anticipated. Pent. Pent. Kill Pent! Kill Pent! KILL PENT!"

Agme dropped the book and approached the orb again. "Master, please! With enough time, we can deal with him. For now, we need to return you to power!" Agme said, thinking of his own return to power.

"Yes, yes of course. Damn this form. We had best move quickly. I fear a... deterioration if we do not act with haste. You need three things to ensure my resurrection. The first is already within our grasp and is why I claimed this dread castle as my keep. The hemites that gather in the rivers below, they are essential."

Agme nodded. "Of course, Master."

"The next is the essence of one from that ancient race. I need the blood of the Scribes to fuel my second coming. As their passion wrote magic and the laws of nature into existence, so will they write my resurrection."

"But Master, the Scribes have not walked the land in centuries. How can I gather such a thing when it no longer exists?"

Yozer chuckled harshly. It sounded as if a sword was being scraped against a stone. Agme trembled. "You fool. You will need to be wiser if you mean to serve me. The Scribes have not walked in this world for years because of men far greater than yourself." Yozer's chuckle became a wheeze as he continued, "Karpas was the first, but I learned his lessons well. We sealed the Scribes away in times long passed, for their power and thirst were more dangerous than any other creatures' in Cinraia. I am standing between two worlds, in the veil between life and death. And so, the last of those seals will be fading. The havoc they will reap may be a horror for the world to behold, but it is a convenience for us. Capture a Scribe, Agme, and bring me its blood."

"I shall do as you command, my master." Agme hesitated, then asked, "And what of the third component?"

The temperature in the room plummeted until Agme could see his breath turning to frost in the air. The mist that was Yozer swirled around in the orb as if he was dancing in delight.

"Why, the last piece is the most exciting of all. You just need a corpse. The corpse of a Crusader!"

CHAPTER ONE

Pent gazed down from the cliff's edge at the village of Somerville tucked away in its natural ravine, taking in the lay of the land. He drew a deep breath, and though he had already spent over a month in this strange new world, the allure of nature still had a certain appeal. The air was fresh, not a hint of trash or pollution. And the sky was full of sounds of life, but no cars or planes. *The longer I stay here, the more it feels like home,* he thought.

He surveyed Somerville—the new Somerville. *Or is this the old one?* He shook his head. The one without technology; the one that a bunch of medieval, fairytale villagers lived in. Not the Somerville with the busted grocery store he used to work at, the Somerville with knights and wizards. *Sorcerers, I guess. That's more accurate. Sorcerers, one of which I killed less than a week ago.*

He rubbed at his face. A bit of curly beard was growing there; it had been awhile since he had had a good shave. His hair was getting unruly, too. "Hey, Hanar. I know you guys don't have barbers here, how do you keep this in control?"

The woodsman shuffled from behind the trees. He scratched at his own beard in his familiar, contemplative manner. Hanar was tall, only a couple of inches shorter than Pent. *But definitely not as big as me.* Hanar's tunic was loose fitting, hanging awkwardly from his wiry frame. He was thin, but strong, Pent knew. *A lifetime of hunting animals with nothing but that bow has kept him in shape.*

"I don't think you need any upkeep there." Hanar said as he continued to scratch his beard. Pent smiled. Of course, he wouldn't see an issue. Hanar's scraggly dark red beard was always disheveled. The man spent so much time in the woods away from others, he clearly didn't see the need for tidying up.

"Let me be the judge of that," Pent said.

"Very well, my friend. You have your blade with you? The one that bends in and out?"

"My folder, yeah." Pent reached into his pocket and withdrew the folding knife. He may have left his jeans behind, but his new pants had pockets sewn in them all the same. *Can't get rid of all the modern amenities, can I?*

"Follow me then. There is a stream back in the forest we can use. The village can last a little longer without our presence," Hanar said, smiling. "It'll give you more time to share your tales of conquest with me!"

Pent sighed, but he followed closely behind Hanar. "Man, how many times do we have to go through this? You've already heard all there is to say!"

"That can't be all there was," Hanar said, deftly ducking a branch. Pent had to sway to avoid it, but Hanar moved swiftly, as if he was born in the woods.

"That's it. I was just one guy, fighting along with everyone in Somerville. All those villagers, they are the heroes here."

"Of course," Hanar said. "And we'll never forget the sacrifice of those we lost. But you, Pent. You toppled the king of the world. You defeated Yozer!" Hanar spoke with a tone of religious awe as he said the sorcerer's name.

Pent shook his head, happy to see the stream that Hanar had mentioned. They approached it together.

"He wasn't ready for me," Pent said at last. "He wasn't ready for this either." Pent tapped on his shoulder holster, feeling the impression of the gun beneath his tunic. "No magic required."

"Every Crusader has their sword," Hanar said.

Pent scoffed. "Oh yeah? Well, swords don't run out of bullets, so I'm not sure about all that."

Pent leaned over the stream, looking at his reflection in the slow-moving water. *Crusader.* He ran a hand through his curly hair and across his beard. He ran his arms down the length of his new outfit. *I've been here maybe a month, and they're already calling me hero names. And all it took was killing a bunch of people I'd never met and barely surviving a crazy battle.*

It was a far step away from his life before. He had gone from bagging groceries to fighting knights, from slamming beers at the bar with his deadbeat friend to parlaying with a hundred-year-old wizard. *A wizard with a bizarre name. Who names their child Gordenthorpe?*

"I look so different in this getup," Pent said. "I wonder if momma would recognize me."

Momma. He couldn't forget about her. Or about everything he had left behind. *I haven't had a chance to search for some kind of way home. But maybe now things will be calm enough. Maybe now I can venture out past Somerville's borders and see if I can figure out a way home.*

He hadn't been the first person to desert his mother without a word. His father had left home, years ago, done with his responsibilities as a parent, as a husband. Or maybe he found something better on the west coast. *I always thought he looked like some kind of surfer bum in those pictures. That punk.* Wherever he was now, Pent didn't know, and he didn't care either. *But I can't do moms like that, can I?*

Hanar rested his hand on Pent's shoulder. "You seem troubled, my friend."

"I guess I am."

"Thinking of the world you left behind again?" Hanar asked, shaking his head. "Or perhaps thinking of your father?"

"I'm like an open book then, huh?"

Hanar stifled a laugh. "You've spoken of your troubles, almost as much as I've asked about Yozer." His expression sobered as he stared into Pent's eyes. "Regardless of what kind of man your father was, you are not him. You are a hero. The hero of Somerville. The hero of the world!"

Pent laughed. "Well help a hero out then." He handed his folder over to Hanar. "Tighten up my hair in the back, would you?"

Hanar palmed the knife, staring at it inquisitively. "I usually handle my hair by myself."

"Hey, this is my first rodeo. And I don't think I'm gonna find a barber who can deal with these curls. So, you're my best bet." Pent shook his head. "Just keep it short. I'll handle my beard."

Pent watched as the shavings fell into the water. They drifted down the stream, following the path of the slow current. Hanar took his time, pulling strands of hair straight out and sawing through them.

I don't know about a hero. But damn, I've already made bigger waves here in a month than I did in my entire life back home. Back in his old home, he was like those strands of hair—just going slowly with the flow. No control over his direction in life. *But now...* He leaned over, scooped up a rock, and cast it into the river. *Now I'm making waves.*

"It would be best to stay still as I work my friend," Hanar said. "I don't want to take off more than you've asked."

Hanar continued uninterrupted, stopping when he felt satisfied. "It is certainly shorter than it was."

Pent ran his hand through his hair, then looked down at his reflection in the water. "Yeah. Yeah, this is good. Good work man, you could have opened a barbershop in my world."

Hanar smiled. "Many shoes, my friend."

"No, no. It's many hats. Not many shoes." Pent shook his head. "Never mind. Let me get that knife so I can touch up this beard."

Hanar handed the blade over. "You'll want to wet it first and go slowly." He laughed, scratching at his own beard, and casting Pent an embarrassed look. "I've since given up the practice! Too many close calls for my taste."

"Looking at that beard you're rocking, I don't find that hard to believe." Pent leaned as close to the water as he could, slowly applying the blade to the month's growth of wiry whiskers. Hanar looked over from time to time to see his progress. Before long he was finished, his face looking cleaner than it had in weeks.

"Much better. I definitely think Ellie will appreciate this," Pent said.

"Ellie? Why would she appreciate it?" Hanar asked. "Is this some kind of matter related to your health?"

Pent shook his head. "Never mind man. Let's make our way back to town."

Hanar nodded. He took point, leading the way past the stream and back to the edge of the forest. Pent followed a step behind and continued to dodge branches, as well as dodge questions about his involvement in the battle against Yozer.

Before long, they were back to the cliffside again, looking down at the village of Somerville.

"Do you remember when we first visited this edge, when you arrived here for the first time?" Hanar asked.

"You know I do—looked like something out of *National Geographic*," Pent said. "I was still in disbelief that all this could be real and was trying to figure out a way to wake up. Part of me still doesn't believe it, if I'm being honest with you.

Hanar looked at Pent, his expression slightly hurt. "I suppose I will never know what it's like to be so suddenly jarred from one life and thrown into another."

Pent shrugged. "It takes some getting used to. But I'm trying to make the best of it."

He took in the village below: the small but well-constructed homes of wood and stone; the village square; the simple people, milling from house to house. *It's like one of those groves from Lord of the Rings, except without the hobbit holes and little people.*

The pole that once held Gilbrand's mark was flagless, the flag burned before their climactic battle with Yozer. Pent couldn't help but stare at the barren pole as they made their way down the side of the hill and into the village of Somerville.

CHAPTER TWO

Pent felt nostalgic entering the village with Hanar. This hadn't been the first time they came in together, but each time he thought of that day he'd come to this world—hurtling from the sky, stripped away from his home. *And finding my way to another.* Somerville. Home.

If Pent didn't know better, he never would have guessed that the town had been ground zero for a battle with a sorcerer only a week ago. The buildings were shabby still, but undamaged. The homes here were made mostly of wood and spaced just enough for each villager to have their own lawn; they were charming, Pent thought.

A broad-shouldered man paced by as Pent and Hanar crossed the bridge to Somerville. *And there's the reason behind all that charm.* Faldo was responsible for most of the structures in Somerville. Builder, architect, and mapmaker, he always had a pensive look on his face as he pondered his next project. His hands were thoroughly calloused from constant work; everything about the man screamed hardness except his face. His features were gentle and soft, a trait he shared with his equally diligent sister, the tailor Daley.

"Faldo!" Hanar called to the man as they crossed paths. Faldo was so absorbed in his planning that he hadn't noticed them.

"Hm?" He looked up from the piece of paper he was carrying. "Ah, Hanar and Pent. It seems you've come back from your hunt... Empty handed again?"

"Indeed," Hanar said. "But sometimes the joy is in the journey, not the destination."

"An entertaining notion, but one I do not share." He gestured to the two towers that had been erected before the battle with Yozer. "I'm setting a plan in motion to have more of these towers set up around the perimeter of the village. If these tidings of danger after Yozer's death are true, we need to be ready."

Pent ran his hand over his recently shaved face. "The towers are a good idea; they helped out for sure in that fight. Makes me wonder why you never put them up before."

Faldo blinked twice. "Before you arrived, we were under Gilbrand's thumb, remember? He banned the creation of weapons; I don't believe he would have been amused by the suggestion."

"Yeah I guess you're right," Pent said, feeling somewhat foolish for not making this connection.

"If the two of you will excuse me," Faldo said, his chest puffed out. "I still have much to plan." He nodded to Hanar, adding, "And I'll have need of your expertise later, to better grasp the lay of the land. You know the forests better than anyone."

"Of course!" Hanar said. "Whenever you need me, Faldo."

Faldo grunted an approval, turned back to his map, and resumed his pacing.

"That guy works too hard," Pent said. "I know Gordenthorpe said things would be different now, more dangerous, but he needs to take a moment and breathe in this fresh air."

Hanar frowned. "I would think he's always breathing, Pent. I know I am."

Pent sighed. "Never mind, man." He clapped Hanar on the back. "Let me get back with you later. I've gotta see Ellie. She'll get a kick out of this," he said, gesturing to his face.

"Ellie? Why would she be interested in your beardlessness?"

Pent stifled a laugh. "You let me worry about that, all right buddy?"

Pent expected to find Ellie in her home, but instead she was in the village square, having a spirited conversation with Faldo's sister, Daley.

Pent raised a hand as he approached. "Yo." They both turned to him. *Smooth talker, as always.*

Ellie clapped a hand over her mouth. "Your face!" She reached up and ran her fingers along his cheeks. "So, it wasn't just game you were searching for with Hanar... Is this for my sake?"

Daley cleared her throat. "I'll not inquire on matters that do not concern me. But don't keep me from my tasks with these childish shows of affection."

Pent blushed, and Ellie stifled a giggle. "Daley you must learn to take things as they come," Ellie said. "Some things are not a matter of life and death."

"You'd know all about that, Doc," Pent quipped.

Daley ignored the statement, continuing the conversation she was having with Ellie before Pent arrived. "Chief Lyle has been in charge for a week; we need to come up with a banner." She pointed at the barren flagpole. "Something must take the place of Gilbrand's vile mark. If this is to be a new world with new powers, she needs a standard."

Ellie shrugged. "When Chief Lyle thinks it's appropriate, I'm sure she will broach that topic. She's had enough to fill her plate already."

Daley turned to Pent. "What do you think?"

Pent blinked. *Forward as always.* "Yeah, I mean, it's a good idea. And if anyone is going to come up with a good design it's you." Pent waited to see if Daley was satisfied with that answer. She stood as unrelenting as a statue. "But I do agree with Ellie. It's not really a priority. And the flagpole isn't going anywhere either. I think we can wait on it."

"Very well," Daley said abruptly, "I'll hold my tongue on this for now. But I would suggest you both think on how the flag should look."

"Probably want to ask Lyle," Pent said. "Doesn't she paint too? She would have some good ideas."

Daley turned to Ellie. "I'll begin work on my other suggestion for you then. It shouldn't take long to craft some gloves for your needs." She swiveled and began to walk rapidly away, her head hung low. She mumbled her thoughts under her breath as she went. *Man, she's just like Faldo. Both of them think about their jobs nonstop.*

Ellie sighed when Daley was out of earshot. "She exhausts me sometimes. When someone is wounded, I never let myself be distracted when it comes to taking care of them." She shook her head. "But if there is no work, why make more for myself?"

"I feel you. Keep work at work. That's the way to do it." Pent studied Ellie closely; she said she was exhausted but didn't look it. Her face still lit up like a Christmas tree every time they locked eyes. She had let her black hair flow freely, getting rid of the ponytail she had when they first met. *Easier to run my fingers through it, that's for sure.*

He spared a glance at her hands, which didn't seem to be any worse for wear. "What was all that with the gloves? Some kind of medical thing?"

She raised her hands, miming the grip of her string instrument. "This is for music, Pent!" She giggled. "I can run a thread through flesh with these fingers, tying up wounds smoothly. But plucking the strings of the viola—doing it for hours on end leaves the tips close to bloody."

"Hours on end? Damn girl, your performances don't last that long."

She tilted her head to the side. "Surely you know how much time I must spend alone, practicing my craft."

"I just figured you were some kind of musical genius," Pent said. "Never heard anything that sounds as good as your playing in my life." He raised his hands when she gave him a skeptical look. "Dead serious."

She walked to him, her stride somewhere between a graceful glide and a dainty step, her eyes on his. "All this praise and this work you've done to your face. What did I do to fall into such fortune?"

"It's cute, the way you crane your neck to look up at me." Pent gestured past the village square. "Let's finish this conversation at your place. Since I still don't have a house, and I don't know if the both of us will fit in Hanar's shack."

"Dear Sister!" Hanar shouted as he barged into the familiar household. His arms were raised outward, in anticipation of greeting her. But Lyle was nowhere to be seen.

The den was a mess, assorted paints and writing instruments strung up and down the table, the chairs pushed haphazardly away. At first glance Hanar thought that perhaps someone had robbed the place. For an instant his blood went icy, as his hand lowered to the dagger at his belt.

His nerves were relieved when his sister turned the corner.

"Hanar," she said, smiling warmly. "When you had not arrived earlier, I assumed you and Pent would be out for the rest of the night." She began rearranging the chairs. "I would have made sure this place was in order at least."

Hanar walked to her and rested his hands on hers. "Sister, you know it matters not this way or that how the chairs look. I'm sure Pent would not care either."

"Still," she said. "It's not becoming of the Chief's home to be in such disarray. Some of us are used to a clean household, brother."

"You can't count me in that number!" Hanar walked around her, to an upright easel. The painting, which appeared to be the shoulders and frame of an older man, was incomplete. A gray tunic hung in loose folds over the body, while the head did not have enough detail to tell who the man was. *I have not seen the likes of this before; at least her new position hasn't stopped her from all of her leisurely pursuits.*

Lyle stopped in front of the painting and frowned. "It's not done of course. I have been trying to claim whatever time I can, to work on it."

"And who might this be?" Hanar asked. Judging from the aged features, he already knew what she was going to say.

"Chief Pohk." Lyle gazed upon the featureless face for some time before continuing. "I'm sure he wouldn't have approved of a thing like this; he always disliked these kinds of sentimentality. But I feel I must honor the man somehow." She shook her head. "And I mean to finish it. Before..."

Hanar glanced at her as she trailed off. "Before what?"

"Before I lose the image of him in my mind. That is what becomes of the dead, Hanar. If we don't work to remember them, they'll be all but forgotten. And I don't want him to be relegated to one of my stories. People should remember him as he looked, in Somerville's greatest moment."

Hanar nodded. He thought about the frail old chief, his hunched over body and his balding head. *He treated me harshly many times, but he was a good man. He cared about this village.* "He will be missed, sister. I don't envy your position, taking his place."

Lyle shrugged. "Someone must lead. And who better than me? Faldo spends his days buried in his maps, and Cenk is no better with his forge. Riven abandoned us. Daley, Marall, Janeen, they're all wrapped up in their various trades. Ellie perhaps..." She scratched at her chin, as she mulled over each person in turn. "She has a spark about her; she could be a leader of people someday, but she is still too green. And Pent, well, he's an outsider." She looked coyly at Hanar as she spoke.

Hanar grinned. "You don't need to say it, sister. We both know I'm in that same field. And I've no interest in leading either." He spared another glance at the unfinished portrait and frowned.

"Speaking of those who we've lost, you should make one of these for Lemen. I never would have imagined that drunkard would become such a hero."

"We all handle our sorrows in our own way," Lyle said as she grabbed a brush from the table. She pushed Hanar gently aside. "Stay with me for a while; we can speak as I attempt to finish this piece. I'll take any moment of quiet that I can get."

CHAPTER THREE

Catherine ran through the halls of her home, trying to ignore the sounds of screaming men and clanging swords resounding through the castle from the gates. *It won't be long now.* She clutched at Peter's hand. "Come on. Come on! I need to get to the armory and grab my sword."

"But... sister!" Peter tried halfheartedly to pull away from Catherine's grip. "Sh-shouldn't we stay where we are? Isn't it safer in our room? Mo-mother will know what to do—"

"I'm not waiting for her advice," Catherine said. "Whatever she says, I'll feel safer with a sword in my hand."

The past few days had been a constant terror for Catherine: Her brother in tears every night; the constant reminders that her father was gone forever. But the castle's calm sadness was shattered when the news of the outside world hit their gates. *Yozer, the true king of the world, had been killed.*

Catherine didn't know how to take the news at first. She felt that the man named Yozer was different from the legend. Her father had been vassal to the sorcerer, and she had heard many tales of his power, and of his justice. In front of the people under

Gilbrand's protection, however, Yozer seemed a different sort entirely; his posturing seemed almost cruel. Catherine wondered at the sincerity of the man. Her mother had later confirmed her feelings.

But none of that mattered. Father was dead, and Master Yozer had led all of the castle's soldiers to take care of this hateful menace, this tall, dark giant who felled her father. Captain Ricard was sure to deal swift justice to the man, and then they would pick up the pieces of their lives.

But that never happened. The soldiers never came back. Yozer fell, just like her father, Lord Gilbrand, before him.

Some of the neighboring villagers came to the castle, reporting news of bandits and of monsters. "If Gilbrand is to tax us our goods and our food, then we demand safety!" When they learned of Gilbrand's and Yozer's deaths, they began to beat at the castle gates. *Barbarians!*

It had only been a few days, but the terror of being trapped in the castle, with who knows what threats on the outside, had been tearing at her mind. *And now...* Now it seemed that there was some new group at the gates, and they had a way to break through.

The armory had been stripped nearly bare. The soldiers had taken most of the stock already; all that remained were a few old and well-worn weapons, and several out-of-place farming tools. Her own blade, of course, was untouched. *Ignored because of the size, as I'd hoped,* she thought.

She reached out, grabbing her sword and its scabbard from the wall. The sword was made for a child, and no grown man would have given it a second glance. *But it's still dangerous in my hands. I can help keep us safe.*

Catherine shuddered for a moment. She had been so certain a week ago; she wanted to join Captain Ricard and his soldiers and dish out judgment to those Somerville killers. But all of the soldiers had been wiped out. *How many were there? Four dozen?* She would have been just another corpse had she joined them.

"Sister..." Peter whined. "I don't want to be here any longer. We're not supposed to be in the armory."

"I just need this, and we can be off," she said, strapping her sword to her waist. "Come, let us go to the courtyard."

"The courtyard? We should go back to our room. Father wou—"

"Father is gone, Peter," Catherine said, perhaps a bit harsher than she intended. Peter recoiled, stung by the iciness in her voice. "You have been alive just eight years, Little Brother, not long enough to become a man, but these days seem fit to age us ahead of schedule," she added in a softer tone.

Peter stared at her, a dumb look on his face.

"Pay it no mind Peter, just come along now." She dragged him down the hall, nearly sprinting up the stairs leading to the courtyard.

The courtyard was sparse of people, sparser than it had been in the weeks past. *Just like everything else in the castle, day after day it all fades away.* The wooden stage off to the side hadn't been used since Master Yozer displayed Gilbrand's corpse to the people. She recalled the performers and bards who used to visit, to sing and dance on the stage for a noble audience. It seemed unlikely that anything so pleasant would grace this place again.

The half dozen remaining soldiers, the only fighting men spared the bloody Battle of Somerville, were lined up along the castle wall near the entrance gate. Another half dozen residents had joined them, looking tense and holding weapons that seemed foreign in their hands. Catherine's mother, Lady Marjen, was standing among the group.

"Mother!" Catherine said as she approached. Peter looked hopefully at Lady Marjen as they joined her.

She glanced from one child to the other, sighing deeply as her eyes locked onto Catherine's sword. "And what do you mean to do with that, Catherine?"

Catherine looked down at her belt. "I just feel safer with this buckled on."

Lady Marjen nodded. There were black rings under her eyes, and her vibrant red hair was in shambles. She had lost the look of Vinalhaven grace that Catherine had always known her for. "That's well enough. Catherine, you've always been a sharp one. Your instincts and that blade—they'll serve you and your brother well." She turned to the nearest soldier and nodded. "I'll only be a moment." The soldier solemnly shook his head, and then checked his blade's edge.

Lady Marjen walked with her children to the stage and sat with them on the fraying steps. "I had planned to call for you in a few minutes, but you've come to me of your own accord."

"Call for us?" Peter asked. "Why, Mother?"

Marjen ran her hand through Peter's short hair. "My dear boy. We are in the midst of a great crisis, and we've run out of people willing to lay down their lives to guarantee ours." She gestured towards the door. "It's been chaos on the outskirts."

"Chaos," Catherine repeated, gripping her sword.

"Some man named Hubard," Marjen said. She stifled a patronizing laugh. "Calling himself Lord Hubard now. He's gathered a sizable group of ruffians, and he's plundered the lands to the north. He is here for our goods now."

"B-but..." Peter said. He buried his head in his hands.

"Why has this man come now?" Catherine asked, but she already knew the answer.

"Without the name of Yozer to keep them in check, wicked men will rise up and attempt to seize power where they can," Lady Marjen said. "And without our soldiers, we cannot defend ourselves." She shook her head, and then turned to the gate. "Those doors will not keep us safe forever, and now they've sussed out that we are undefended."

"If only father was here," Catherine said, wiping the tears from her eyes.

"Your father—" Lady Marjen began. She struggled to find the words. "He was a damned fool, and he signed our damnation with his greed. And that man, Yozer..." She shrugged, standing slowly. "It matters not; whatever they wished they are all dead now. Lords and sorcerers and their whims, and now a fool knocks at our gates, armed with blades and death."

"I've never even heard of this Lord Hubard before," Catherine said.

"One of the women here is familiar with him," Lady Marjen answered. "A fisherman from Seward. He moved on to thieving when he was unable to survive off of his fishing line. Too many desperate men have been swayed to his way of thinking and joined his lot."

Lady Marjen wrapped her children in her arms and hugged them tightly. "What I ask you is too much for a mother to bear, but you must flee, my children." She lifted the staircase slightly.

Catherine stared past the stairs, under the wooden stage. *The hidden passage out of the castle.* She had used the passage before while playing with Peter. *And, on more than one occasion, to avoid a lecture from Father.* "Mother, wha—"

"Don't play coy with me, Catherine, or did you think only you knew of this passage? You must flee the castle grounds. We will attempt to parlay with this Lord Hubard, and failing that, we will attempt to repel him. But if we fail..."

"I won't leave you!" Catherine shouted. "I won't abandon you now, you and my home!"

"Listen to your mother!" Lady Marjen said, her voice rising in a shrill shout. Catherine hung her head. "This is easy for no one, Catherine, but think of your brother! This is not a place for children. Flee the castle for now. Don't look back, and in a few days' time you may return. Take each step with thought and care, lest ye be sorry ever after." A hint of a smile played around Lady Marjen's lips as she repeated the old saying, but her eyes were wet with grief.

Catherine pushed a weeping Peter through the staircase and under the stage, following closely behind. "Mother—"

"Do not look back, Catherine," Lady Marjen said. "Be safe, my children. And know that I will always love you." She lowered the staircase back into position, concealing the entrance to the stage.

Catherine, leading Peter by the hand, followed the familiar path to the stone wall of the castle, where a section of stone had appeared to be placed haphazardly. Catherine heaved it aside, revealing a hole large enough for someone of her size to crawl through. The underground passage would take them to an opening nearly a half mile away from the castle.

"I want you to wait here, Peter." She gestured to the entrance of the passageway. "Don't move from this spot."

"But what about mother?" Peter stammered.

"She'll be fine," Catherine said. "Just wait here for now and be silent. I'll join you in a moment."

Sulking, Peter dipped into the hole, his blubbering whines echoing up and down the length of the passage.

Catherine waited a moment to make certain he stayed put in the mouth of the passageway, and then turned and ran to the edge of the stage. She found a thin gap between the planks through which she could see Lady Marjen and the soldiers.

The wooden gate shuddered under heavy blows. Once, twice, and then a third time. It swayed on its hinges.

Lady Marjen nodded to the soldiers. They stepped away from the wall and took a fighting stance, along with the remainder of the castle residents. Catherine stared at them all from the hole in the wall; they all seemed to tremble at each thunderous knock. *Except for mother. Does she know something they do not?*

The sound of splintering wood exploded through the courtyard as a sharpened tree smashed through the wooden gate. Wood scraped against wood as the battering ram was pulled back, leaving a sizable hole behind.

"You'd best let us in," shouted a gravelly voice through the hole. "We'll have this gate down in less than an hour, and then you'll wish you had listened."

"Lady Marjen," one of the soldiers called out. "We're at the ready, by your command."

She raised a pacifying hand. "No. No, open the gates. We'll let them in."

"My lady?" the same soldier asked. His voice rose sharply, clearly bewildered by the request.

"Look at that hole," Lady Marjen said softly, so that Catherine had to strain to hear, "they'll have their way whether we open the gate or not. Our best chance is to reason with them."

"But my lady, what if they're less than agreeable?"

She shrugged. "All of the children have gone from the castle; it's only us now. Let's make an end to this, one way or the other."

At her signal, the gates were opened. Catherine counted as twenty haggard men cautiously entered into the castle. Their coats were torn, and their boots had holes in them. Most of them had weapons, but Catherine could tell even at a distance that they were in various states of disrepair.

"Kind of you," said the man in front. He was a thin man with long, brown hair tied in the back in a ponytail. He had a deep gash in his upper lip; he ran his tongue through it as he spoke. "My boys were awfully tired, what with all the knocking."

"And whom," Lady Marjen began, "do I have the pleasure of speaking with?"

"Lord Hubard will do," he said as he raised his sword, laying it over his shoulder. "And it seems the lord of this keep is missing."

"My husband has sadly departed from this world," Lady Marjen replied stiffly. "So, Lord Hubard, what is it you want?"

Hubard sneered. "This castle and all of its goods for starters. The lord of this castle is gone; the lord of Cinraia is gone. And I don't see a reason for good men like us to work the fields and seas for the likes of you lot."

His men all raised a cheer at that. Catherine blinked, and in that instant, she heard one of the bandits cry out.

The bandit fell to the ground, an arrow sticking out of his chest. One of the castle's residents had let his bow hand slip. In the blink of an eye, any chance of a negotiation slipped away.

"You uppity whore!" Hubard shouted, leveling his sword at Lady Marjen's chest. "You think you can ambush us? I'm privy to you Vinalhaven snobs. I'm not just some green fisherman!"

"No! Wait!" Lady Marjen shouted. But even as she called out, the soldiers were rushing towards the bandits, and her yells were cut off by the clash of swords.

Lord Hubard approached Lady Marjen with his sword raised. Catherine closed her eyes and cried out. She turned and ran for the hole, the image of her mother falling to the ground, covered in blood seared into her mind.

CHAPTER FOUR

Following Yozer's unexpected death, Agme found himself deeply conflicted. He walked the long halls of Yozer's keep, his head swaying, searching for some insight, some sign of the way forward. Where the walls once seemed to shift and stir as he walked them, they were now completely still. *They used to move, as if in response to the breath of their master. Now that his breath has stilled, so has this place.*

He placed a hand against the cold stone. There was nothing to distinguish this castle from any other structure now. The magic had already begun to fade away.

He had his objectives, set by Yozer himself. The hemites would be easy enough. He was familiar with their alluring charms; they would not lead him to a watery grave, as they had led many others. The heart of a hemite could be excised within the span of an afternoon, and he would not have to trek far to achieve that goal.

The Scribes, that was another matter entirely. "They have not walked the land for years upon years, for an entire age." He shook his head. "It is difficult to believe that they would rise again after all this time." *But perhaps...*

If the magic that had once coursed through Yozer's haunted halls was fading, perhaps he spoke truly about the Scribes—that they were sealed away for all this time, and that they would reenter the world stage again now that he'd gone. "The Scribes... the supposed builders of the world. If what I've read is true, they're ageless creatures." *And what concern does an immortal have with waiting an age to take power again?*

He crossed the hall, finding himself at a familiar staircase. As he descended, he ran his hand along the drab, wooden banisters. He had taken this path countless times before. It took him to the most important room in the castle. *Yozer's study.*

He flung open the door. With a snap of his fingers, the candles adorning the circular room burst into flame. Agme breathed deeply, savoring the musty air. *Infinite knowledge.*

"But not infinite time," Agme said aloud, a deep frown carving his face. He could scour Yozer's library for ages and never find the secrets to his master's powers over life and death. "And he has proven himself in that regard. Even after being killed, his body destroyed, he seems to have retained his consciousness in a form I have never seen before." He shook his head. "No, I need my master. These sorcerers, they're the only ones who know how to maintain life forever. I shall do as he heeds, at least for now."

He extinguished the flames and left the library. He would take care of the hemite, at the very least. The Scribes would come in time. The Crusader, though, would take planning. *I don't believe finding him would be that taxing. Master could help me in that regard.* But this was a man who was capable of killing Master Yozer. *I cannot act too hastily. I cannot afford to lose my life so haphazardly.*

He hurried along to the entrance of the castle, heaving at the stiff doors, which opened reluctantly. The air was refreshing, but the sunlight forced his eyes to water. "It's been some time since I've wandered the world outside these walls..."

Agme looked deep within and attempted to summon a power, once so easy to reach, but now it eluded him. Strands of darkness fluttered in the air around him, but try as he might, he could not conjure his crows, his far-reaching agents of the night. The crows were made of shadows and could cover large areas in a short amount of time. The intelligence they provided was invaluable, but now it was beyond him. The strength with which he had summoned them before had not been his own. *An augmentation, by Master Yozer.* It was another sign pointing him to the need to resurrect his master. *Without him, my hopes and dreams are finished. I will pass on from this world, like all the rest of this chaff.*

He glanced to the end of the land bridge, frowning at the sight of a beast of burden. A horse was strung up to a tree.

Agme strode along the bridge without casting his glance down to the creatures below. *The hemites—their powers work only against lesser men.* He smiled at his own prowess. *I am not so useless without Yozer after all.*

The malnourished horse recoiled in fear at his presence. It had been there for a few days at least, but no longer. "I see. A gift from dear Gilbrand, is it not?" Agme laughed into the chasm below, his chuckles resounding from the sides of the cliff walls. "This will make my journey to the Scribes easier." He glared at the horse. "I'll be with you in a moment. There's just a small matter to attend to first."

The river below Draemar Castle fed out into the ocean to the east. A small pathway down the cliff was hidden on the castle side, obscured by a false rock that could be pushed aside with a gentle tap. Agme followed the path all the way down to the edge of the river, where he stared into the swiftly flowing depths.

The wait was not long. As one of the hemites drew near, Agme looked deep within, searching for a semblance of his once formidable powers. He breathed in and out slowly, summoning an icy wind. He whipped the cold around like a lasso, pulling the hemite from the water and freezing it on the spot.

Agme fell to his knees, gasping for breath, instantly fatigued. His eyes, tired and weepy, fell upon the frozen form of the hemite, and he couldn't help but shudder. Even in ice, its slimy blue skin repulsed him. The long, thin body was the length of two men, and razor-sharp claws grew around its midsection. Two beady red eyes glowed faintly through the ice. It was still for the moment, but, when free, the wild contortions and erratic movements of these creatures could bring bile to any man's stomach.

"And now Yozer needs one of these dread beasts," Agme said, drawing a knife. As he began chipping at the ice, he felt as though the hateful red eyes followed him. He would have to free the monster and carry it all the way back to the castle. *A difficult bit of labor ahead of me.* But with this, the first piece to Yozer's resurrection would be in hand.

"He'll be pleased with this, at least. And it'll give me time to plan on how to get the next two pieces..."

CHAPTER FIVE

Ellie's home was a very different from Hanar's. The man lived in what could only be described as a shack, and even that was generous. *When he even lives in it,* thought Pent. Unsurprisingly, the woodsman spent most of his time in the woods, hunting, fishing, gathering, and perhaps, just a little, hiding from the rest of the townsfolk. That had changed somewhat since Pent's arrival and Lyle's promotion to chief, but Hanar would always be the type of man who preferred to sleep under the boughs of a tree. Pent, on the other hand, wasn't comfortable unless he was sleeping with a roof above his head.

For this he was grateful to be spending time with Ellie. Her home was clean and organized. Her light wooden furniture was immaculate and well sanded—pleasant to the touch. And aside from her viola and some spare strings, not a thing was out of place.

All around them, Ellie's home was adorned with flowers and plants. Pent had asked her how she found the time for three trades, as if being a doctor and a musician wasn't enough, but she had laughed at the question. "Pent, where do you believe my medicines come from? The power to save a person's life comes from life itself. Or more accurately, from the ground." Whenever Pent asked her a question, she always had a quick answer at the ready. *She's good for that, keeping my on my toes.*

Pent was sitting at her table, running a hand through his shortened hair. He took a swig from his drink, then shook his head and gasped. "This has got a real kick to it," he said, his voice hoarse.

Ellie was carefully adjusting the blanket on her bed. "It's Lemen's stock. I still have some on hand. Who knows whether the distillery will open again?"

Pent nodded, taking a much lighter sip of the liquor. *I should have known by the smell of it. This is that rotgut bourbon all right.* "I don't know if anyone will be able to make it as well as he did." He lowered his mug to the table, swiveling in his chair. "That battle really showed us his true colors."

It was only for a second, but Pent noticed the grimace on Ellie's face. She tore the blanket off the bed, unsatisfied with her efforts, then began again.

Pent crossed into the bedroom and stood behind her. "Let me help." He grasped the blanket and folded it over, laying it immaculately over the bed. "Didn't think those delicate hands would have so much trouble with a thing like this," he said, smiling.

"It's not that, and you know it." She turned away. "Is everyone from your world as obtuse as you can be?"

"I don't know what that word means."

"Is that not a word where you're from?" She tilted her head. "Like dense, doltish, thick—"

"All right, all right," he said, raising his hands defensively, "I get it now. You don't need to throw the dictionary at me." Pent pointed at himself. "Yeah, I make jokes, maybe too much. It's easy to play around when things are getting too serious. But I'm not a doctor. I'm not some musical prodigy. I just bagged groceries and played football in my home. You don't have to insult me for making a joke."

"All this death..." Ellie shook her head. "It's hard for me to joke about."

"You realize who you're talking to here, right?" Pent said. He sat on the bed, looking up at her. "I got Hanar asking me every ten minutes about how I slayed Yozer, about how I led everyone in battle... I didn't come here to become some hero and kill people. How many of those soldiers we fought... how many of them had kids they aren't going back to?"

Ellie sat next to him, resting her hand on his leg. "You did not have much of a choice. It was either run and leave us to our fate or fight with us. You've saved more lives than you've taken, Pent."

He snorted. "In my world, I bet people wouldn't be very sympathetic to that line of thinking. Like, is it okay to kill a murderer as a baby, so they don't go and kill a bunch of people when they grow up? Would you kill Hitler as a child?"

"What?" Ellie asked, looking blankly at Pent.

He shook his head. "Never mind."

"A battle like that, you learn a lot about a person by how they act," Ellie said. "You stayed and fought, risking your life. Lemen stayed and fought. And yet others—"

"You mean Riven," Pent said. *Now I see why she got mad when I mentioned true colors.* Riven was the doctor of Somerville, and Ellie's mentor, before Yozer attacked the village. He was a brilliant doctor, hard-working and thoughtful. He was also an outsider, with his well-groomed hair and stylish coat, hailing from the city to the north, Vinalhaven.

When the situation in Somerville became desperate, he announced that he would parlay with Gilbrand and Yozer. And that he would turn Pent and the former chief over to save his own skin. Pent and Hanar sent him packing, and they hadn't seen him since.

"Perhaps he's too ashamed to show his face again," Ellie said. "He was more interested in protecting himself and furthering his own power than to protect the people here. It's a sacred pact that those who heal make, that we will protect and cure everyone under our wing. He clearly had other things in mind."

At the time, Ellie had taken his abandonment in stride, but Pent could clearly see how she shook with anger now. He wrapped his arm around her. "Let's just leave all the talk about killing and abandonment on the sidelines for now. Let's try and live in the moment."

"In the moment, indeed," she said. Getting up, Ellie crossed over to the other room. After a minute, she returned holding a large case from which she withdrew her viola and bow. "I know nothing of sorcerers and their tricks, but from where I stand, music is magic."

She began plucking the strings at a slow pace, letting the somber tunes fill her home. She lingered in that melancholy mood for only a few seconds, though, before quickening the tempo. The bow seemed to fly across the strings while her fingers danced upon the neck of the viola, and she swayed from side to side, letting her hair play freely atop her shoulders.

Pent was mesmerized by her performance. *Music is magic, you got that right girl.* It was always a treat seeing Ellie like this. Her many worldly concerns almost seemed to fade away, her mind consumed by the music as she let instinct take control. Medicine and healing required all of her concentration and her mental focus, while the music freed her and let her mind be at ease. *I could use a hobby like this too, I guess. Gotta find something to do, at least until I make my way home.*

The thought of home drew Pent's mind to the life he had left behind. He hadn't had much of a chance to search for a way home during his time in Somerville. *Hopefully with Yozer gone, I'll be able to make that happen.*

Pent was hauled roughly back into the present by a yell from outside, which cut through Ellie's performance like a dull axe.

"What was that?" Ellie asked as she lowered the viola to the ground.

"I don't know." Pent darted to the door. "But it didn't sound like a celebration. Let's go find out."

. . .

Pent ran to the village square. He scanned for where the yells were coming from, but after a second he didn't need to use his ears. Black smoke was billowing up the southern cliff, near the fields. "Fire!"

He sprinted toward the smoke, running right through the fields. Near the farthest corn field, Pent found Marall, one of Somerville's farmers. His son Bart was lying several yards behind him. Marall had a shovel in his hand and was waving it threateningly at some kind of beast. Pent had never seen its like before.

"What the hell is that?" Pent shouted. He looked around for something he could use as a weapon, cursing himself for not grabbing Faldo's sword before coming out here.

"I-I do not know!" Marall shouted. "But it means me and my son harm, and it's burning our crops!"

Pent looked at the fire that had already claimed a dozen stalks. *But... how?* He studied the lizard beast for the first time. It was as big as two men, and close to the ground on all fours. It was a darkish brown-red, unlike any lizard Pent had seen before. It had a long, flat head and a thick tail that trailed several feet behind it.

The creature locked eyes with Pent, opened its mouth, and began to hack like a cat with a hairball caught in its throat.

"Pent, look out!" Marall shouted. Pent saw a light emitting from the lizard's mouth; the light became a ball of flame, and the creature spit up a gob of rolling fire.

Pent barely had time to react, diving to the side with only inches to spare. His arm tingled from the heat, and he smelled burning hair follicles where the fireball had grazed him.

"Screw this!" he grunted as he jerked his gun out of his shoulder holster. With the gun held steady, Pent lined the sights up with the creature's head.

BAM!

BAM!

Two shots tore through the air; the first tore through the lizard's throat, the second striking it right in the eye. It slumped over, motionless.

Pent panted for breath as he turned to Marall. "You all right? Your kid?"

Marall was hovering over Bart, jostling the boy. "He's fine. Just fainted from the sight of that ghastly thing." When Bart began to stir, Marall clutched him close to his chest. "Oh, thank goodness. My boy is everything to me. I don't know what I'd do without him."

"I'm glad he's all right," Pent said. Although he sometimes found Marall's child to be a handful to deal with, he was glad the boy wasn't hurt.

Pent checked his gun, shaking his head before he holstered the weapon. *I shouldn't have fired twice. I'm gonna run out of bullets if this happens just a few more times.*

"Here comes the chief!" Marall said, cradling his son in his arms.

Chief Lyle approached the corpse of the monster, with Hanar close behind. The village blacksmith Cenk rushed in a moment later. Short in stature with massive arms and a thick brown mustache, with eyebrows to match, Cenk was carrying two large buckets, one in each hand. He scurried along the field, dousing the flames.

"Good call with the buckets," Pent said. "But I would have thought bringing someone with a weapon would have been smarter."

Hanar raised his bow. "Does this not cover your needs?" Hanar joined his sister, studying the creature. "And if I'm speaking true, I thought it was an accidental fire. This is a surprise indeed."

Pent walked next to them, leaning over and examining the wounds he inflicted on the lizard-beast. It was hard to tell where the blood had fallen, since it matched so closely with the red scales. *Definitely dead though. I'm still a good shot.* Now that he was getting a better look at it, Pent recognized the creature, which appeared similar to something from his world.

"I've only seen them in the zoo before," Pent said. "A Komodo dragon."

Hanar stared at him, furrowing his brow. "No, no. It's kodomo, not Komodo. This is most curious, to see one in such a state."

"Kodomo?" Pent asked. "No, I know that's not right. They're

called Komodo dragons. But I don't think they're red in my world. And they definitely don't breathe fire."

"You are mistaken, my friend. The name is kodomo."

"Well," Chief Lyle said, cutting Pent off before he could respond. "You may call it a kodomo or Komodo, it makes no difference. Such creatures feature prominently in the tale of the Dragon Queen, Tamiat, but I've never seen one in person before. Hanar?"

"I have. Only once," Hanar added quickly as the others turned to him in surprise, "on a beach to the southeast. I have not traveled far from the forests of Somerville, but I have gone that far at least. I saw one of these beasts there."

"And did it try to roast you alive?" Pent asked.

Hanar shook his head. "Upon seeing me, it turned and ran. I asked Gordenthorpe about the creature, and he told me the name. According to him, they like arid, sandy environments, and they are able to burrow under the earth and stay there for long stretches of time. Above all else, they are afraid of man. They turn and run from any encounter with a two-legged creature."

"Tell that to my boy!" Marall shouted. "That thing damn near killed us both. And we weren't being a bother, just tending to the corn! Didn't seem very afraid to me. It came looking for a fight."

"This is a bad omen," Chief Lyle said. "This creature behaving in such an odd way... We have enjoyed peace in the week following Yozer's death, but I worry of the implications here. Your sorcerer friend seemed sure that the natural order had been disrupted by Yozer's death. Maybe we are seeing the first ripple of that shift here and now."

They all stared in solemn silence at the dead creature.

"Perhaps I will help Faldo attend to his guard towers," Lyle said at last, breaking their silence. "Whatever else is lurking in the outside world, I would rather not be surprised again."

"That's a good call," Pent said. "It's always best to be prepared."

CHAPTER SIX

Although Pent never lost his desire to return home, life in this new Somerville was so constant, so involved, that time passed without his consideration. Six months had gone by, and Pent had grown more comfortable in this new world. There were parts of it that he genuinely enjoyed; he'd never been called a hero in his own world. Pent often considered all the things that had happened in this place: his fall into the Cinraia, meeting Hanar, standing up to Gilbrand, and, of course, battling Yozer. He thought of that battle often.

Pent could still clearly feel the jerk of the gun in his hand, the sharp crack of both shots, the shocked look on the sorcerer's face... In that moment, Pent felt like he'd saved the world. After what he'd seen since, though, he could no longer be sure.

It had become clear that Yozer had been doing more than just oppressing the masses for his own amusement. According to Gordenthorpe, he had been holding back the tides of chaos, and with him gone, long-forgotten beasts and threats had emerged.

The first few months after the fall of Yozer were full of joy and hope for a new future. The damage done to the town had been limited, and the town builder and architect, Faldo, had managed to get it all repaired in due time.

Faldo worked hand in hand with Somerville's blacksmith, Cenk, to create a new, more long-lasting village. They had expanded out past the river, which served as the old entrance to town, and even into the mines that lay in the chasm walls to the west. Tall guard towers had been assembled on the outskirts of the village, and the paths in and out of town had been leveled and covered with gravel.

The previous leader of Somerville had fallen in battle. Though the people mourned Chief Pohk, they welcomed his successor, Chief Lyle, who had overseen the expansion of Somerville. She had taken the danger of a post-Yozer world to heart; the defense of the town was made paramount, and it had mostly been effective.

But after a few months, their fears became reality. Monsters had reappeared as if fallen from a fable, stirred from the graves of history. Travelers began to appear at the gates of Somerville, sharing tales of treacherous travel and dangers abroad, of bloody battlefields where the dead were left as carrion for the beasts. These people came in hopes that there could be some safety to be found in the world, and Somerville's defensive towers spoke of more promise than they had seen elsewhere. The town had grown as the months passed.

But Somerville wasn't immune to the chaos that threatened to spill across the world like a flood. The children of Somerville had begun to disappear. It was this mystery that had drawn Pent and Hanar out of the village in search of answers.

Pent rubbed at his shoulders as they walked. The months had treated him well enough. He hadn't been this fit since high school; his calves were huge, his muscles bulged in his chest. But his eyes were bloodshot, and his hair had grown wild.

The woodsman, who walked at his flank, had a similar fatigued look to him. Deep black rings lined his eyes, and his beard had gone ragged, even more ragged than before. Unlike Pent, who had grown bulky in their labor, Hanar grew leaner; the woodman was as thin and wild as the trees he spent his life under. Pent knew they were both being overworked physically, to the point of mental exhaustion.

Their search had brought them nowhere closer to their goal. They had wandered far through the forests, but Hanar could not make head or tail of the trails they found.

"There's every manner of tracks surrounding us," he said, scratching at his beard. "Monsters and man—the forest is teeming with life as it never has before." He stopped suddenly, staring at the tops of the trees.

Pent clutched his M1911 and took a controlled breath as he released the safety. He raised it, pointing it at the trees. "You're making me nervous, stopping like that."

"Fear not my friend. The forest is, as always, completely at my mercy," Hanar laughed. He cleared his throat after studying the treetops. "We should continue our search. My previous hunch may have been off the mark."

Pent holstered his gun and walked on. They had been searching the woods for hours, and he was beginning to get a handle of the woods himself. The leaves had turned brown and orange, many falling off the branches, obscuring their trail. And the noise—Pent was certain the forest had not been so loud before. It was a constant reminder that they weren't the only creatures here.

"I'll defer to your judgment," Pent said, "but I swear we've been around here before."

"You are not wrong for that, Pent; I've been attempting to backtrack. Trying to mix up our trail."

"Mix up our trail, why?" No sooner had Pent spoke than there was a deafening roar from the trees to his right. His gun was in his hand before he realized what he was doing.

"For that!"

Pent glanced in the direction Hanar was pointing. The monster was broad in the chest, with thick, furry arms. The claws on its fingers were a half foot long each.

Hanar nocked an arrow, drew, and let it fly. The arrow pinned the treehopper to a branch, but that only seemed to anger it, and it tore free a moment later, vaulting over their heads and onto a tree to their left.

"The stuff of nightmares," Hanar muttered under his breath as he nocked another arrow. "It seems I've led us into another ambush."

Pent aimed at the creature. A shiver ran through him as the treehopper's beady red glare locked onto him. Pent squeezed the trigger.

BAM!

BAM!

Click!

The treehopper tumbled through branches and landed on its back a few feet away. It shuddered and then drew its last breath.

"I thought you said those things were rare, man. We've seen at least a dozen since we started this search." Pent wiped the sweat from his brow. "That was way too close."

"They were rare once. Recall back to when we wandered the woods for sport and game, before all that has happened? We never encountered a single treehopper."

"Things have changed around here."

"It is as Gordenthorpe warned. The world is different now. More dangerous than it once was." He gestured towards Pent's pistol. "What of your mystical head cannon?"

Pent smiled and shook his head. "Hand cannon man, hand cannon." He pulled the magazine from the M1911, already sure of what he would find. "Damn. Empty." His time traveling with Hanar had exhausted all of his ammunition. *And no chance of a gun store here.*

"Damn." He slid the magazine back into the gun. "Think we should take that as a good sign to head back. Maybe someone in Somerville has had more luck."

. . .

Back in Somerville, Pent and Hanar approached Chief Lyle. She seemed a husk of her former self. Pent remembered when he first met her, how her beauty had stood out against the haggard appearance of the other townsfolk he met. Now she looked malnourished, her facial features sunken in. She had cut off much of her red hair; it was nearly as short as Hanar's now. Her body betrayed a lack of sleep.

She was flanked by Faldo, who had also grown weary in the passing months. His cheeks drooped, and his hair had grown too long. His expression was grim.

Although Lyle smiled to see them, there was a certain sadness in it. "I see only the two of you; I suspect you don't bear any good fortune."

Pent spoke first. "Yeah. No luck, Chief." He rubbed at his eyes. "We've been searching off and on for days and nothing. We haven't found any sign of the children."

"Still missing then, still vanished from their homes..." Lyle sighed and hung her head.

CHAPTER SEVEN

"Peter! Peter, come back to me! I'm sorry for what I said, come back!"

Catherine trudged through the woods, clutching her sword, and cursing under her breath. *How could I have lost him? How could I have been so stupid?*

It had been a few days now, and her brother seemed to be long gone. She thought of what she had told him; how he had been dead weight, a whiny, useless bother; how he had been holding her back for months. *And how I couldn't even see him as my own brother. How surviving in the wilderness was hard enough without having to lead him around on a leash. How he didn't take after mother, or after father.*

"Mother and father." She rubbed at her misting eyes. Less than half a year had passed, and all she had to remember of them was her own thoughts. *That's all I'll ever have of them, if I can't find Peter again.*

Father had been a brutal man at times—rough around the edges, she had heard him spoken of—but he had taught her many lessons in life and shared his love in his own way. His lessons had become true to life; life had taken a hard turn. Being strong was your only means to survive in this brutal world.

Mother had shared other lessons, one of which Catherine had foolishly forgotten at the worst moment. Lady Marjen, so brave and so dignified, truly a great lady of a noble house. Thinking of her made Catherine shiver. *For you to be killed in such a way... 'Lord' Hubard, what noble oaths did you swear to claim such a title? A promise to bloody your sword? The loyalty of men is a farce in this hell of a world.*

Loyalty. Service. Her mother had warned her every step of the way. Marjen had known somehow, known that the world would turn to fire.

Father's broken, mangled corpse trapped in that melted armor for all time. Catherine had cried at the sight, but Lady Marjen had moved to ensure their safety. She had told Catherine that day to never let her brother Peter from her sight. All they would have was each other, and she would need to keep that relationship secure to guarantee their lives.

"And I abandoned that," she whispered to no one, her shoulders slumped, "because of my lack of patience for my own flesh and blood." A tear rolled down her cheek, but she wiped it away angrily. *The time for tears has ended. The time for panic and tears, that's long gone.*

Through the quiet, her ears caught the sound of a stream babbling in the distance. She approached the sound cautiously. Wandering the forests alone was treacherous these days, but there were advantages to going alone. The burly, clawed beasts known as treehoppers only seemed to be drawn to lumbering groups, stalking them through the night. She had seen them attack travelers who walked carelessly, but she had always been light on her feet and proficient with a sword. *I can thank father for that at least.*

None of her wilderness training had prepared her for life outside the castle, so she picked it up as she went. She grabbed a branch off of the ground and began to sharpen the point of it with her small knife. Before long she had a crude spear and took position at the edge of the stream. She stood as still as a statue, waiting for her moment, then jammed the spear downwards, striking true.

She retrieved the flopping fish, and then ran it through mouth first with the spear. She would have to risk a fire to cook it, but she was hungry. Perhaps the smell of fried fish would attract her brother back to her. *Or maybe it'll attract something else entirely.*

It took some time, but she was able to strike a fire with her flint and knife. She wouldn't spend much time here. *Peter has to be gone from here; it's been several days already.* His departure had been a shock. They had fought, but for him to leave without a word made no sense.

They had wandered far in the months that followed their escape. She had initially considered traveling to her mother's home, the city of Vinalhaven, but it was a long walk, and they'd had too many close calls with robbers on the road already. *It seems to only become worse as we head farther and farther north.* They had ended up spending most of their time treading familiar ground, ultimately not making much progress.

For several minutes Catherine turned the rough wooden spear, her mouth watering and her stomach aching as the smell of cooking fish began to fill the air. As she ate, she pondered where Peter could have gone. *Surely, he has made his way back to Gilbrand Castle,* she realized. *It's the only home we've ever known.*

When she'd sucked every scrap of meat from the thin bones, she flung the spear to the ground, snuffed out the flames, and gathered her things. Hopefully she was right, and Peter had gone back home. She dreaded traveling back there. *The smell of blood. The despair of silence.* It would be some days' worth of travel by foot, and nothing great awaited her there.

"Wherever you are, sweet brother, please be safe."

CHAPTER EIGHT

Pent made his way to the end of Lyle's dining table, taking a seat next to Ellie. They shared a look, and Pent found her hand under the table. They laced their fingers together, and he ignored Hanar's probing glance.

"How's it hanging, Doc?"

She smiled. The rings under her eyes were as thick as anyone else's, but she looked as beautiful as ever.

"I wonder if I'll become used to your manner of speech, some day," she said.

Faldo cleared his throat, and then sat as well, letting his broad shoulders slump as he leaned back. Chief Lyle slowly made her way to the end of the table and sat down with a sigh.

They all stared at her, waiting for her to speak. Pent remembered being in a situation like this before, sitting around the old Chief's table, hanging on him to make a decision. The last Chief, Pohk, was a terse old man, without Lyle's trademark patience. He had been a hard man, but his care for the village was paramount. It was clear that the burdens of his people weighed heavy on him, as they weighted heavy on Lyle now.

"These past few months have been a dismal series of tragedies," Lyle said. "For all our want of protecting Somerville and making a more secure home, those of us who are the most vulnerable have slipped from our care."

She spoke at length of the situation. With no warning signs, Somerville's children had begun to disappear. At first it was one or two, forgotten among the hustle and bustle of activity. So much time was spent on erecting new buildings that they had been forgotten, until it was too late.

The issue became known, and the children still managed to be plucked from the village's grasp. The farmer Marall, always so watchful of his rambunctious son, Bart, had fallen asleep, and all at once the boy left the village. He seemed to be one possessed, as he sleepwalked out of town and into the forests.

"Half the children now are gone, taken away from us," Lyle continued. "An unknown fate awaits them, and we have failed to stop it." She trembled slightly. "These events don't speak well of me as a leader. Chief Pohk would be ashamed."

Faldo slammed his hand on the table. "These are horrible times, Mother Lyle. You cannot say that, we need boldness now. Not weakness and self-pity."

"Chief Lyle," Ellie corrected. Lyle had gone by Mother in the days when Chief Pohk was still alive. Pent noticed some villagers still call her that from time to time. *Old habits die hard.*

"Chief Lyle," Faldo said, accepting the correction. "That is the truth. You are our chief, and we shall follow you."

"Boldness," Lyle said. "Perhaps I should step aside and let someone bolder take charge."

Hanar rose from his seat and walked to Faldo. He rested his hand on the builder's broad shoulders, calming him down. "There's no one I know bolder than you, dear Sister," Hanar said. "You have been doing a fine job; I don't think there's a person here who doesn't believe in your good intentions. But there is a darkness in the air, one that lingers in the forest like the stink of a fetid corpse. Some evil is ferrying the children into the night... how could this be your fault?"

Lyle rose from her seat as well and began to pace. Despite the situation, Pent smiled at the similarity between brother and sister. *When they need to act, they jump upright.*

"I once chastised Chief Pohk for holding these secret meetings, keeping council with a select few to decide the fate of everyone in Somerville. And here I am, doing the same thing, while Marall and others bang on my door, screaming that I return their children to their homes."

"We'll figure out what's happening," Pent said. "And you're talking about stepping aside? Well, I don't know who you expect to take your place. You're the best we've got. If there's anyone's at fault here, it's me."

Faldo brushed Hanar's hand aside. "When a bridge begins to crack, you don't sit in a circle for hours and debate who laid the foundation wrong. You figure out how to fix it." He knocked on the table with the palm of his hand. "What's done is done. Now we must create a plan, and act."

There were nods around the table. Their faces were grim but determined.

"I know you have been having difficulty, Pent," Hanar said. "But I am happy you have joined us. We would all be dead, without your aid."

Ellie squeezed his hand under the table. "I'm happy you've joined us as well."

Lyle nodded. "All spoken true, what's done is done." She turned and studied Ellie. "You've been quiet, aside from heaping attention onto Pent." She let the comment linger for a moment, before continuing. "I must be honest, it tries my nerves to see our doctor sit on this small council but not speaking to the issue at hand. Riven's betrayal has soured my taste for pensiveness at this table."

The mention of her old teacher made Ellie flush red. "You wound me, Chief. No one was hurt more by Riven's betrayal than I. I don't sit in silence, plotting over how to usurp you and take control of Somerville. I could never do what you do; your burdens are too stressful for my shoulders." She shook her head. "Not that I don't have my own stresses. We are heavy with stresses in Somerville these days."

"Indeed," Faldo said. "My belief in your leadership is unfaltering, Chief Lyle. I'm a man who works with his hands, and my mind is focused on new creations, not the workings of people. But even I can see that the villagers are growing restless."

Ellie nodded. "I've checked all of the children, and they all seem sound of mind. It makes no sense, almost as if they were simultaneously possessed by some kind of illness. If I had a patient, I could perhaps yield more information, but without that, my hands are tied."

"Speaking of that," Faldo began, "why don't we do that with the kids? If we chain them all at home, then they cannot escape our sight."

"I mean, that's an idea," Pent said uncertainly, "but I think you're gonna piss off a lot of people, what with the villagers growing restless thing. I mean, have you seen Marall? Dude is on the warpath. I'd hold off before you start shackling anyone."

"Someone already tried that," Ellie interjected. They all turned to her. "Janeen had Bri tied in her home while she tended the fields during the day. Bri broke through the rope and clawed her way out of the house—in the brightness of daylight."

Faldo frowned. "That's the first I've heard of that. I knew Bri had gone, but not under those circumstances."

"She showed me the tear in the rope," Ellie said. "I think Janeen was ashamed that she couldn't handle things herself. This mess has people behaving irrationally."

"Ellie and Pent are both right," Lyle said. "We need to keep the people calm while we solve this problem. Throwing all of the children into a house and locking the door might help for a time, but we cannot keep them shackled like cattle forever, and I imagine the villagers who have already lost their children would soon come knocking, and for more than answers I fear."

"We must tighten the watch then," Hanar said. "That is what the situation demands. I fear another sleepless night awaits us all."

"What of your tracking, Hanar?" Ellie asked. "Were you able to find signs of the children as they left?"

"The tracks, I can follow them for some time." He leaned on the table, tracing two paths from the center. "But north and west of Somerville, there is more foot traffic than I have ever seen before. Beast, man, and child alike, the trails become confused outside of town."

"Fatigue is taking a toll," Faldo said as he rubbed his eyes. "I mean no insult to either of you. Hanar, I know, is an expert in the forest. But we've been sharing too many sleepless nights. A blade grows dull with overuse."

"It's not just that. Things are getting pretty wild out there," Pent said suddenly. "More signs that with Yozer gone, things have gone to hell. And to make matters worse," he withdrew his gun and laid it on the table, "I'm out of ammo. Consider this magazine the quiver for my arrows. It's empty, and Somerville lacks any way to craft new bullets, so far as I can see."

Chief Lyle stared at the gun with reverence. "We wait day after day for things to change, and our resources diminish slowly. But what recourse do we have?" She turned to Hanar. "I'll put this in your care, Brother. Tighten the watch tonight." She rose slowly. "We've spent enough time speaking of this for now. You're all dismissed."

As Pent was leaving Lyle's hut, Marall blindsided him. The farmer's eyes were glossy and wet from tears. "P... please!" he sobbed. "Please save my son! I was a fool, I let sleep take me, and then he was gone! Please, Pent. I work the fields every day to keep us fed. I'm a good man. I know I've called him a bother, but I miss my boy!"

"We're doing everything we can," Pent said. *Children getting swept up in the night, sounds like some movies I've seen...*

Marall continued as if he hadn't heard Pent speak. "Monsters roaming the forests, sorcerers throwing fire and lightning all around, and now the children vanish from their homes. And my son among them! Please, I put my faith in you to protect us. I've spoken of my disdain for the way things have run under Chief Lyle, but please! Please save my son!"

"You have my word, man," Pent said, trying to put confidence he didn't feel into his tone. Marall's face was a mask of desperation. "I don't know how, but I'm going to do everything I can to get your son — every child who has left Somerville—back." He clapped Marall on the shoulder. "For now, let's follow Hanar's lead. Help us with the watch tonight."

"Do you believe I can really be of help?"

"It's either that, or wallow in sadness. And I'm done wallowing."

CHAPTER NINE

Hanar rubbed at his dreary eyes. Night had fallen. *It's been at least three days since I managed a night of good sleep.* He took his rest in the day now, and even that was fleeting.

He had settled for the night in a familiar spot—the branch of a tree—not far from Somerville's fortifications. The towers surrounding the village gave a great vantage point of the surrounding areas, but Hanar stayed with what was comfortable, lamenting the amount of wood used to construct them. *The forest seems diminished, but I suppose it is for the best.*

He surveyed the line of watch guards from his perch. They looked as tired as he felt. *I need to keep my wits about me.*

He wiped at his eyes again, then was forced to scramble for his footing as he nearly slipped from his roost. The brief moment of panic served him well enough to wake him up. Shaking his head, he stared out into the woods, then back into town.

Somerville. His home. It had changed so much since the arrival of the dark-skinned stranger, the huge man who fell from the sky.

When Hanar thought of Pent, he could not help but smile. *Everything is different now, but altogether better.* The change brought him some pause—he was used to a slow pace, to things staying as they were—but he felt more purpose than he ever had before. *And I'm sure Pent feels the same way.*

Hanar's smile wilted into a frown as he felt a pang of guilt. *I should not be counting this as a positive change. Not while the children are missing.*

Hours passed before Hanar heard a rustling in the bushes below. He gripped his bow and slowly pulled an arrow. He studied the bushes; the rustling was not a predator; it was shambling and without stealth. He nocked an arrow and shot it wide of the target.

There was no reaction from the creature. It either hadn't heard the arrow thudding into the ground, or it hadn't cared. *The time for boldness is now then.* He vaulted down and into the bush.

Reaching blindly through the thick foliage, he grabbed onto the creature within and pulled it from the bush. It was a small child, the girl Fen, her dainty dress torn from her travels. Small cuts and scrapes covered her arms and face. Her eyes had glazed over; she attempted to walk through his grip, exhibiting an impossible amount of strength for a child of only eight years.

He held her tightly and yelled out into the night. "Help! Someone. Come to me! I have one in my grasp!"

The burly figure of Pent lumbered through the foliage. He stared at the small child with a look of compassion and gently shook her. "Come on girl, quit playing around!"

Fen ignored his request. She continued to struggle with inhuman strength. Pent grappled with her, lifting her off the ground. "What in the hell? Fen, wake up!" he shouted into her face, but to no avail. "What do you make of this?" he asked Hanar.

Hanar shook his head. "It is unlike anything I have ever seen." When Hanar saw that the other watch guards were approaching, he called out. "This is not meant to be a show! Return to your posts, we don't know what controls her, or if others have the same ailment!"

The guards grumbled as they turned back the way they'd come. To Pent, Hanar said, "Perhaps Ellie can make sense of this. She did mention needing a patient, after all."

The journey into the village was not as easy one, as the girl fought with Pent the entire way. Hanar knocked on Ellie's door as Pent cradled the child in his arms. It was some time before the door opened. Ellie looked at them blankly, rubbing at her eyes, and yawning. "What is it you need, Hanar?"

Hanar envied the little amount of sleep she had seized in the depths of night. Before he could speak, she gasped. "One of the children? What has happened to her?"

Pent spoke through gritted teeth as he fought to maintain hold of the child. "No clue, hoping you can help us out with that, Doc. She won't calm down."

They rushed into Ellie's home, and she began to examine Fen. Pent tried to hold her still, but her thrashing made it all but impossible. She briefly broke free and walked to the door, but she only clawed at it, clearly unable to figure out how to unlock it.

"It makes no sense," Ellie said. "She moves as if in a trance."

"A trance," Hanar repeated thoughtfully. "Some kind of spell perhaps?"

"Perhaps, and nothing seems to be jarring her from it." Ellie splashed water on the child. "If it was merely sleep, that should have been enough. Her arms and face are torn from the woods. And look at her eyes." They were glassy orbs; the pupils had faded and were nearly unperceivable. "This is no sickness, not one I have ever encountered."

They all watched as Fen continued to try and claw her way out of the house. Pent shook his head. "Wish I had her energy. I'm exhausted just watching her go at it." He pointed at the door. "She keeps this up, she's gonna tear the door off its hinges."

"It's just as Janeen described... If only Riven was here," Ellie said suddenly. "My skills are so limited. Riven was a master doctor, perhaps he would have known what this is."

Hanar clenched his fist. Every mention of the man tried his nerves. He had abandoned Somerville at its most desperate moment. "Riven is a master of nothing but treachery. Wherever he snuck off to, we're better off without him." He gestured to Fen. "And besides, this does not seem to be a matter that medicine will solve."

"The chief of the village of Seward, Darson. He could solve this," Ellie said. "I remember Riven speaking of him—another medical prodigy from Vinalhaven. They received refined training in the city. All I have is my herbs, and whatever Riven was able to bless me with."

"Come on El, all that self-defeating talk? It doesn't suit you," Pent said. "I'm not an expert, but I think Hanar is right. This isn't a cold or a stab wound. We need to seek out Gordenthorpe." Pent walked to Fen and held her gently by the wrists to stop her scratching. "You said it was a trance, right? Maybe of the magical variety?"

"A sorcerer does seem fitting here. But, Pent, you know that he has been gone the past few times I have paid him a visit. He seemed to disappear after all of this started." But Pent was right, it was the best chance they had. "I am unsure if we could convince him to come all the way here."

"Then we go to him." Pent scooped Fen up. She began to scratch and bite at his arms; he did his best to ignore it. "What other choice do we have? We can't just sit here twiddling our thumbs."

Hanar nodded. "Spoken wisely as always, my good friend. Let us depart at once." He motioned to Ellie as he opened the door. "Please send word to Lyle. Chief Lyle, rather. Tell her we've gone in haste, in search of Gordenthorpe's counsel."

CHAPTER TEN

The forests south of Somerville were dense with foliage; the paths were not nearly as well maintained as the ones to the north. Pent and Hanar marched as quickly as they could. Pent struggled to hold Fen, desperately trying not to hurt her, but fearing that she would hurt him at the same time. *Hopefully Gordenthorpe has some spell or potion to calm the poor girl.*

Gordenthorpe. Pent had mixed feelings on the man. At this point, he was their only shot, but he had been known to disappoint before. "What are the chances that he actually helps us out this time?"

Hanar hurried along the trail to Gordenthorpe's hut. He spoke without losing focus on the path ahead. "You speak of his failure to aid us in the battle with Yozer."

"Uh, yeah. That was kind of a big deal. We could have all been killed, while he was living lavish in his forest getaway."

Hanar ducked under a branch, then said, "Pent, you're a brave man. Brash perhaps, but brave. You might be slow to admit it but risking your life for the lives of people you've only just met—it's a brave act."

Pent stopped, fighting to hold Fen still as he formed his response. "And you may not admit it, but I didn't have much of a choice. I put Somerville between a rock and a hard place, and I had nowhere else to go."

Hanar turned and regarded his friend. "There's always a choice, there are always places to go my friend. You don't have to accept the compliment. I know your temperament well enough now. Begrudge Gordenthorpe all you want, but he had no horse in this fight."

Pent smiled. "It's horse in the race, not fight. But I've seen horses in war now, so maybe they should change the expression."

"A horse in the race! That is what I was going for."

"Horse or not, the man is a coward."

"Perhaps. But we've come this far on your suggestion already. And this coward could have the answers we need."

Soon they reached the clearing where Pent had first met the whimsical sorcerer. Pent watched as Hanar rummaged through his pack, pulling out the familiar stone he used to call Gordenthorpe.

Hanar raised the stone into the air. As the stone began to light up, he shouted, "Gordenthorpe! Reveal yourself!" The wizard's hut began to shimmer in from nothingness. The familiar, quaint hut stood in the field. A ramp, which was held up with a few weak-looking twigs, led to the entranceway.

Before they could even approach the ramp, the door shot open. A small, round man glared at them from the inside of his hut. His eyes narrowed at first, and then widened when he realized who had arrived.

"Hanar, and Pent as well! Come in at once. I imagine you have many things to discuss." He popped back into his home, and Hanar sprinted up the ramp. Pent followed more slowly, still struggling with Fen.

. . .

Pent winced upon entering Gordenthorpe's home. "I forgot how damn bright it is in here." Without a free hand to shield his eyes, he had to resort to squinting at everything. Magical artifacts hung from the walls, sat on shelves, and overflowed from every tabletop. The odor of tea hung around his nostrils, and, despite his discomfort, Pent was filled with a sense of relaxation. All at once, days of fatigue were washed away.

Gordenthorpe had danced over to him and was studying the small child who twisted and turned in his hands. He tugged on Pent's tunic, beckoning him deeper into the hut. The old man gestured to a chair; Pent carried Fen over to it. Gordenthorpe waved his hands over the arm rests and restraints appeared, buckling Fen in.

Pent scratched his head. "I appreciate you taking her off my hands, but we could have tied her up back at Somerville." She continued to struggle in the chair. "What's going on with her, Gordenthorpe?"

"In due time, in due time. I would suggest you take this moment to catch your breath," the pudgy old wizard nodded towards Hanar, "as your friend is, anyway."

Hanar was sitting down in a wicker chair, his head slumped over. He was snoring loudly, lulled into sleep by his own fatigue and the whimsical ringing that filled Gordenthorpe's hut. Pent took a moment to look at the artifacts that adorned the walls and tables, the magical items Gordenthorpe called tokens, which he had spent a lifetime of adventuring to collect.

"I could use the sleep, that's for sure. I really could..." Pent felt his voice trailing off as he found his way into a chair and passed out.

CHAPTER ELEVEN

"Killer."

Pent turned to the voice that had spoken. It was familiar, and one he hadn't heard in a long time. A tall, black man stood across from him, facing in the opposite direction.

"There's no way this is real, give me a break," Pent said.

The man turned then. James hadn't aged a day since Pent had seen him last. The bullet hole where his eye should have been still leaked blood. He mouthed the word again, "Killer."

"I've done what I've had to do, man." Pent said defensively.

"And you think that makes you better than anyone else?" James nodded to the weapon in Pent's hand.

He hadn't noticed the gun. He dropped it and backed up a step. "I did what I had to do. I had to defend myself."

"That's what everyone says, everyone who takes another's life." He pointed at the hole where his eye used to be. "How do you think this feels?"

"Please, man. Just stop. Stop this, whatever it is." Pent shook his head.

"Let's see how you think it feels." Pent blinked, and the gun was in James's hand. He aimed down the sights with his missing eye and pulled the trigger.

BAM!

"Wha-what?" Pent shook his head. He awoke so abruptly that he tore himself from his chair and crashed onto the ground.

"Easy my boy, easy." The gentle hands of Gordenthorpe brushed his shoulder. He helped Pent to his feet, and then back into the chair. "Easy now."

"Finally awake!" Hanar said, scratching at his beard. "But not the most graceful move I've seen from you, my friend." Hanar had turned away from the magical tokens to face him. He was passing a perfectly round stone, engraved with the symbol of a sun, from one hand to the other. Gordenthorpe glanced at him nervously.

Pent heard a child's giggle from somewhere nearby. "Everyone is always making fun of Mr. Pent for being such a heavy sleeper!" Fen darted in from the other room. "But you snore so loudly! Your own snores should wake you up!"

"Fen!" Pent got up, feeling the blood rush to his head. He swept the girl into his arms, "You're all right!"

"She's been recovered for some time," Hanar said. "Gordenthorpe has the answers to some of our woes, but there are matters we need to discuss." His face took on a grave expression.

"Wait, how long was I out for?" Pent asked.

Gordenthorpe glanced out the door of his hut. "It's been hours, the sun has made its way high in the sky." To Fen he said, "My child, would you please leave us for the moment? The adults have matters to speak of." He smiled and hunched over her; he was only a foot taller. "Boring things, nothing a small girl would be interested in."

With a smile and a bow, Fen took her leave of the three of them. Gordenthorpe beckoned for Pent to sit down again.

Pent watched her leave, surprised again by the size of

Gordenthorpe's hut. *The hut seems way bigger on the inside than it does on the outside.*

"I'm sure I've gotta hear what you have to say," Pent said, addressing the wizard, "but is it a good idea for us to wait here for a whole night?" He shrugged at Hanar. "I bet Lyle is worried about what has happened."

"I'm sure you're right, my friend. But you'll be thankful you listened to what he has to say," Hanar said. "There's little in the way of answers back with Lyle. There are two puzzles at our feet. The first was what has been happening to the children, and we've solved that. Or rather, Gordenthorpe has."

"And the second..." Pent began, "where have the children gone? The ones who vanished before this happened to Fen." He glanced at the aged sorcerer. "Go ahead old man, surprise me."

Gordenthorpe looked wounded at the remark. "An audacious response, for someone who just saved a child from a horrible fate. What will it take for you to warm to me?"

"Hey, don't get me wrong, I appreciate the help. I've just got a thing against wizards. Last one I met sent an army of skeletons to kill me."

Gordenthorpe winced at the mention of his old master and friend, Yozer. *And he's probably not happy about getting reminded that he didn't do a thing to help either.* "That's... I suppose that's fair. I'll have to walk a long path to make amends with you, Pent. I don't resent your judgment. It's the judgment of a Crusader's heart after all."

"A Crusader..." Pent said, trailing off. *There's that word again.* "I don't know anything about that. I'm just a guy trying to make it work in this crazy world."

"Your desire to change the world, to act on your own convictions and against your own fears—that's what makes you a Crusader. You're like the heroes of old, Pent. You refuse to let the world choose your fate; you forge your own."

"If you say so." Pent thought back to all of his time spent bagging groceries. *I mean, I didn't really choose to come to this world of monsters and wizards. How is this forging my own fate?*

"You speak of old heroes and fates. My jealously is rising," Hanar said. "But perhaps the talk of old heroes could wait, so we can wrestle with our current problems."

Gordenthorpe danced over to a cloak that hung from the wall, waving his hand over it. "The stories of old heroes and your current problems are intertwined," he said. Abruptly he went off into the other room, then returned with a book in hand. "It took me some time to locate them, but I've been studying old texts. My memories alone aren't enough to serve this new world you've helped create."

"This post-Yozer world, you mean," Pent replied heavily. *And all the turmoil to go along with it.*

"Precisely. Yozer was a complicated man, in many ways an evil one. Why, I remember the first time I met him. Even then, people spoke of the darkness in his heart. Darkness wielded by a powerful man with deep ambitions, a man motivated to tame the world... what a powerful weapon indeed." Gordenthorpe looked up, glancing at Pent. He cleared his throat. "My apologies. The point is, his passing was a good thing, but there have been consequences to his passing as well. In killing Yozer, you've managed to rile a long unseen danger. The blood of the Scribes has begun to boil over."

"The Scribes?"

Gordenthorpe handed Pent a book and flipped ahead several pages. Pent stared at a drawn picture of several tall, rail thin men, with ears that looked like a cropped dog's. "When I glanced at the girl you brought to me, I feared that this was the case. My ability to raise her from her trance—it only confirms my thoughts. The Scribes have awoken once more. And they are strong enough to plague the world again."

Pent observed the picture more closely. "Scribes... they look like elves." Gordenthorpe raised an eyebrow at the comparison. "Or at least the ones I'm familiar with. Real *Lord of the Rings* stuff." The men in the picture looked oddly familiar to him. *I can't place it, but I know I've seen someone like this before.*

"I know nothing of elves, but whatever you must call them, the Scribes are an old race. The oldest, in fact. The legends in that book speak of them, and how they created the material world around us." He tugged at his long, white beard. "I'm not sure how true that is. People always seek to find answers where they have questions, and sometimes no answers can be found. But the Scribes use a dangerous and ancient form of magic." He sighed, pausing for a moment. "Long ago, I wandered the world with the Crusaders of old, my long-cherished allies. The Scribes had already been mostly wiped out before I even entered the fold of the Crusaders. Yozer, alongside our mentor Karpas, did battle with them. But Karpas, in his mercy and, perhaps, lack of wisdom, sought not to finish them off. They were sealed away, but the last of those seals has vanished." Gordenthorpe sighed again, his shoulders sagging as if under a heavy weight. "Brave Karpas. Brave, kind Karpas. He did not want to exterminate an entire race of people. He always saw the best side of the world…"

"What do they want?" Hanar asked.

"Blood," Gordenthorpe said, trembling. "They use an ancient power, the power of creation. The forge is one's own imagination, the fuel is blood. They lure the unwitting to their lair and drain them of their blood, to power their creations."

Hanar went pale. Pent felt his own heart beat faster in his chest. "Blood? You mean the children are…"

"Yes. I removed the curse from Fen, but I fear she will be entranced once again. Hanar told me of all the children who have already vanished. There is still time, but if you delay, they could be lost."

"Why children? What kind of horrible beast would prey on children?" Hanar stood up as he shouted. Gordenthorpe glanced at him, concern plastered on his face.

"They are vulnerable. And the Scribes, their power has been sealed for decades. They must still be weak. At the height of their power, their spells could ensnare men and women alike. Only the strong of heart and conviction were able to resist them." He laced his fingers together. "This is a bad omen; the Scribes bring tidings of dark times with them."

Pent shuddered and looked down at the book. The passage spoke vaguely about the origins of the world and the power of the Scribes. "I'm not seeing much in here in the way of a weakness, or a secret lair. Lots of doom and gloom, pretty light on hope."

Gordenthorpe frowned. "Yes, the people who wrote that tome had a flair for the dramatic. Or so I assume. I was not there to witness their powers in person. But make no mistake, the Scribes are dangerous." He looked again at the cloak that was mounted to the wall. "The meaning of danger for me might be different from yours. I believed Yozer was the most dangerous being in existence, but you handled him. Perhaps this is within your capabilities as well."

Pent rose up, unclipping the gun from his belt. "Don't give me too much credit. Yozer didn't see this coming." He dropped the gun unceremoniously on Gordenthorpe's table. "The gun is useless now. No more bullets."

"It was not your magical bow that saved us, Pent," Hanar said. "It was your bravery and courage."

"Thanks for the vote of confidence, buddy, but I'm pretty sure it was the gun." Pent was certain of that. If he hadn't had the pistol, he never would have even gotten close to Yozer. He breathed in deeply. "Well, gun or not, I think we all know what the deal is here."

"Hm?" Gordenthorpe said as he turned. Hanar was smiling, sure of what Pent would say.

"We're gonna have to take care of these Scribes. That's the only way we're getting the kids back." He glanced up and down Gordenthorpe's wall. "I don't suppose you've got anything I can use? How about that cloak you keep eyeballing?"

"Oh, this?" He grabbed the cloak and stretched it out before them. "No, this would be useless against the Scribes. A magical cloak, able to dispel the effects of a wizard's magic. The Scribes use a force that is of a different design entirely. Much darker magic than I'm capable of."

"A magical cloak that dispels magic?" Pent clenched his fist. "That sounds like it would have been real helpful, if we had it when Yozer attacked us." His anger towards the cowardly wizard was boiling over again.

"I'm afraid it would not have been. The cloak is only effective if it has the blessing of the specific wizard. This is my cloak, not Yozer's."

"That's counterintuitive," Pent said.

"Indeed." He looked at Pent's bewildered face. "We made them ourselves to help train new sorcerers. Much easier to practice if you're not in danger of being burnt to a crisp." He shook his head. "There is no help upon my wall. But I can share a bit of knowledge with you.

"I have seen your builder's maps. They are most impressive. I recall some words of wisdom I shared with Karpas and Yozer about the Scribes, many, many years ago. Their last lair should lay in the west—far in the west—outside of range of your Faldo's maps. And they do have a weakness."

"Something we can carry, I hope," Hanar said.

Gordenthorpe nodded. "Milk. The byproduct of cattle. It disrupts their ink and stifles their ability to use their dread magics."

"Milk..." Hanar scratched at his beard. "Somerville has no cattle. I remember years ago we traded for milk with traveling merchants who visited our lands. We haven't had milk to drink in a long time."

"Maybe Lyle has an idea of how we can get some. There's nothing else? What kind of weakness is milk?" Pent asked.

Gordenthorpe pondered the question for a moment, mulling it over in his head. "I can vaguely recall something else. The foundation of life? The essence of life? The forge of life?" He tugged at his beard. "Something of two components with which to foster life, perhaps the other component is a weakness as well, but I do recall milk being spoken of." He smiled sadly and lowered his head. "Yozer had similar reservations about the weakness; he wondered how such a powerful race could be felled by such a thing."

"Glad to hear I've got something in common with that psychopath." Pent nodded to Hanar. "I guess we've got what we came for. We shouldn't keep Lyle waiting any longer than she has already."

"Just a moment," Hanar said. "Gordenthorpe, we mean to put an end to this, as it seems to be a grave threat. Will you not join us in this struggle? Your powers would be invaluable."

Gordenthorpe shuddered in place. "Forgive me. But the Scribes can be resisted by only those of strong conviction. I am a Crusader no more. You had it right at the start, Pent. I am a horrible coward." Pent felt a pang of guilt for the man, but it quickly faded. "I shall go to your home and help protect those who are still there. I can be more helpful removing the trance from those who have been ensnared; I would only be in the way of your quest."

Pent shrugged. "I'm not gonna hold a gun to your head. We'll have to make do with what we've got." He called for Fen, who came running to his side. "Oh, speaking of guns..." He reached down and lifted up his M1911.

He studied the gun, turning it over in his hand a few times. "Man. It's harder to give this up than I thought it would be. I still wonder, if I had this on me that day, I wonder if James would still be alive." His friend's murder was the whole reason he started carrying the gun to begin with. His friend met an early death for no good reason.

If it hadn't been for the gun, Pent would have died instead of Yozer. It was because of the gun that he was able to turn the tide of their battle. *I don't think anything I learned on the football field would have helped, and his magic would have beaten back any sword or arrow.* And now here he was, standing in a wizard's home, next to his friend, the gruff woodsman. *An empty gun won't help me play my part here, will it?*

He lowered it slowly onto Gordenthorpe's table. "This has been one of the most reliable things I've ever owned. I always carried it around, thinking I would need it just walking through the streets. And can you imagine that, I saved an entire medieval village with the squeeze of a trigger." He shook his head. "But it's useless to me now. I want you to hold onto it."

"Me?" Gordenthorpe reached forward and plucked it from the table.

"You were curious about it when you first saw it. Besides, I think it would look cooler floating on your wall than collecting dust in my hut. I can't cling to the past forever."

Gordenthorpe stared at the gun with reverence before slowly nodding his head. "Indeed. I wish you both the best of luck. Travel quickly and carefully; these are dark times that have come. The old age of Crusaders has passed, and the order of Yozer's rule is gone as well. Go, Pent, and show me what you will make of this new age."

Pent glanced back at the wizard. "We'll see," he said simply, then he turned and walked out into the sunshine.

CHAPTER TWELVE

Pent followed Hanar's lead on the return to Somerville. They were hunched over, walking slow and low to the ground. They made their way down the cliffside and to the edge of the bridge easily enough.

Fen looked from man to man with confusion. "Why are we being so sneaky?"

"Just treat it like a game, Fen," Pent said. "If we tiptoe into town, it'll be like we never left." Raised voices echoing from the center of town told him this was the right call. *We didn't exactly tell Lyle where we were going.*

"HALT!" A shout from one of the towers overlooking the bridge stopped them in their tracks. "You three, stop where you stand!"

They did as commanded. "There was no one watching the bridge when we left," Hanar said. "Perhaps we've caused more concern than I thought we would have."

Pent squinted. "Monty, is that you up there?" He thought he recognized the slim farmer-turned-soldier, a man he had been particularly hard on during his training of Somerville's villagers in the art of war. *Or at least the art of war told by Stanley Kubrick...*

"Is that Pent and Hanar?" the voice called back. The figure

leaned out for a better look; it was Monte, as Pent had guessed. He pointed to the town square. "I would make your way back as Chief Lyle is at her wit's end. And she's not the only one. People were speaking about how you two were swept up by creatures of the night!"

Pent and Hanar glanced at each other, swept Fen up in their arms, and dashed over the bridge and into town.

As they ran through, passing the quaint houses, the villagers of Somerville turned and gaped at them. Some shouted cheers of joy, and others cursed under their breath. They stopped in their tracks when they reached the town square, coming face to face with Chief Lyle.

Lyle glared at them, her eyes a blistering inferno. "I hope there's an explanation for this, a good one at that. Have you forgotten who the Chief is here?" She stomped her foot on the ground. "You can't just leave in the middle of a crisis! You've made whatever panic we had even worse."

"Sister, please..."

"Don't sister me you fool!" Her face had gone as red as a strawberry.

Pent stepped in front of Hanar, dragging Fen with him. He gestured to the small girl. "Look, we had one good reason for leaving right here. Let's talk."

They met in her home, along with Faldo. They laid Fen to sleep in Lyle's bed; she was exhausted from her travels throughout the night. Hanar explained what they had learned from the wizard Gordenthorpe, and how he had managed to release Fen from her trance.

"The Scribes?" Lyle said doubtfully. She tapped her fingers anxiously on the table. "The Scribes... I used to tell the children a story involving the Scribes."

Pent's ears perked up. Before she was Chief Lyle, she was

Mother Lyle, best known for being a guiding hand to the villagers—particularly the children. He recalled the story she had shared about the desert mole Forterzo, and the Freewalkers of the western part of the world.

"I don't recall that one, Sist-, I mean Chief," Hanar said. He was still reeling from her reaction to their arrival.

"It was not a tale about the Scribes exactly. It only mentions them. The story itself is about the scourge called Pyrious—the Crusaders called him The Deceiver—and the story only mentions the Scribes once."

"And what of them?" Faldo asked.

She closed her eyes as she tried to remember. "How does it begin... 'And then Gerontius marched off to meet The Deceiver in battle. For he had spent his time cast away from the first people, turning men's hearts with his foul speech. Where the Scribes changed the world with their mythical quills, Pyrious worked a forked tongue.' Most of the length of the story talks about how Pyrious rallied people to fight for his cause, and against their own." She smiled. "Maybe I can tell you the rest someday. I miss being able to share stories with you all."

"It's a fine story," Hanar said. "But isn't that tale about this man Pyrious? It mentioned the Scribes but did not give us much information."

"Perhaps there is some other connection between Pyrious and the Scribes," Lyle said. "All of these stories about the Scourges tend to focus on just one of them. That the Scribes are mentioned alongside the Deceiver... Well, why else would they be mentioned in the same tale?"

"That's not much to go by," Pent said. "These Scribes, they can pull Somerville's children away to serve their needs. But all we have to go by is 'west.'"

Lyle rubbed her forehead. "Well, the story goes along with that. Pyrious rallied his forces far west of here, but not as far north as the

Freewalkers. If Pyrious has some kind of connection with the Scribes, then maybe... Could you fetch your map, Faldo?"

He nodded and rose up from his chair.

"The west seems a dangerous place," Hanar said. "Every other story I've heard, either from you, Chief, or from Gordenthorpe, speaks of some kind of horrible monster or demon from the west. Evil spreads like a plague from that area."

Faldo returned to the table and began to unroll his map. "That's part of the reason why Somerville was settled where it was. The founders wanted to put as much distance between this village and the center of all that chaos. The proximity to Castle Draemar was considered as well. They believed no one would dare pillage or revolt so close to Yozer's domain."

Pent laughed. "Well, so much for that plan. Sorry to disappoint your ancestors, Faldo."

He shrugged. "All an architect can do is build the foundation. What people do with it is their own affair." He tapped on the left side of the map. "My map ends just at Gilbrand Castle, but I suspect you will have to travel much further. From the castle, you can head south to reach the coastal village of Seward, or northwest to Brighton." He frowned, tracing his finger to the edge of the map. "It's not as complete as I would like. I've been busy enough here as is, but someday I will chart a map of this entire land..."

"The castle is a decent enough place to start," Hanar said. "But I don't think we would receive a very warm welcome. We should travel wide around it."

"Yeah, I don't think Gilbrand's people are gonna be happy to see us," Pent added. "Hanar can probably get away with it, but if these other villages or that castle are anything like Somerville, I'm gonna stick out like a sore thumb."

"Agreed," Lyle said. "If you're to head west, you'll have to tread carefully." She looked around the table. "All right, what else?"

"We've learned of the Scribes' weakness from Gordenthorpe,"

said Hanar, "and it is cause of some concern. Milk—and Somerville has no cattle."

Lyle shook her head slowly. "No, we do not. And milk curdles if kept, so we do not store it. She looked towards the door. "These times don't invite much in the way of traveling traders. You'll need to find a merchant outside of Somerville."

"So, we're heading out with nothing," Pent said, "hoping to find a cow somewhere in the woods." He glanced at Hanar. "You know how to milk a cow? 'Cause I sure don't."

"We've learned a little," Faldo said. "We know more collectively than we did before. A week ago, we were completely in the dark."

"We should have asked your sorcerer friend earlier, Hanar," Lyle said.

Hanar raised his hands defensively. "I have been attempting on my own to reach him, but every time I have gone to his home, he has either not been there, or has simply not answered his door. I cannot force him to speak with me."

"He mentioned something about old books," Pent said. "Maybe he was going to grab those? Don't know where wizards store their old crap; it already feels like he lives in a magic shed."

"Whatever the cause," Hanar said, "it was fortunate that we were able to grab hold of him this time. A stroke of good luck."

"Luck is all we have to rely on, apparently," Pent said. "So, we need to get our hands on a glass of the white stuff. And then we need to find the Scribes and hope that the children are with them." He stared at the map. "That's a lot of hope. We're pretty much just throwing a Hail Mary here."

"My brother is an expert tracker, is he not? Hanar should be able to pinpoint them somehow."

"Through the children," Hanar said at once. "They're being pulled into the wilderness against their will, running through bushes and getting torn to shreds. Their march is unlike any animal. If I can find just one of their paths, I can lead us to the Scribes. I'm sure of it."

"Perhaps..." Faldo began. "Perhaps we can wait for another child to be ensnared, and then follow it to this nest of vipers?"

"Vipers kill, Faldo," Chief Lyle said, straightening up in her seat. "We do not know what happens to the children when they are gone. I'll not use one of our children as a hook at the end of a line, putting further people in danger."

"Considering how pissed off everyone is already, I don't think you're gonna get a lot of takers from the parents on that one," Pent said.

"And Gordenthorpe should join you all soon," Hanar said. "Offering his protection. He can ensure we don't lose more than we already have." He spoke in reverence of the wizard's awesome powers. Pent shook his head slightly. *That's if he actually bothers to help this time.*

There was a lull at the table. Faldo examined the map, as if squinting would reveal a piece he hadn't charted. Lyle's glance darted from Pent to Hanar, and back again.

Pent broke the silence. "So, what's the play here? When Yozer came knocking, he forced everyone in town to get involved. But we're not playing defense this time, we're taking the fight out there."

"We can't march the whole of Somerville to the west in search of the children. We need to keep the people from panicking. And we'll have to meet with Gordenthorpe as well." Lyle looked from Pent to Hanar. "The two of you—you've spent plenty of time together, scouring the forests. Pent, you manage somehow to keep my brother safe. And Hanar, there is not a more reliable navigator and woodsman among us. Certainly, you know what needs to be done."

Pent gestured for her to stop. "We'll get this done, Chief. We'll get those kids back home."

Hanar stood up. He clapped Pent on the back. "I suppose the buck stops with us." He raised an eyebrow, waiting for a response.

Pent laughed. "You got that right, for once. My coach used to say that one."

"Then we're all settled," Lyle said heavily. "You should make a quick round through Somerville and grab what you need. And I imagine Cenk will want to see you out. I would be quick and quiet, if I were you. We don't want to make another scene as you leave."

"Make certain to visit me as well before you leave, Pent," Faldo said as he rolled up his map. He got up and left without another word.

Lyle rose to her feet and blocked the doorway. "I don't know what you're walking into, or what kind of dangers you will face. But I know they will be treacherous. We'll have the strength of Somerville behind us, as well as Gordenthorpe when he arrives. But you'll be alone, with no one but each other. So—"

Hanar embraced her. "Dear Sister, all of this emotion for me?"

"You need the warning, Hanar. You'll fall into trouble if I don't look after you." She tightened her grip. "You always do."

"We'll be all right," Pent said. *At least, I hope we will. Damn if I know what we're getting into this time.*

"Take care of my brother, Pent." She released her grip from Hanar. "Just be careful, both of you. I can't afford to lose either one of you."

Pent made his rounds around Somerville. It was a nostalgic moment for him; he felt as he had six months ago when he'd toured the village, preparing everyone for their battle with Yozer. The townsfolk took little notice, unaware of the danger he and Hanar were walking into.

Hanar; he couldn't remember having a closer friend in all of his life. *When you cut out the TV, and the glitz and glam of the modern world, all you have are the people.* Without all those distractions, you had to fill your day with people you cared for. *And I care about the people here.*

He passed by the site of the old graveyard. Where once there were many headstones and graves, now there was only a single monument to Somerville's fallen. The battle with Yozer was the most horrific thing Pent had ever experienced. He thought of the dead, crawling free of their graves, and attacking their descendants. When the battle had ended, the corpses of the fallen had all been gathered and burned in a funeral pyre.

Even now, the village felt like something straight out of a fairy tale: the stone and wood homes, the quaint village square, the bridge over the gently flowing river. And the people. *The people here are simple, with simple needs. But they're real too. More real than most of the clowns I knew in my old home.* He had to do what he could to set things right here. *It's because of me that their simple lives are all screwed up.*

He passed by the old distillery, where Lemen had made his rotgut. The front had been shuttered. It had been Lyle's intention to reopen the distillery when things had calmed down in Somerville, but things had never calmed down enough. "Wish I had a glass to pour out for you, man," Pent said. Lemen had been sloppy drunk the entire time Pent had known him, but he had proven to be a true hero in the end, giving his life in the fighting against Yozer.

Cenk, on the other hand, was just about the soberest person Pent had ever met. Pent walked up cautiously to the smith's smoldering hut. Smoke billowed out of the top of the conical roof. He banged on the door.

The stout man poked his head out. "Aye."

"Hey, Cenk. Don't have a whole lot of time to chitchat. Me and Hanar are gonna be heading out pretty soon, seeing if we can put an end to this whole missing children thing." Pent nodded towards the interior of the house. "I was wondering if you had anything to help me out."

Cenk glared at Pent, and then returned to his home. Pent had no interest following him in there. *Don't feel like choking half to death on all that smoke.*

He didn't have to wait long. Cenk returned, carrying several items which he dumped on the ground at Pent's feet.

Pent looked over the pile of gear. There were two sets of chest armor, one for a thinner frame and made of links of chain, the other a solid plate with extensions on the shoulders. Pent smiled down at the familiar armor. *Looks like he's made some adjustments.* He lifted it up from the ground and was surprised to find that it was significantly lighter than he remembered. The armor was thinner as well; it looked like it would give a greater range of movement.

There was also a short sword on the pile, with a fitted sheath made of wood. Pent frowned when he picked the blade up. "I can handle something bigger than this, man, and I think you're missing one sword."

Cenk shook his head. "Not here. Faldo." With that said, he turned back to his work. After a few moments of waiting, Pent shrugged, scooped up the equipment, and moved on.

As he neared Faldo's home, he spotted Hanar approaching. The woodsman was carrying a bundle of cloth with him. His quiver was filled with arrows.

"So, you've made your way to Cenk's then." Hanar gestured to the items in Pent's arms.

"And you? You picked that stuff up from Daley, right?"

"Indeed. I asked her for these cloaks some time ago. The weather is changing; the later seasons will bring more rain. These will suit us well."

"I wonder if the lands to the west have different weather?" Pent said. "It's been mostly temperate here; I wouldn't mind a change."

"We shall see. There are many days of walking ahead of us, and I've never traveled this far myself. A blessing to Daley for having completed these; they feel warm to the touch."

They both turned their heads as they heard yelling coming from inside Faldo's house. The door swung open violently, and Faldo emerged, his arms crossed. "You come bearing ill enough tidings, spare me of having to hear you discuss my useless sister."

"Faldo, whatever issue you have with your kin, perhaps you

should let those feelings die off," Hanar said. "These times are hard enough without family members at each other's throats."

Faldo pointed a finger at Hanar's face. "You live your life as you choose, and I'll live mine. Don't presume to tell me what is right or wrong." He waved them both in. "Now come on in already. You were both meant to leave without fanfare, yet here you are, standing in the wide open, carrying bundles of weapons and armor. Any longer out here and people will begin to ask questions."

Faldo's home was as Pent remembered it. A few candles were dimly lit on the windowsill, and there were stacks of crumpled pages all over the table. Faldo returned to them immediately. Pent and Hanar exchanged a look, and then dropped their new gear on the floor.

Hanar bent over and lifted up the chain mail that Cenk had expertly crafted. "I see what he's been up to. This is light to the touch. I imagine it won't encumber me as much as plate mail." He slipped it on over his tunic and jumped in place, illustrating his point.

"This is pretty light too," Pent said, hefting the plate armor. It took longer to don than Hanar's chainmail, but Pent felt immediately that Cenk had outdone himself. He lifted his arms over his head. "Got a lot more give on the shoulders." He tapped his finger against the shoulder plates. "And I bet I can I tear someone up with these."

Pent rummaged through the clothes that Hanar had brought. "All right, so some kind of cape? I guess you guys have awhile to go before you start making bomber jackets."

Hanar slipped one of the dark brown cloaks around his shoulders. "A cape, a cloak. I'm no tailor myself, but this will cover you from the elements. And the hood may help a bit to shield us from the eyes of the outside world."

He picked up the remaining cloak, which was a dull green color. *Makes me look like an olive.* The idea of a cape and hood masking his identity made him chuckle. "Not a chance that this is gonna keep anyone from noticing me." He slipped it over his armor. It was just big enough to cover all of his features. The shoulders jutted out slightly, making him look like a broad-shouldered ogre.

"Hm, still quite conspicuous." Hanar grabbed the sword and strapped the scabbard around his waist. "I'm not so used to carrying a blade of this size, but a knife and bow alone might not serve us on our whole journey." He shifted in place, swiveling the scabbard until it hung loose on his side. "It's more weight than I'm used to, but at least Cenk made a sword of reasonable size."

"Speaking of that..." Pent glanced at Faldo, who was still engrossed with the array of maps on the table. "Cenk sent me away without a sword of my own. I'm strapless, gun or otherwise. He mentioned you, so I was wondering—"

"Yes, my family's ancestral sword. Cenk has sharpened it to a razor's edge," he said without raising his head. Faldo had given him the sword after the battle with Yozer, but claymores weren't much help in their search for missing children. They had agreed to store the sword on Faldo's wall, where it hung as an ornament.

Faldo rose up, made his way across the room, and pulled it from the wall. "The sword is yours, of course." He held it reverently in his hands. "It's painful to part with, even after my promise. You understand, don't you?"

Pent recalled Faldo's story; the sword had been passed down from his grandfather to his father, and then to him. *I don't have anything like that in my family, but I get it.* "I feel you. I'll treat it as delicately as I can."

"It's a fine blade. I mean no insult to Cenk's craft, but steel from the old age seems to cut deeper than the ore we forge from our cliffs." He handed the long, heavy blade to Pent. "It will do more in your hands than it will collecting dust on my wall. If it helps to save the lives of Somerville's missing children, then I will be happy."

Pent gripped the sword tightly in his hand. There was a heaviness to it beyond its own weight. *I feel powerful carrying this around.*

"Hold it with care. Here is the scabbard to go with it," Faldo said.

Pent sheathed the sword and clipped it to his waist. It dangled mere inches from the ground.

Pent glanced at Hanar's much shorter sword and laughed. "People are gonna think I'm overcompensating for something."

"Hm? What was that, my friend?"

"Nothing, man, nothing at all."

Faldo stared at him with his eyebrow raised. "Another quip from that odd world of yours. Here's something to help ground you in this one." He handed over one of his maps, pointing at a spot on the edge. "I've only been able to draw this based on guesswork, but your goal should lie west of Gilbrand Castle. This should aid you as far as the castle, but after that..." He shrugged. "That's all the help I can offer. Hopefully it's enough."

"It's more than enough, Faldo," Hanar said. "Thank you for all you've done."

"Yeah, man. We'll bring the map back, along with the sword and all the children."

They embraced, and left Faldo to his maps as they marched back into town.

CHAPTER THIRTEEN

"Give me a second, man, just need to check out the homestead," Pent said. He left Hanar alone for a moment, as he ducked into his own small hut.

Standing in his home now made him think of the time he spent living in Hanar's hut. *Nice to have a room where I don't crick my neck lying down.* This wasn't the fanciest home; the furniture was shabby, half-melted candles sat on the windowsills, his clothes—from both worlds—were set about untidily. His jacket hung from the back of a chair. He placed a hand on his chest, feeling the cold hardness of the plate. He'd traded his jacket for armor, his sneakers for leather boots made from the tough hide of the local wild boards, called minches, and his jeans and T-shirt for a flowing woolen tunic.

He rummaged through the wood dresser next to his bed—there wasn't much left for him to use—and felt a pang of remorse for handing his gun over to Gordenthorpe. He knew it was useless without bullets, but still there was a pit of emptiness in his stomach; he felt incomplete without it strapped to his waist or resting in his shoulder holster. "I should have been more careful," he said to himself. *Wasting all those bullets shooting at forest critters, so stupid.*

He shook his head. That was the wrong mentality to have. *Be prepared for anything, and I was prepared.* The creatures they had run into, particularly the treehoppers, had been dangerous. If he hadn't acted then, he or Hanar could have been seriously injured. *I did what I could with what I had.* "No use worrying about what has already passed."

He swept up his Bic lighter and shook it in his hand; it was about half full. *Or half empty.* He loved these things; they were so cheap, and they lasted for a long time. He pocketed the lighter, and then grabbed his Kershaw folding knife. Cenk had sharpened it, after admiring the modern craftsmanship. The blacksmith had found the idea of a folding knife to be novel and clever. "It might come in handy, who knows?" *It's always best to be prepared.*

"Just one more stop to make." Pent gave his new home one last look before exiting into the village.

Pent knocked on the door to Ellie's home, before letting himself in.

"Are those the manners of everyone from your world?" Ellie said. She was mixing herbs together, her back to the door. She turned, a coy look on her face. "I assumed only you would be so audacious. Or is that some other knight in shining armor that has walked so boldly into my home," she quipped, taking in his armor, cloak, and sword.

Pent smiled back to her. "Audacious is what I'm all about, though I don't know about 'knight in shining armor.'" He crossed the length of the room and grasped Ellie in his arms. "There's something going on, something I need to tell you about."

"Is this about Fen?" she asked, her smile fading into a look of concern. "I heard there was some kind of commotion." She led Pent to the bed and sat him down. She laid a hand on his knee.

"She's fine, El. The sorcerer was able to release her from that trance. He told us a lot, and we've got a plan to get all of the missing kids back." Pent scratched at the back of his head. "I mean, sort of a plan. It's not really that much of a plan if I'm being honest. But we've got more to go on now than we did before. And Fen's safe. Gordenthorpe is coming here to help protect the rest of you. If he even shows up, I mean. He wasn't really that helpful the last time we needed him. If you ask me, his punk ass—"

"Shhh..." Ellie pressed a finger over Pent's lips. "You're rambling like you have a fever." She passed her hand over his forehead to be sure. "So, Fen is safe then, I heard that at least. Just take a deep breath and speak clear."

Pent exhaled deeply, and then drew in a long, slow breath. "Thanks El." He unclipped his sword and placed it on the ground. Then he lay back on the bed, dragging El down with him. She giggled as she fell. "Feels like I'm being thrown to the wolves here a bit. Everything is happening so fast."

"Then slow it down, talk it out," Ellie said. "There's no need to face the wolves alone."

He stared at the ceiling. One of the wooden beams holding the roof up seemed damaged. *I've been meaning to get up there and fix that.* He hoped that things would calm down, whenever he got back from this new journey. *If we get back, that is.*

"Looks like I'll be going away for a bit," Pent said, breaking their shared silence. He gave her the story up until that point: about catching Fen in the woods, the conversation with Gordenthorpe, and Chief Lyle's decision.

She absorbed it all, staring pensively at some of her medicinal herbs. "So, west then."

"That's right," Pent said. "Not much of a plan, if you ask me. Just the two of us, stumbling through the forest." He shrugged, pushing his sword along the ground with his foot. "Don't get me wrong, I think Hanar will lead us there. But it's a mess—what good am I gonna be without my gun?"

"You have more value than any single tool, Pent."

"I've just never done something like this before. It was different fighting Yozer. That was live or die, and I had all of you behind me. This time it's all on me."

"You can do anything," she said, her head resting on his broad shoulder. "I believe in you, and I believe you'll come back to us, safely, and with the children in hand."

"I wish I had your confidence. But that helps, El. I feel like everyone just knows what to do, and I've fallen into this role without having a chance to breath. I feel like I did when I first landed in this world." He met her eyes and wished he could just stay here in bed, forever. No adventures, no Scribes, no sorcerers... just a man, a woman, and a bed. "It's nice to talk to someone about this."

"Have you not shared this with Hanar?" Ellie asked. "You spend so much time with him as is; this can't be your first time expressing your reservations."

Pent shook his head slowly. "He's a good guy; I've got a lot of love for him. But it's awkward talking to him about this. He's got it in his mind that I'm some kind of great hero, always asking me about the battle with Yozer. He wouldn't take any kind of reservation like this seriously."

"But is that him not willing to listen, or is that you not willing to disappoint these expectations you believe he has for you?"

Pent paused, considering. "Maybe a little of column A, little of column B."

"Hanar is your friend first and your fanman second. You should not harbor these feelings, nor keep them to yourself. It is not healthy." She planted a kiss on his cheek. "That is, if you trust the opinion of this doctor."

Pent smiled. "It's fanboy, by the way."

Ellie narrowed her eyes. "But Hanar is a grown man. I don't know if I'll ever understand your manner of speech."

Pent stood up, grabbed his sword, and clasped it to his waist. "It's been half a year, I'm sure you'll figure it out eventually," he said with a wink.

She giggled. "So, you're off then, Mr. Crusader." She rose, her eyes level with his chest, and embraced him, holding him tight. Pent hugged her back, his eyes closed, and he hoped against hope that he would make it back from this journey. *Is it worth it, risking this, risking it all?* He sighed, already knowing the answer in his mind. When he opened his eyes, she was staring back at him.

"Yeah, I'm off then."

"I'll walk you to the bridge," she said, lacing her hand with his. They stepped out of Ellie's home together.

CHAPTER FOURTEEN

Hanar was waiting at the edge of town. Pent had spent a fair amount of time in his new home, while Hanar hadn't even spared his own home a second glance. *He has been living here for half a year, and he already has more of an attachment to the village than I.*

Above him, Faldo's fortifications cast a long shadow. The sun was already beginning to set. He had one foot placed on the bridge, and he watched the water flow slowly past. His heart thumped with excitement. *This is a far step from spending my days fishing and my nights among the trees.* He had never ventured out as far as they planned to go now. *But for Lyle and these children, I'll walk to the ends of the world.*

He saw two figures approach the bridge. Pent, wearing his cloak and armor, with Faldo's long sword hanging from his waist, and Ellie by his side. Hanar scratched at his beard. *Did Pent have need of medicine? Surely Ellie is not joining us on this quest.*

Pent lifted his hand in greeting. "Looks like you're ready to roll," he laughed. "At least one of us is excited for this. You look about ready to dance out of those boots." He turned and embraced Ellie.

They stared in each other's eyes as Hanar shuffled in place.

When they finally let go, Ellie addressed Hanar. "Please take care of him. He's not as flippant about the dangers of this world as he appears to be. And be careful yourself. Come back together and in one piece."

Hanar smiled. "Funny, I was just given the same advice from the Chief. But we intend to, Ellie. I look forward to playing music with you when all of this mess is handled. I've missed the sweet sound of your strings as of late."

"I've had my plate full, as the only doctor in this village. Hopefully when you return, you'll bring some normalcy with you."

"To normalcy then. Goodbye, Ellie."

"Bye, El," Pent said. Ellie leaned forward and gave him a peck on the cheek, then ran off without another word.

Hanar and Pent began their march to the outskirts of town. Hanar looked Pent up and down, but waited until they had neared the edge of Somerville's new fortifications before he spoke. "So, there are some secrets to you that even I wasn't aware of! You've been speaking to Ellie about *personal* matters, have you?"

Pent went a little red around the ears but let out a good-natured laugh. "I'm surprised, man. You're usually more observant than that."

Hanar furrowed his brow. "If the two of you have been sharing a bed—well, maybe it's not my place to say."

"We've got a long walk ahead of us." Pent said. "May as well get it off your chest now."

"That was not a very touching goodbye, my friend. I would have expected something more... touching."

Pent continued to walk, pretending to not hear the comment. Before Hanar could repeat himself, he said, "I dunno man. I'm just not good at goodbyes, I guess. I didn't get a chance to give one to anyone from my old world." He shook his head. "I don't know what's wrong with me. Damn, making stupid excuses. I'm just like my dad."

Hanar eyed his friend thoughtfully. "Drag those thoughts from your mind, Pent. If your tales of the man are true, you are nothing like him. He has not a hint of your courage."

"I hope you're right. We're gonna need courage by the truckload for this."

Hanar led the march. After leaving the outskirts of Somerville, they came upon a path that had not been maintained in some time. Hanar glanced about, smirking at the place they had come to. "This is where I laid in wait for Yozer to arrive." He pointed at a tree off the path. "I camped out there. My pack was down here, and I called to you from that branch with my horn." He scanned the forest. None of his handiwork seemed to be present any longer; the forest burned by the flames he had set to slow Yozer's army down had been overgrown with new brush. *These forests are resilient,* he thought.

Pent grunted his approval, staring at the branch Hanar had pointed to. They admired the calm of the landscape. Hanar reached down, feeling through the grass. *No tracks, at least nothing notable.* Somehow the children had managed to come up and around the bridge to Somerville, but then veered off the normal path and cut through the woods. *Broken stems all around, but are these from the children, or something else?*

He scratched at his beard. *It's too soon to make assumptions. We must keep searching.* He had to trust in the advice of Faldo, Lyle, and Gordenthorpe. "They had to have kept moving west. Surely there will be more signs as we approach the castle."

"I hope so, man," Pent said. "We should keep going, while it's still light out."

They walked for some time; Hanar stopped every few moments to scan the ground for tracks. The forest was alive with the cawing and rumbling of animals, but they heard no man-made sounds, child or otherwise. The tracks told a different story. "A lot of activity, even this close to Somerville. It's a wonder we don't see more visitors."

"I guess the kind of people out here aren't looking for a stable home life," Pent said. "Probably looking for trouble."

"I pray we don't have to give them any." Hanar rubbed his hand against the trunk of a tree. It came back sticky. "Speaking of trouble…"

"What is it?" Pent rushed forward to have a look. "Sap? What's the problem with that?"

"Not just sap my friend, look here." Hanar pointed at a horizontal line carved into the tree. "A blade's edge did this." Hanar glanced around, making note of the pieces of shrubs by his legs. "No doubt cut through by someone frustrated with the heavy brush of this forest."

"I got you, someone using a sword like a machete." Pent glanced at Hanar and then shrugged. Hanar admired many things about Pent, but his constant references to his old life were confusing. *I suppose it takes time to get used to living in another world. I should be patient.* "Never mind," Pent said.

The cawing of a bird in the distance drew Hanar's attention. The trees were dense still, but not quite as dense as the forests south of Somerville. He studied the land through the forest and could see a river in the north that ran from west to east. They had already traveled a ways from Somerville, and the sun had nearly set. Hanar glanced at Pent, considering their options for the night. He was nervous of traversing the woods in the darkness. "We've made good distance already. Let us do our best to find a place to raise camp."

CHAPTER FIFTEEN

Pent yawned loudly. It had taken them another half an hour to find a decent spot to hunker down. The woods grew denser as they traveled farther north, providing the adventurers heavy cover as they marched on. Tucked away in the forest they came upon a small clearing with a creek running through it. It was narrow, with two sides covered by prickly thorns. They took their time setting up camp.

Hanar had brought a small axe along, and he got to work gathering logs for a fire. Pent gathered up smaller sticks to get the fire started. He glanced at Hanar, chopping away diligently at a fallen tree. "You need a hand with that?"

"That's all right my friend," Hanar replied, without even pausing for breath. Pent got right back to gathering twigs. *We're strapped for time, and he doesn't want me holding us up. I get it.*

Before long, a low, smokeless fire smoldered at the heart of their camp. Hanar knew which wood to burn and just how much to set on the fire to keep it from blazing out of control or boiling with smoke. Although Pent had learned many of Hanar's survival tricks, he would have been lost without the woodsman now.

Hanar was staring grimly at the flickering flames. "There may come a time when we can't brave even a small fire. We don't fully understand yet the dangers of this new world, and it's likely to grow even stranger as we move westward."

Pent shivered. "It's not like we're new to camping out here, but there was always Somerville in the background. If things went south, we could always hightail it back to the village. That's not an option anymore."

Hanar nodded. He began to rummage through his pack, checking his things. "You speak true my friend. But you also speak as if we have walked to the end of the world. Somerville is still less than a day's travel away."

Pent pulled out his folding knife and flung it into the dirt, where it stuck easily. "Nah, we can't think of it like that. We can't go back there, not without the children." He pulled the knife from the dirt. "I promised Lyle we would sort this out."

"Indeed," Hanar said, then flicked his head to the side suddenly.

"What's wrong?" Pent asked.

"Hm... The wind perhaps." He stood up abruptly. "Or perhaps not," he continued, lowering his voice to the point where Pent had to lean forward to hear him. "The forest is lush with life, and I fear what drives some of these creatures. I'm going to do a sweep of our surroundings." He gathered his bow and quiver and strapped them on silently. "When the fire begins to dim, cast the sand on it. We'll turn in for the night when I return."

"You sure you don't want me to go with you?" Pent asked. There was no answer, as Hanar had already vanished into the forest. "Who does he think he is, Batman?" Pent muttered to himself.

He took a seat by the fire and flung in the remaining sticks, humming softly to himself. It was a moment before he realized he was humming at all, and when he did, he was almost startled to hear the tune of a song from his past life. He tried to recall the name of the song he was humming, but he couldn't place it. *No internet in this place. No rap albums either, for that matter. Damn, who even sings that song.*

He hummed louder, trying to place it. *Something about an estate, and missing probation...* He closed his eyes as he nodded his head to the beat. He hummed louder still, as he began to sway from side to side. *Really should have burnt some CDs before I came through here. And brought a player for them. And I guess a Costco size case of batteries.* He chuckled to himself at the absurdity of his wish. He hummed from the verse to the chorus. *Damn it, who is on that track?*

His head snapped up in realization, and his eyes opened wide. "Jadakiss!" he said aloud.

Drawn into his own mind, he hadn't noticed the rustling around him. When he glanced up, there were three shadowy figures glaring down at him. *Ah shit. Stupid, stupid!*

He sprung to his feet as the first man lunged at him and slammed his fist into the man's face. The attacker crumpled into the dirt, his nose a bloody mess. Pent fumbled with his sword as the second one grabbed at him.

"Geth him! Before he pullth that thword!" The man on the ground muttered between labored gasps. The second man, much larger than the first, had his hands around Pent's throat. Pent groaned and reared back, then brought his head sailing forward.

He smashed his forehead into the other man's eye, sending him reeling backwards and onto the fire. The man rolled away from the hot coals, screaming in pain, and flailing at his cloak, which had caught fire when he fell.

Pent had only a moment to savor his moves before the icy sharpness of a steel dagger touched his throat. "Easy, easy now," he said, his hands out and his voice barely a whisper. He swallowed hard and felt the edge of the blade move against his skin.

"That's enough out of you! You crazed giant!" There was a note of hysteria in the woman's voice as she began ordering her companions about. "Greil, if you're done flitting with that cape of yours, help Walter with his damned nose."

Pent watched the man she named Greil get up slowly and attend to the other man, Walter, who was still lying on the ground, both hands over his nose. "He smashed my eye, the scum. I'll be lucky if I can see out of it again," Greil said.

The woman cursed under her breath. "A single man gives the two of you this much trouble—this was meant to be a quick affair," she yelled into Pent's ear. "That was a pleasant greeting from you, giant. Now then, let's have your name, where you're from, and what you're doing out this way."

"You'll have an arrow from me, and nothing else," a voice shot out from the darkness of the forest. Hanar stepped silently through the brush. The two men on the ground eyed him, panic gripping them. "That's if you don't release that blade from my friend's neck."

The woman's grip on his arm tightened, and Pent felt the blade press deeper into his flesh. He didn't dare to speak. The woman was less inclined to be silent. "I'll drop him here, I mean it! It would only take a second to slit his thick throat." Pent could feel her gesture towards the two men on the ground. "And you're clearly outnumbered. How about you drop that bow instead?"

"I could put an arrow through each of their skulls in the time it took you to run that knife along his neck." Hanar narrowed his eyes and pulled back his nocked arrow. "Or maybe I should try for yours? How much faith do you have in your friends to avenge you?"

They stared at each other in the darkness. Pent could feel the woman's grip become clammy. He didn't dare try to break away. After several tense moments, the woman let out a desperate groan and dropped the knife.

Pent stepped away as she cradled her head in her hands. "To have come so far, only to fall into another robber's trap. Damn you brigands. Do what you will."

"Uh, excuse me," Pent said. "What the hell are you talking about? You just had a knife to my throat. And we're the robbers?" He glanced over at the two men. The darkness had made them seem very threatening, but in the light of the fire, he could see the fear plastered on their faces. The one with the broken nose was short, thin, and had a thick moustache. The other man was taller, and portly. His hair was light in the fire—it could have been gray—and hung over one of his eyes. They weren't carrying any weapons.

The woman studied Hanar cautiously; he had yet to drop his bow. Pent gestured for him to lower the weapon, which he did slowly. "Pent, I wouldn't trust this woman at her word. These are dark times."

The woman was taller than either of her companions; she was nearly as tall as Pent. Her dark hair was cut short. Pent stared into the woman's eyes and saw no malice there. *I've been wrong before, but—* "Let's not make them darker than they are. I'm giving you more credit than I should, lady, I hope you respect that." He waved to the fire. "Let's sit down for a moment, talk things out. And I'll hold that knife for you in the meantime."

She trembled but did as he asked. Her two companions joined her; Pent and Hanar sat across from them.

"How can you call this a robber's trap?" Pent began. "You were the ones who snuck up and jumped me."

"I'm thorry for that thir, really I am," the broken-nosed man named Walter said through hands still trying to keep back the blood. "Wathn't Aisa who thaid to do it. She thaid to thteer clear of the fire, she did. But we've been awfully hungry ath of late, and I chanthed we could parlay for some food."

"So, you thought you could steal from my friend, since he was half-asleep?" Hanar asked.

"I wasn't asleep," Pent cut in. "I was... deep in thought."

Walter hung his head in shame. "I'm thorry thir, if I could take it back I would, believe me I would. I thaw the man thitting there, in sthining armor, with a sthining thword at histh hip. I panicked!"

The one called Greil shook his head. "Walter, for the sake of all that is good, please stop talking." He leaned over and examined Walter's busted nose. "Grab hold of this, it's still bleeding. And don't speak again." He turned back to the fire. "We've seen the sharp end of enough swords. It was foolish to come here at all; we should have heeded what Aisa said."

"That's right, you should have," she said sharply. "There's trouble around everywhere these days, and no matter how far you travel, you can't seem to avoid it. Monsters in the brush, and thieves lurk the forests for easy marks. Even in what was once Yozer's realm, men carry swords and mail, as if equipped for war." She gestured towards Pent. "Not unlike what you're carrying beneath that cloak."

"Thieves... We've run into trouble before, but not thieves." Pent frowned. "Yozer's realm? Isn't the entire world Yozer's realm?" He cleared his throat. "Or it was, before—"

"Before he was killed, there was calm under his rule," Greil said. "But Aisa speaks of the forests outside of Yozer's home. Draemar castle, and the rivers below it—no man would dare to pillage so close to his home."

"Thieves so close to Draemar castle, it's unheard of," Aisa said.

Greil nodded before continuing. "Word has it that he died at the hands of mere mortals, not far from Draemar castle itself."

Pent coughed in his hand and looked away. "Yeah, imagine that."

"So then, it's not known who killed Yozer? How he fell in battle?" Hanar asked.

"The rumors are as plentiful as they are unlikely," Greil said. "But what's known for sure is that he was defeated in this area."

"I see," Hanar said. "Very interesting. You would be surprised to learn tha—"

Pent punched Hanar in the shoulder, silencing him mid-sentence. "Lots of interesting things all around. I'm Pent, by the way. And this is Hanar. Sorry for roughing you up. You got the drop on me though, and I wasn't gonna wait to ask questions."

"It's fine," Aisa said. "If we can sit in peace for a moment, then no one among us will hold a grudge."

"It's a chance encounter for both sides," Hanar said. "We've been sent from our village in search of several missing children. Would you have any news on their whereabouts?"

The three would-be-robbers looked at each other. "Ill tidings," Aisa muttered. "Even the youths are vanishing from the world. Dark days." They all lowered their heads and there was a moment of silence.

"We hail from a village to the north," Walter said into the quiet night. Though his voice was still thick, he seemed to have stopped the flow of blood. "Much farther north, there are not so many trees and not so much sun. I miss the weather; it's swelteringly hot here—I can't stand it."

"The ruins of the Tower of Eccue are a short trip away from our home," Greil said. "But the tower fell long before any of us were born. Travelers would come through on occasion to comb through the rubble. One of them spoke of a library or some such." He shook his head. "Can't read myself—was never very interested in the problems of the past."

"You're rambling, Greil," Aisa said softly. "They don't care to hear your feelings on books."

Greil glanced at her and nodded. "There's a river that runs through the middle of our town, all the way to the north end of the world. Brighton is the name, great place to live." Greil trembled as he spoke and shifted closer to the fire. Pent threw another log on to stoke the flames. "At least it was."

"What about the kids in your village? Did they vanish too?" Pent asked.

"This matter with the children must be new, if you're searching for answers only now. Brighton was reduced to ashes months ago," Aisa said bitterly. "Pirates. With large paddle boats. They've claimed all the waters they can reach."

"Pirates? That's great. We have pirates to deal with now?" Pent turned to Hanar. "What is wrong with this world? You can't blame me for pirates now. You can't."

The three strangers exchanged a curious look. "You speak oddly," Aisa continued, "and look odd as well. But I will hold my tongue to questions, as you have shown us mercy."

"Not many places with mercy these days," Greil said. He raised his hands towards the fire. "Perhaps north is the answer. Have you heard of the Umbro Mountains? The Vampire Lords once ruled it. After they died out, the people of the coasts near the mountains thrived. I've never been that far north myself. If you run along the river far enough, you'll reach their great city, Vinalhaven. They have plentiful resources and great need for ships."

"Vinalhaven," Pent repeated. "That's where Riven was from, right?" Hanar nodded an affirmation. "I wonder if he snuck back there, after... well, after our disagreement."

Aisa nodded absentmindedly. "For years the mountains were inaccessible by the coast or rivers due to the hemites—dread creatures, controlled by dark magic, with horrible powers. The hemites seem to have followed Yozer from this world, which has allowed for travel on the rivers."

"That doesn't make sense. So what, some weird sea creature is gone. How does that make pirates appear?" Pent asked.

"There have always been men of crude ambitions in the north, stymied by the rule of Yozer," Aisa answered. "Perhaps you live too far to have heard, but when Yozer passed, his vassal in the north immediately sprang to action—a fierce man who goes by the epitaph Brownbeard. He gathered a crew, enslaving many of the villagers on the outskirts of Vinalhaven. He has waged a bitter battle with many rivals in the world of piracy. There's blood in the water to the north, and everyone wants to take their place on the throne."

"And it's the little people who suffer!" Walter blurted out. "Pirates, pah! Call 'em what you want, they're nothing but thieves and murderers! Brownbeard, Golding, J'ilardus, and even Hesh." He laughed bitterly, holding his nose, and wincing in pain. "The nerve of the last, to name himself after the hero of old. He doesn't have a drop of noble blood in him."

Pent tried to take it all in. *Pirates now? I didn't sign up for all this.* His actions had consequences that he had never even considered. He pitied the travelers for the pain they had experienced. "What kind of name is J'ilardus, anyway? How do you even spell that?"

"He's a dangerous man, they all are," Aisa said. "Wherever the water flows wide enough for their ships to pass through, Brownbeard and J'ilardus are names to fear. The pirates have sacked each town in turn, taking the people as slaves, and stealing anything of value they can hold onto." Aisa hung her head, breaking eye contact with Pent. "Brighton burned before our eyes. I was forced to leave my things behind, hopefully hidden from their plundering—but nothing that would help us in our plight. We've been on the run ever since."

"The pirates aren't the only thing to deal with," Greil said. "We've traveled far enough to avoid them, but there are dangers everywhere you turn. And if you've been around, I'm sure you've seen it for yourself. Just yesterday a thief snuck into our camp, making off with most of our food and drink."

"That's why I was so jumpy," Walter said, remorsefully. "I thought when we saw you, perhaps justice was at hand. A chance to recover our food." He shook his head. "I was wrong to think that. We just want to be left alone. There needs to be safe spaces in this new world, there just has to be."

Pent and Hanar shot a glance at each other. Pent shimmied next to Hanar and whispered into his ear. "What do you think, do you trust these guys?"

"It's hard to trust anyone I've never met. But if I followed that to its end, then you and I would not be friends."

Pent nodded. "Yeah, I feel you. But I'm not asking if you trust me, I'm asking if you trust them." He glanced at the group. They had fallen into a sullen silence. "I think we should point them to Somerville. They would be safe there. Well, safer anyway."

"But will our people be safe, Pent?" Hanar asked. "Would you put their lives on the line for three travelers you don't know?"

"I trust Lyle's judgment at least. And with her and Ellie, and Faldo... I think they'll be able to see through these dudes if they're not being sincere." Pent turned to the newcomers. "We know where you should go, if you all need a place to rest your heads."

Hanar nodded hesitantly. "There's a path, not far from here. It's been neglected as of late, but if there's a tracker among you, you should uncover it. Follow it, head south and then east. You should find the village of Somerville, if you keep along that route."

"Greil is a competent tracker; we can make our way," Aisa said. "It's a blessing to have found you after all. Thank you for your great kindness."

"You won't consider it great, if we come home and find that you've made trouble," Pent said. "You hear me? I'm just trying to do my part to fix all this mess that I... well, to fix this mess with the dark days and all that. But if you hurt our loved ones, we'll hunt you down."

Aisa, Walter, and Greil looked nervously at each other, but agreed wholeheartedly. It was pitch black outside and not well suited for travel, so they all decided to camp together for the night. They huddled around the fire, basking in the warmth. Pent and Hanar took turns keeping watch, with one eye open to the newcomers.

When the sun rose over the horizon, nearly everyone in the camp was up, already breaking down the site and preparing for travel. Pent woke last. He had strained his neck while sleeping and stretched out the soreness as he rose.

"Heavy sleeper, that one is," Walter said. Pent glanced at him and winced to see his swollen nose and the bruises forming under his eyes. "Started to think you wouldn't wake up."

Hanar laughed. "Careful, he can be sensitive about that." He rummaged through his pack and handed out some bits of jerky to the group. "Break fast with us, before we're on our way."

They ate around the ashes of the fire. Walter was virtually in tears from the offering of food. Hanar gave him a bit more to eat, with the promise of more food at Somerville.

"I've known it my whole life," Hanar said. "This is a new ordeal for me. I've never traveled this far from the village before."

"Hard to imagine, given your light steps," Greil said. He tugged at his jerky with his teeth. "I would have thought you were born in the woods considering how you stalked us silently through that brush."

"Well, that's only a step away from being true. But it's the woods of Somerville I'm most familiar with." He looked around. "The farther we go west, the more spread out the trees seem to be. I wonder what awaits us at Gilbrand Castle."

"Well, hopefully we can veer wide of the place," Pent said. "That punk—all of this is his fault if you think about it."

Greil raised an eyebrow. "We have heard word of a deserted castle to the west."

"Deserted?" Pent asked.

Aisa turned away from Walter and joined their conversation, while Hanar seemed to grow distracted and stared off into the trees. "Rumors travel farther along the river," she said. "There are bound to be many deserted homes across all of Cinraia now."

"It would make things easier for us if it was deserted—more of a straight shot to the west, instead of having to go around." Pent studied Hanar, who had stood up and was scanning the forest. "What's going on, man?"

"Hm? Oh, nothing. I thought I heard a rustling, but it must be my imagination."

"I trust your imagination."

"And I yours. But we can't jump at shadows forever. We must press on." Hanar began to pack up his stuff. Pent took the cue to join him, and the others rose to their feet.

"So just on south a bit, and then east," Greil said as he made his way through the bushes.

"Indeed. Just try to mind the massive footsteps of my friend here. They should give you a good map to our home." Hanar grinned at Pent, who shrugged in response.

"I'm not gonna apologize for the size of my feet." He patted Walter on the shoulder. "Again, sorry about your nose. When you get to Somerville, mention Pent and Hanar. They should treat you kindly."

"We're greatly obliged. Best of luck and safety on your travels ahead," Walter said.

With that, the two groups departed. Pent walked deliberately behind Hanar, letting him take the lead. His friend was more pensive than usual.

"What's going on man? You're so quiet."

"You can call it my imagination again. I fear we're not alone in our travels."

CHAPTER SIXTEEN

Catherine watched the group closely as they shared jerky to break their fast. Her stomach rumbled at the sight of food. From her perch in the tree, she had a good view of the clearing. A group of four men and a woman—a dangerous crowd. *A pack of adults is always going to be dangerous to someone like me.*

She had skulked close to their camp during the night, hoping that she could take them unaware and grab some of their food. Three of them she had seen before; they didn't have any more food to spare. But the other two were new. *New travelers, new meals.* Her stomach growled as she stalked her prey, but the one with the thick beard was too alert. He kept glancing into the forest, and she was sure he had spotted her at least twice. *Must have thought I was just some small animal. He's not that far from the truth.*

The night had passed without her having a chance to eat. The travelers had staggered their sleeping, so she was never able to sneak in without risking being caught. She had slept, or tried to sleep, on the tree branch, hungry, cold, and frustrated.

She almost fell from her perch when she heard her father's name mentioned. The bearded man had said it: "I wonder what awaits us at Gilbrand Castle."

She leaned over and listened more closely. The huge man had spoken of her father with a disrespectful tone. She studied his features. *He's a giant, and with dark skin.* It made her think of that day six months ago, when she had lost her father. *The day my life changed forever.*

The sorcerer Yozer had displayed her father's corpse for all to see, and told them that a huge, dark man had slain her father and reduced him to that terrible form. She squinted at the man now. He wore thick plate armor with broad pauldrons and carried an ornate sword. *Some kind of foreign knight? Could it be the same person?* She began to grind her teeth as she considered the man. "Is he the one who murdered my father?" she whispered to herself.

She clasped her hands to her mouth. The red-bearded man stood up and began to scan the tops of the trees. *That was foolish!* She needed to be more careful. A false step with these people could spell the end of her. *And before I've found my brother. I can't let that happen.*

Catherine attempted to focus on her brother and let her mind wander from the strangers and their encampment. But when they all rose and spoke of separating, she felt her anger boiling over. "When you get to Somerville, mention Pent and Hanar," the huge man said. Catherine's eyes widened. *That name. That's the same name!*

She could never forget that name, not as long as she lived. *That beast, that murderer!* She climbed down from her tree slowly and followed them like a predator stalking its prey. It wasn't a difficult thing to do; the killer named Pent had bigger feet than any man or beast she had ever seen. She glared at him through the brush, wondering if she should attack them now. *Not a chance I walk away alive, not in the woods.* The bearded man was too fast and alert; he would catch her for sure. *But I could end Pent. In a flash, I could finish him off, my blade through his neck.* And then there would be peace.

She followed them as they marched on through the day. The sun ran across the sky, and she realized where they were leading her. She studied them as they left the forest and approached the entrance of her home. They stopped at the broken gates and stared. She felt her heart trembling. *You murder my father, and now you've come to disgrace his noble home. My home.* She clutched the hilt of her sword so hard that her nails pierced the flesh of her palm, drawing blood. She held the wound to her mouth, sucking at the cut.

She came to a decision then. She was fine with death, but she would have her revenge. "I'll make sure you pay for what you've done." In this harsh world that was lacking in justice, she would deal it out. *Justice for you, father. At least this I can manage to do.*

She watched as they walked through the castle gates, and she grinned. *Thankfully I know of another way in.*

CHAPTER SEVENTEEN

"This place is giving me the creeps." Pent glanced up at the castle walls, which were devoid of any movement at all. *No guards, no lookouts.* Aisa and her group had shared the rumor that the castle was deserted, but they still walked carefully. *Feels like I've got eyes glued to the back of my neck.*

Only when they saw the front of the gate did they realize the truth of the rumors. The castle had seen better days. The walls looked as if they had been smashed and beaten with large stones. One door of the gate, which lay on the ground at the front of the castle, had a massive hole smashed through it. The hinges had been sheared free from the walls by force.

The inside of the castle wasn't much better. The smell of rotting food and death assailed them as they walked into the courtyard. *This is really killing the fairy tale vibe for me.* It looked the part of some fantasy castle, with its darkened stone walls with towers at each corner, one of which cast a shadow over an old well with a crank. To the right of the entrance was a wooden stage; it seemed oddly out of place to Pent. *I can't imagine Gilbrand putting on puppet shows. More likely it's where he had people executed.*

Pent glimpsed a pole protruding from one of the towers. What remained of a piece of cloth was fluttering in the wind. *I guess that's where Gilbrand's flag once was.* Pent remembered the flag that hung from the old Chief's home; it was white with a black and yellow cross. They had ripped it down and burned it after Gilbrand had threatened to burn their village to the ground.

"Could still be a trap, you know," Pent said. Hanar was pacing in a wide arc, regarding the features of the castle.

"I don't think so. It doesn't seem like this castle has been lived in for some time." Hanar walked over to the raised wooden planks on the north side of the courtyard. "It's a bit of a surprise. The castle is in bad shape, but it's still four mostly intact stone walls. Someone would take it over if it was abandoned."

"Maybe they didn't want to deal with the smell. It's like a kennel." Pent held his nose at the odor. It was disgusting, and he had unfortunately realized the source. "There's dead people in those towers, gotta be." He never thought he would become so familiar with the smell of dead people.

Hanar nodded, gesturing towards the towers that adorned the corners of the castle walls. "Whatever happened to these people, it was violent and sudden. Dark days indeed." He coughed into his hand. "We should explore the grounds a bit. Perhaps we can find somewhere this horrible smell hasn't reached."

"You're not suggesting we stay here for the night," Pent said incredulously. "This place is horrible. I'll be vomiting all night if we stay here."

"You'll become used to the smell. We have four stone walls around us. I feel safer here than I do surrounded by woods on all sides."

"Never thought I'd hear that from Mr. Outdoors."

Hanar grunted. "It's only for your benefit my friend. I assumed you would prefer the bed of a nobleman to a pile of dirt clumps and rocks."

Pent scratched the back of his neck. An actual bed sounded really nice. *Six months in, and I'm not used to this lifestyle yet.* "If we can do something about the smell, then maybe I'll consider it." He glanced up to the sky. The sun was beginning to set. "It is getting late though, and we've just about reached the western tip of Faldo's map. We don't know how much longer we'll have to travel."

Hanar nodded. He frowned at the map in his hands. "And we don't know exactly where to go either. Our path branches here. South perhaps, down the hills, in hopes of finding one of those towns Faldo mentioned. But west, and with hope to spot a trail, is our best chance for finding the children."

"And the Scribes," Pent added.

"Yes. And either way, I'd rather travel with a full day's worth of light to work with."

Hanar sat down on the edge of the wooden stage. Pent had just turned to look at one of the towers across from them when he heard a pained yelp.

He drew his sword as he spun toward the sound, just in time to deflect a blow aimed at his face. He cocked his arm back, preparing to drive the blade down on his attacker, but was forced to check the blow when he saw who was trying to kill him. *What the…?*

A small, dirty child—a girl, he thought, though it was hard to tell under all that filth—who couldn't have been older than thirteen, bared her teeth at him like a cornered dog. She was panting and brandishing a thin sword. Blood dripped down its edge.

"Hey, easy there. We're not here to hurt you," Pent said softly. "If you want food, we can help you out, little girl." He glanced at Hanar, who was cradling his arm, trying to staunch the heavy flow of blood.

"He won't be helping you, not with his bowstring snapped in two," the girl barked at him. She lunged forward, stabbing at Pent's midsection. He dodged to the left twice, and then brought his sword down on her, stopping short of her head.

"Calm down! Calm down!" he yelled at her. *Jesus, I almost killed a little girl.* "I don't want to hurt you; we don't want to hurt you!"

She ignored his words and continued to stab. Her strikes were wild, grazing against Pent's blade and then shifting mid-swing, aiming at his shins instead. She thrust up and then slashed down as quickly as Pent could blink. *She's so fast.*

"Just die! You murdering bastard!" She dove at him recklessly, cutting at the side of his leg. He didn't fully manage to step out of the way of the blow and felt the warmth of fresh blood trickling into his boot.

Pent barely kept pace with her, backing up and blocking her slashes, always moving. He had occupied her long enough for Hanar to circle around. His arm still dripping with blood, he clenched his short sword and joined the fray.

She looked frantically between the two of them, panting heavily now, with sweat muddying the grime on her face. She shifted from one to the other, spinning in place like a top, then started backing up until she was pressed against the wooden stage.

"All right, how about we just relax, drop our swords, and talk about all of this?" Pent asked. Hanar had taken up a place by his side. His wounded arm was drooping.

The girl let out a desperate cry and sprinted forward. She charged into Pent, with her sword out like a lance. He dipped into a crouch and tanked the blow. Her sword scratched the side of his armor and slid off harmlessly. She cursed, and then dashed out of the front gate of the castle.

Pent trembled as he stared after her, waiting for some time before sheathing his sword. "What the hell was that?" He glanced at Hanar. The woodsman was covering the wound with his other hand. When he pulled it away, it was red and damp with blood. "Damn, you gonna be okay? That doesn't look too hot."

"Yes, I shall be fine. A glancing blow." He sat on the wooden platform, grimacing as he tightened a bandage around his arm. "Just... a glancing blow," he repeated. "I'm more concerned for my bow. I'll need to restring it." Hanar palmed the bow and frowned. "That little girl was able to wound me and snap this line before turning her attention to you. She fought with great determination and skill. That was no simple thief."

"How did she get the drop on you? Was she hiding behind that stage thing the whole time?" Pent walked over to the elevated wood planks and lifted them up. There was a small hole behind them, just big enough for a child to fit through, that led into the wall and out of the castle. "A secret passage. She knew this place."

Hanar nodded. "That seems likely." He sucked air in through his teeth, and then cursed under his breath. "I need to act as you do more often—trust my gut. I was certain there were eyes tracking us."

"But a little girl? You were just talking about jumping at shadows. We can't be afraid of everything out here."

"A little girl with a sword," Hanar replied. "More dangerous by the virtue of her intelligence than any wild beast we've seen. And perhaps just as vicious."

Pent rubbed his fingers along the cut on his leg, confirming Hanar's observation. The fingers came back dyed in red, but the wound had already stopped flowing. *What do they call it? Déjà vu?* He pictured his fight with Gilbrand. He had taken a cut along his shoulder. On the walk to Gordenthorpe's hut, the wound had already been scabbing up.

"What is the matter my friend?" Hanar said.

"It's weird. I don't know how to say this. It's like... wounds heal quicker here." He pointed to the cut. "This is already sealing up. In my world you would need some disinfectant, a bandage, maybe stitches." He looked at Hanar. The man was clearly confused by the notion. "I guess that's another two-worlder thing I'm gonna have to get used to."

"I'm more concerned about that girl. Maybe you were right to fear staying here for the night."

"I mean, I didn't want to stay because of the smell. I'm used to it by now. All these distractions helped." He thought about the look of the girl; something was off about her. "She knew this place. She had to, to have figured out that secret passage." He marched towards one of the towers. "But I still think we'd be better served resting our heads here. Alternate watches, we should be all right."

"Even knowing that she's familiar with this castle in ways that we are not?"

"Better this," he gestured to the stone walls around them, "than being surrounded by forest in every direction. At least we have an idea of what we're up against now."

They made their way to one of the guard towers across from the castle entrance. The tower overlooked the south and western parts of the forest. Pent gazed out over the landscape and admired the beauty. In the tower they found a small room with two child sized beds. The room, like most of the others they had found, was a complete wreck. Clothing lay in tatters, candles had been knocked over, and small sculptures were shattered in each room.

Anything that was too heavy to take had been destroyed. Broken chunks of stone littered the walkways, creating an obstacle course of wreckage everywhere they went. To make matters worse, there were human remains left to rot throughout the castle halls. Bodies had been dropped seemingly at random.

"These wounds were not dealt by the claws beasts and monsters," Hanar said, gesturing to the cuts and gashes on the bodies. "This is the work of men, with swords and axes."

"That group we just met, they talked about pirates. But there's no river close to the castle." Pent said.

Hanar scratched at his beard. "Vandals and thieves don't need a ship to steal. Who knows what caused this? We may never learn the truth, and it might be that it isn't our concern."

The tower they had settled on was devoid of corpses, which was a great relief. There was a room that looked to be a library, but the books had been thrown into a pile and burned. Pent frowned as he thumbed through one of the charred tomes. "Books of poetry, stories for kids. Why would you burn all this?" He had considered combing through the books for anything he could use but most of them crumbled at a touch. *Not finding a way back to my world here, that's for sure.*

They had chosen to spend the night in the children's room. It hadn't been spared from the ransacking, but the beds at least were unspoiled, unlike those in other rooms, which had been cut open and rifled through. They pushed the two beds together, as one alone was too small for an adult to rest in. Pent lit the candles that had been left on top of the destroyed wooden dresser.

"Alternating watches then, that's how we do it," Pent said. "Don't want anyone to come in here and slit my throat."

"Yes," Hanar said as he inspected the chambers. "Yes, I shall take the first watch, if you're not up for it." He rested his hand on the wounded arm, massaging it gently.

"I'm up for it, man. You should lie down. Give that arm of yours a rest."

Hanar nodded his appreciation and sat down on the bed.

Pent reached over to Hanar's pack and withdrew Faldo's map. "This isn't much help at this point. You have any idea about how you're going to pick up a trail to the west?"

"Hm? We'll need—some time—to pick it up," Hanar answered.

"That was the most half-assed answer I've ever gotten from you."

"So much death," Hanar said suddenly. "You couldn't have known what would happen, Pent."

"What are you talking about?" Pent asked. But he was already certain what Hanar was thinking. *I've been thinking it since the moment we stepped in here.* Whatever walls had held the world up before had crumbled when Yozer died. *When I killed him.*

Everywhere Pent looked he saw constant reminders of the death and darkness that had swept over the world: missing children, plucked away by elven monsters; travelers jumping at shadows in fear; little girls turned to banditry; and now, a castle that was drenched in blood and death. *Not just any castle. Gilbrand's castle.*

"I beat Gilbrand and sent him packing, and then he went off

somewhere. I guess to meet with Yozer? Because Yozer admitted to killing him." Pent kicked away a chair leg, watching it clatter across the room. "He wasn't here to protect his people. They all got killed because he wasn't here to protect them—because people were taking advantage of Yozer being gone—because of me."

"These deaths aren't on you, Pent." Hanar was attempting to restring his bow. His face had gone pale, and he was shivering slightly. He was clearly not ready for sleep. "You can't blame yourself for every bad thing that happens."

"I had this screwed up dream earlier. My friend James, do you remember me telling you about him? He got shot for no reason, straight out of high school?"

Hanar nodded slowly. "What was your dream about?"

Killer. Pent recalled the word James had used. "It doesn't really matter. But man, you've put arrows into people. You've watched them fall down and stop moving. How do you live with that? I never killed people in my world. It's horrible, man. The screaming, the blood..." He shook his head. "It's not like the movies."

"It is a horror," Hanar said, his bow forgotten in his hands. "But I am not a murderer, and neither are you. We've fought people who have meant to do us harm, to kill us."

"Self-defense, sure," Pent said skeptically. "Lyle told me once that I don't really think about the consequences of my actions. Well, I'm trying to do a better job of it." He began to sharpen his sword. It didn't need it, but it gave him something to do. "I'm not brooding. People die every day, there's not much you can do to change that. I don't know, man." He flung the sword to the ground, stood up, and began to pace the room. "What the hell am I even supposed to think about all this? Cleaning blood off my damn sword—and all of this chaos—is it my fault? Is it not? That little girl sure seemed to think something was my fault. Did you hear what she called me? Murderer! Damn it, man, all I wanted to do was stop a fairy tale knight from killing your sister!"

Hanar stared at Pent. After several long moments, he burst out laughing. Pent frowned, and then started chuckling himself. "What the hell is so funny?" he wheezed.

"My friend, you have two world's worth of questions and problems, but I have no answers! The world is a confusing and scary place, and all we can do is live in it. You've tried to do what you believe is right, and that's the best way to live." He waved his hand as if to swat Pent's words out of the air. "Let's leave our crises of morality for the morning. We've had a long day, with longer still ahead."

Hanar was out like a light within minutes. Pent took the first watch, staring out into the stone hallway and wondering what the next day had in store for them.

CHAPTER EIGHTEEN

As night fell around her, Catherine stared up at the guard tower, straining to hear the voices of her quarry. *I was so close, so close!* she thought, her jaw clenched so tight it hurt.

Now her father's killer had joined the ranks of dozens of other strangers who had intruded on her birthright and her home. *Bastards, all of them. Especially him.*

She found it hard to believe that this man named Pent could have beaten her father in a fight. He was slow and sloppy. *Perhaps father was drunk.* It wouldn't have been the first time, but it was a shame for him to fall in battle to such an inferior swordsman.

She should have been patient. Had she waited until they had gone to sleep, she could have cut their throats in the night and watched as Pent drowned in his own blood.

Slumping down, she fell into the dirt. Catherine rubbed at her tired, moist eyes. She couldn't wait; she didn't have that kind of patience. Seeing the two of them in the courtyard speaking with such a lack of respect—her blood had boiled over. "But I'm no killer," she whimpered.

That was the sum of it. She could do things now that had never been possible for her before: she could rob the innocent of things they needed, she could hurt others with her cold steel, she could hunt animals in the wild. *But I can't murder someone. Not even the man who killed my father.* She sobbed at the thought of it—her father never being avenged. *There's no justice in this world.*

"I guess some people are monsters," she said as she glanced up at the guard tower. "Some of us can't steal away lives so easily."

She rubbed at her eyes again and fresh tears assailed them. *This is stupidity. What am I even doing?* She remembered the guard tower, her and Peter's bedroom. *Peter.* Her mother had spoken to her that day, the day her father died. She had warned of the days ahead and told her to never let her brother out of her sight.

"And here I am again, letting my own desires come before his needs." She swept up her sword and stomped away from the castle, refusing to spare it another glance. *I'll come back someday. Me and Peter both. We'll come back and reclaim our home.* She had ventured north before, but perhaps west was the answer. She would scour the world if she had to, to find a clue to his whereabouts.

As long as he was out there alone, she had work to do. And that was more important than her own vendetta. *But I'll come back for you someday too, Pent.*

CHAPTER NINETEEN

Awake, Pent rose from his bed, cracking his neck and his back as he did.

"Don't think there's any breakfast waiting for us," Pent said. He looked around the room, gathering his bundle of goods together. Hanar sat in a rickety little chair, his back to Pent. His head lolled slightly to the side.

Looks like someone was skirting on their guard duty. He approached Hanar and shook him. "Get up man."

Hanar groaned and straightened slowly in the chair. His face was pale and covered in sweat. "Must be trouble... if you've woken before me."

Pent looked at his friend, a wave of panic washed over him. "I was gonna make a joke about you being lazy on your watch, but you look like hell. What happened?" Pent stepped back as Hanar coughed violently He placed his hand on the woodman's forehead. "You're burning up."

Hanar's breathing was labored. He struggled to rise out of his seat, making it halfway before his legs started to give out. Pent pulled Hanar's arm up over his shoulders and half walked, half dragged him to the bed, where Hanar collapsed with a groan. He shook his head slowly. "It appears... my wounds... were more serious than I thought. Pent... I don't know if I can continue."

"No, not a chance. Not on my watch." *Didn't people used to die because of minor injuries and diseases?* Pent was never the best at history class, but he remembered that much at least. *And I'm not a doctor.* "Ellie. We need Ellie, man. We need to go back to Somerville. But how the hell am I even supposed to get you back there?"

Hanar raised his hand slowly, pointing a single finger at his pack. "Th-the map..."

Pent rushed to the pack, turning it over and spilling the contents out onto the floor. He picked through everything until he found it. "All right, great, it's a map. What good is this supposed to do? We just need to head east to make it back to Somerville."

Hanar laughed harshly. "You... wouldn't make it back without me. Even... with the trail." He shook his head. "We move forward."

"How are we gonna move forward? I can't do that tracking crap you do." Pent shook the map in Hanar's face. "I have no clue where to even go from here. All they said back in the village is 'west.' West isn't gonna do it for me."

"Not west... south..." Hanar said, his labored voice sounding more like a croak.

"South?" Pent looked down at the map. The drawings were crude; Faldo was not much of an artist. But the lay of the land was clear. Somerville to the east, Draemar castle to its north, and Gilbrand Castle to the west. And south of Gilbrand Castle was the village of Seward. "Seward..."

Pent spared another glance at his friend. Hanar had passed out. *He said that the children were likely west of here, so we're not going to find them in Seward.* But they had talked about the village before departing, and Ellie had mentioned that the chief there was supposed to be a doctor, and a doctor was what Hanar needed now.

Pent began stuffing Hanar's things back into his pack, talking to himself as he did. "I dunno if this map is to scale, but it's maybe the same amount of time to that village as it is back to Somerville. And there's not a giant forest in my path." *Less chance of getting ambushed again, but no place to hide either.* He folded the map and put it in his pocket. *Hanar is feverish, but maybe he's got better judgment than I do.* Hanar had wanted him to go south.

"Okay. Okay. Doctor to the south. Let's roll with that. But then what?" Pent wiped the sweat off his brow. *What am I supposed to do, sprint down there and beg someone to come back with me?* He shook his head. *It's either that or sling him over my back and walk him down there.* Pent paced from one side of the room to the other. He was strong, but that would be a tall order. It wouldn't be a comfortable trip, and Pent wasn't sure either of them would make it to Seward.

"I should at least try to make him comfortable now," Pent said. He shot Hanar another worried glance as he left the room.

Pent had spotted the well in the courtyard earlier. He hadn't used it before, but Hanar's head was burning up like a barbeque, and he needed to cool him down. "Get a rag, a bucket—at least I can cool him off some."

Pent dashed down the stairs, tripping on the last step and tumbling to the ground. He cursed violently. *Get a grip man. I can't afford to lose my composure. Not now.* He turned down the stone hallway, happy that he hadn't twisted his ankle in the fall.

It was a simple well. There was a crank on the side to raise and lower the bucket of water. Pent began to turn the crank, winding the rope around an axle and lifting it up out of the well.

He slapped his head when the rope reached the end. The rope was not connected to anything. He looked over the edge of the well; it went down into darkness, but he couldn't tell how far, but he could hear the slow sloshing of water at the bottom. *At least there's definitely water down there.*

He headed back to the hall, searching for a storeroom. They had passed one while searching the castle earlier, he knew. He found it—

the door had been battered down—and scanned the contents of the room. The storage room was nearly empty, only some shovels and farm equipment remaining, as well as a few weapons that no longer seemed functional. Pent rubbed his hand over a rusty sword. *I bet Cenk could make this shine, if he could get his hands on it.* He wondered at how the sword was made initially. *I didn't see a forge like Cenk has. Did he make all this stuff for them, and Gilbrand just stole it with his taxes?*

The object he was looking for was in the far corner. A metal bucket with a handle made for the well. He scooped up the bucket, checking it for holes and finding none.

As he turned to leave the room, his eyes locked on something else he could make use of. "Speaking of Gilbrand's taxes—" A wooden cart with four wheels was turned on its side, propped up against the wall of the room.

When Gilbrand had visited Somerville to collect from the people there, he had brought a cart with him. He would parade the cart, along with his horse, around the town, and when he was done harassing the townspeople, would load the cart up with barrels of Lemen's alcohol. Pent scoffed, looking at the cart and all it represented. *But it could help me get Hanar to Seward.* If he could get Hanar down the stairs and onto the cart, he could move him much farther and faster than he would without it.

He laid down the bucket and pushed against the cart. His muscles strained as he heaved against its weight, but he managed to tip it over. "It's not exactly light, but I think this could work." He put the bucket on the cart and started to drag it out into the hallway. *Damn, what are they called? Rickshaws? This is like some crap out of the Flintstones—can't believe I'm gonna try doing this.*

But abandoning Hanar here was not an option. And he couldn't wait forever for his fever to break. *If it even will.* He could try going back the way he came, all the way to Somerville, but that would be admitting failure and defeat. It would be the same as saying to Lyle and Marall, "Sorry, it was too hard, we couldn't save the kids."

And not only that, but all those trees... Pent felt his neck, remembering the cold steel pressed against it. They had already been ambushed once on the way over, and Hanar was the one to get them through that mess. According to the map, there were fewer trees to the south, only low, rolling hills. *At least, I think those are hills.*

Pent reached the edge of the stairs leading up to the room they had slept in. He let the cart down gently. "Either way, I gotta get Hanar some water, and then get him on the cart." He scratched at the back of his neck. "Maybe I'll have a better idea by then."

Several minutes later, Pent had successfully filled up his bucket and made his way back to their room, where he sat pressing a damp cloth to Hanar's forehead.

Hanar stirred, tossing from side to side. "What... what has happened?"

"Here, drink this." Pent lowered a mug of water to Hanar's lips. "I think you're dehydrated—all that sweat—the body needs water to heal," Pent said. *And medicine, probably.*

Hanar drank deeply. He opened his eyes when the mug had been emptied. "Ah, thank you, my friend. My carelessness has cost us dearly it seems." He stifled a cough. "If I am confined to this bed, I don't see how our journey to find the children can continue."

Pent shook his head. "You should think more about yourself, man. That fever is no joke. I need to get you to some kind of doctor. I need your help to save the children, so getting you taken care of is the priority."

"A doctor—" He coughed again, much louder this time. "You mean to go south, to Seward."

"You're the one who suggested it," Pent said. "You don't remember that? It was like, thirty minutes ago, if that." He forced his hand on Hanar's forehead. "You're still in rough shape. Happy to hear you talking though, I thought you'd be out for a while."

Hanar stared absentmindedly into space, his head wobbling back and forth, as if he had not heard what Pent had said. Several moments passed before he seemed to register Pent's words. "You could go back to Somerville. At the very least, you know Ellie will come back with you. This Darson she spoke of, we know nothing of him." He coughed harshly, hacking up phlegm before continuing. "And don't forget of our dealings with Riven."

How could Pent ever forget the man? He had left Somerville high and dry when they needed him most. A self-interested man at best, a traitor at worst. *Looks like he wasn't so interested in that "do no harm" thing that doctors are supposed to be about.* "I'll be honest, that wasn't my first thought. But I'm fresh out of options. You really think I can make it back through those forests by myself?"

"I've seen stranger things. I've seen a man fall from the sky once," Hanar said dryly. He paused and wiped at his own forehead with the wet cloth. "Ah, that was you. But you're likely right. The forests seem treacherous these days, especially without a tracker. Going alone would not be wise." He frowned. "Perhaps that's what happened to Riven?"

"You're still thinking about that punk? I think we've got other stuff to worry about right now. He probably hightailed it back to that fancy city of his."

"But have you ever pondered it, Pent? He never returned to Somerville. I'm sure we would have turned him away, but he never tried. And he did not join with Yozer's army, right?"

"Okay, so we never saw him again. That doesn't mean he's dead. He said he traveled from Vinalhaven, right? How did he make through the first time?"

"It was years ago," Hanar said. "Riven was always a bit of a dandy, not a drop of woodcraft in his blood. He traveled with a caravan. We used to see more of them, but that well dried up. I'm not sure why." His voice faded off as he began to zone out. "Lyle would know more, I'm sure." He mumbled the last, almost as if he was speaking to himself.

Pent sat down on the edge of the bed, running his hands through his hair. He hadn't spent much time considering Riven's fate. He just assumed that Riven had made his way back to Vinalhaven and was out of their hair. *Maybe he did make his way up there. That little girl who ambushed us was by herself, but I guess she was pretty scrappy. Maybe she's working with a larger group of people.* But Hanar knew these forests, and if that was his judgment, it was hard to argue with him.

Pent shook his head. "Look. Whatever happened with him, it doesn't really matter right now. We need to focus on this," Pent gestured around them vaguely, "Getting to these children, and getting you the help you need."

"I fear I cannot walk a step," Hanar said. He lifted his head slowly, to illustrate his point. "I seem to have little strength left."

"I think I've got us covered there. You know those carts Gilbrand used when he was robbing Somerville of its liquor? Well I found one in the storeroom down there. Four wheels on it. I slap some bedding in there—you've got a comfy ride."

"And..." Hanar began, then paused. "I don't understand. There are no beasts of burden in the castle that I can recall. Did you find a horse, or a mule?"

"I'm the mule here, I guess. I'll drag it to Seward. It might be a bit bumpy, but I'll get you there."

"That's madness, Pent," Hanar forced out, through increasingly raspy coughs. His voice began to fade out.

"Maybe. But like I said, I'm fresh out of options." Pent leaned over, scooping Hanar out of the bed as gently as he could. "I'm not gonna leave you here to rot. I've gotta get you to a doctor."

CHAPTER TWENTY

"How's it going back there?" Pent called to Hanar. Getting the woodsman set up in the cart was easy enough. It went just about as well as he planned. He lined the cart with the least moldy hay he could find, then put every blanket in the castle over that. Carrying Hanar down the stairs had been far more difficult, as he had to move his friend without further injuring him. But, all in all, it hadn't taken long for them to get moving.

Hanar mumbled something under his breath. He hadn't spoken much since leaving the castle grounds. Pent couldn't blame him. Although he kept re-soaking the rag to keep the water cool, Hanar was still burning up. *That burst of talkativeness was a one-off, I guess.* Pent kept moving.

He dragged the cart on for an hour, not willing to stop. *We left in the morning, so there's that at least. I've gotta make good time here.* Even after an hour's march, Pent could still see Gilbrand Castle far behind them, a gray crown atop the distant green hill.

The forests Pent had become so accustomed to gave way to grassy, sweeping mounds. The hills were as green as a well-manicured field, but the grass was wild and untamed. In some parts it had grown as high as Pent's shins, and he found himself wading through it slowly. *It's weird. The land just kind of shifted. It was covered in forests, and now there are barely any trees.*

Pent had not been much of a wanderer back in his world. Still, he couldn't recall ever seeing a place where the land transitioned so sharply. A park could be a drastic change, but a park was maintained by people: rangers and wildlife workers. This was abrupt, as if someone had plucked all the trees from this part of the world and decided that hills were better suited here.

He turned, ready to ask Hanar what he thought of the new landscape, but his companion was still sound asleep. "I'm no geologist, so maybe this is just how hills are sometimes. Maybe he'll have a more profound explanation when he wakes up."

Pent grabbed the straps for the cart and hefted them up. He walked slowly, dragging the cart up the hill. *Gonna have to take it slow going down.* It wasn't easy work, and as he marched on, Pent found himself stopping more and more frequently. The straps were meant for a horse, and the cart was heavy enough without Hanar on it. At least he didn't have to haul it by the rough wooden handles like Gilbrand's servants had. *Servants whose corpses were probably among those at the castle,* he thought darkly.

At the top of the third hill, with no end to the rolling green mounds in sight, Pent plopped down on the grass, easing his grip on the straps. His shoulders throbbed and his back ached. He had only made it an hour since his last stop, but he felt spent. "This—might—be the worst idea—I've ever had—in my entire life," he panted to himself. He looked up at the cart and, for an instant, he considered abandoning the man. *If he had been paying more attention back at the castle, we wouldn't be in this mess. This isn't even my fault, so why am I lugging him around like a mule?*

Thirst override his desire to not move, so Pent forced himself up and grabbed a waterskin from the cart. After gorging his thirst, draining more than he should from the skin, he leaned over Hanar's sleeping body and rested his hand on the woodsman's forehead. Guilt burned in him, as hot as the fever that still raged in Hanar's body. *It's not his fault, it's that damn girl.* Pent rewet the cloth from the nearly empty bucket and replaced it on Hanar's forehead. *Dude already saved my ass once on this trip, and now I'm blaming him for getting hurt. What the hell is wrong with me?* He grabbed the straps and moved on.

Sweat ran down Pent's back like a river, soaking through his tunic. He found himself gasping for breath, pushing forward in twenty-minute intervals and resting in between. He had to hold the cart back as he reached the bottom of yet another hill. Once back on flat ground, at the point between two hills, he let go the straps and dropped heavily to the ground. He pushed a finger to his neck, checking his pulse, and marveled at his rapid heart rate.

"Pent," Hanar said from the cart, his voice a weak croak.

Pent nearly yelled out in surprise. He'd gotten so used to silence... "Damn, man, scared the hell out of me."

Hanar lifted his head over the side of the cart slightly, just enough for Pent to see his bushy beard. "The castle is nowhere in sight. How long have you been dragging me along?"

"I don't know. A few hours now." In truth, Pent had no clue how long he had been pulling the cart. It felt like an eternity.

"You look miserable," Hanar said.

Pent laughed. "That's really something, coming from you right now." Pent was sweating and gasping for breath, but Hanar was deathly pale, and his skin was clammy to the touch. "I don't have a mirror on me to show you how ridiculous that sounds."

"I will take your word for it, my friend," Hanar said. "I have been listening to you gasp, as if you were on the brink of death, for some time."

"And you didn't say anything?"

Hanar let out a harsh cough. "I did not know what to say." He paused. "I still don't. You're killing yourself for my sake."

Pent got to his feet and rested his hand on Hanar's shoulder. "I get the feeling you would do the same for me—if your wiry ass could even lift this cart."

"I may not have your muscles, but I am no slouch. I would certainly try." Hanar grimaced and turned away to cough. Pent sucked in his breath when he saw the blood in Hanar's phlegm.

"All right, enough chitchat, let's keep it moving." Pent reached down to grab the straps. *Blood in his mucus... that can't be a good sign.*

"I feel better than I did before, Pent, truly," Hanar said when his coughing fit had subsided. "Do not harm yourself on my behalf."

"Don't worry about me, this is nothing." Pent forced a laugh. "You should have seen some of the stuff my coach put me through in high school. Varsity football is no joke. I could haul this cart in my sleep. Speaking of, you lay down now, get some rest."

Hanar did as he asked. "You have a few hours more of daylight, Pent. When the sun is closer to setting, you should consider sheltering for the night. I am not familiar with this area, and I would not want to see what dangers lurk in these fields after dark." He closed his eyes, muttering, "Thanks," before falling back to sleep.

Pent marched on, pushing himself to a near-reckless pace. He rose over one hill, and then another. A small hut, assembled from straw and light wood, came into view. Excitedly, he rolled the cart to the hut's door, but as he approached, it became clear that the hut was abandoned. He investigated briefly, but it appeared to have been some time since anyone was here, and there was nothing useful to him left behind.

Another hill came and went, and this time he saw three small huts. These too, were abandoned. *They don't look damaged, just like whoever lived here up and left.* The homes were too sparse to be called a village, and Pent was perturbed at what the abandoned huts meant for his chance of finding a doctor. *If I keep going and Seward has also been abandoned, then this whole trip was a waste of time.* He spared a glance at Hanar, not wanting to think about what that meant for his friend. It wasn't clear how long the huts had been vacant. *A lot of cobwebs on them, but not a lot of dust.*

Pent's muscles were worn to the point of tearing. His breaks were longer than his periods pulling the cart now. A five-minute burst of energy, followed by five minutes of labored gasping, then sitting in the grass for as long as his conscience would allow. He stretched his arms and legs with every break, drank several mouthfuls of water, and twisted his back. It wouldn't have been half as bad if the entire route was downhill. The fact that he had to continually overcome mounds of different height wore on his body, and on his mind. *Wasn't there some story I read in high school about this? Some guy, cursed to push a boulder up a mountain for eternity?* He wiped the sweat off his forehead. *Sure feels like an eternity right here.*

The sun was beginning to sink, and with it went Pent's hopes of finding Seward in a day. "If this area wasn't so hilly maybe I could see some semblance of this village." He ground his heel into the grass in frustration. This lack of any sense of scale for their journey was defeating. He had no idea how close to his goal he was. All he had seen to give him any indication of progress were the abandoned huts, scattered across the hilltops like carrion bones. "It might be time to claim one of them. I don't want to chance these slopes at night."

He dragged the cart over the next hill with the last bit of strength he had left. Another two huts awaited in a clearing at the bottom of the hill. Pent pointed to the nearest one. "Sold."

He pushed aside the door, which was made of straw and twine, and scanned the interior of the room. Cobwebs covered the corners of the cylindrical room; a simple bed was across from the entrance. Pent swatted the webs around the bed away, and then went to retrieve Hanar.

He jostled him slightly. Hanar's fever was just as bad as it was when they had begun their journey, and he didn't stir at Pent's probing touch. "Guess there's no point in waking him. May as well let him sleep." Pent lifted him as gently as he could manage, feeling the muscles in his arms near to giving out. He walked him into the hut and laid him down on the bed. "You can take the bed, I'll take the cart, buddy."

He sat on the dirt floor, breathing deeply. *If I can even make it to the cart.* There wasn't anything in the hut with which to occupy his mind. He imagined the people who lived in these small homes were simple, with simple desires. *Not much in the way of food out here. I wonder what they ate.* He felt his stomach rumble as he reached into Hanar's pack, withdrawing some jerky to satisfy his own hunger. *I'm sure Hanar would have a better answer for that, with his outdoors skills.*

He yawned and lay back on the floor, thinking of all the things he should do to prepare for the night ahead. But his head was heavy, and his arms and legs throbbed. Within moments, even his eyelids were too heavy to keep open.

It was not the break of day or the sound of his friend that woke Pent up. Instead, he abruptly jerked up at a repetitive but unfamiliar chittering sound. The sun had fallen, and it was nearly pitch black in the hut. Pent felt a soft, cotton like substance on his legs that broke away as soon as he touched it with his hand.

He reached in his pocket, withdrawing his lighter. The first flick produced a spark. On the second he got a flame.

A thousand gleaming eyes stared at him; it was a spider as big as a bulldog. Pent shrieked and dropped the lighter, and darkness encased him again. He tugged awkwardly at his sword until it slid free of the scabbard, then stabbed wildly into the dark. There was a crunch as his sword struck something solid, but he did not let up his attack, instead swinging wildly, forgetting for a moment the ache of his arms. When his panic subsided, he reached down and felt around for his lighter. Several long, terrifying moments passed as he slapped at the dirt floor in desperation, then he had it, and the flame was again casting dim, flickering light through the room.

The spider was dead. It had been trying to wrap Pent up in its webs. *I woke up at the right time.*

He shot a glance at the bed; Hanar was gone. *Oh god. All the cobwebs—how could I be so stupid?* He darted out of the hut, waving his lighter around. The light it produced barely extended past Pent's hand, but there was still just enough to make out a figure being dragged in the distance. "Hanar!" Pent called as he dashed towards him.

A dozen of the huge spiders had surrounded him and were blocking his path to what could only be Hanar, trapped and encased in a web. Pent swung at the first spider, cutting off three of its legs and killing it swiftly. He turned to the next and drove the sword through its fat torso.

The sword was heavier than a boulder, and his back was as stiff as a board. His legs shook and he went involuntarily to one knee, cursing under his breath. *I spent the better part of a whole day dragging Hanar and that cart. I can't even move anymore.* He roared like a wounded beast as he rose to his feet, swatting at the nearest spider with all his strength.

The rest, however, had darted inside the reach of the long blade, and two of them worked in tandem, rapidly spinning webs around Pent's legs. He attempted to bat them away with his sword, but as he did another spider leaped onto his back and he was knocked off his feet. Before he could recover, the creatures had begun to tie off his arms. "Damn you!" he yelled. *This can't be it. I can't go out like this.* But his struggles were futile; the spiders pinned him down and continued to enclose him within a cocoon of webbing.

He was so fatigued that he imagined seeing a bright light in the distance. All he could think of before he passed out was the light at the end of the tunnel.

CHAPTER TWENTY-ONE

Pent shot up, batting at his chest and legs. "Spiders, oh god, spiders!" Slowly, he realized that his body was free of the webbing that had bound him before he passed out. Sighing, he let himself fall back into bed, his pulse still pounding in his ears. The bed on which he lay was comfortable. *Probably the nicest bed I've been in since I've come to this world. Where am I?*

The room was similar to the hut he had fallen asleep in before the spider attack, but much larger. The entire building was made of straw and thin wooden supports. Unlike the hut, it appeared that someone lived here. Intricately designed sculptures made of glass filled the room; he saw many small creatures and trees, some of which he recognized, although some he didn't. Pent had never seen such delicate work in person before. He tried to get out of bed, but his muscles were stiff to the point of agony.

"You'll need to take it easy, young man." An older man stepped into the room, letting in sunlight as he opened the door. He was a thin man with neatly kept hair which was graying at the edges. His voice was unusually high and made Pent think of a singer in a boys' choir.

He glanced around, noticing his sword and pack propped against the wall to his left. *Wouldn't be smart to let my guard down, even with that goofy voice.* But springing for his sword was gonna be a tough move to pull off. *I could probably take him hand-to-hand if I had to. If I could move...*

The old man backed up a step, perhaps sensing something in Pent's demeanor. He too glanced at the sword on the floor. "Is that the sword of a bandit or an honorable man?"

"I'm no bandit," Pent said. "But the last thing I remember was being tied up by spiders, and now I'm here. You'll understand if I'm a little on edge."

The man crossed the distance in an instant, moving swiftly to join Pent at the bed. He offered his hand to Pent. "Then allow me to relieve you of some concern. My name is Darson, and this is my home."

"Darson?" Pent grabbed his hand and shook twice. "So, this is Seward then?"

Darson nodded. "That's right. One of our villagers heard the sounds of a struggle, not far from here. He went to investigate and found you in the clutches of those dread spiders."

"Found me..." Pent felt a jolt of fear. "What about my friend? I was with someone! Where is my friend?"

Darson raised his hand, palm out. "He is fine. The spiders had him as well, and he was in a dire state. But he has been under my care for the night and should be all right."

Pent sighed in relief. He moved to get out of bed, but Darson gently pushed him down. "I know not where you strangers are from, but I must have you know that I am an esteemed doctor."

"Yeah, I know about that. That's the whole reason we were headed this way. Hanar got hurt really bad, and this was the only place I could think of."

"Then you must know that I am not speaking for my own sake. You need rest, son, if I'm to believe you've been carrying your friend all this way." He shook his head. "He certainly did not move under his own power, considering his feverish condition. You must have been traveling for days."

Pent leaned back down into the bed. *I guess not everything out here is hostile; the villages at least have nice people.* "It was just a day, actually. And I was dragging him in this rolling cart. We ran into trouble at Gilbrand Castle."

"Gilbrand Castle," Darson repeated. "I was under the impression that it was abandoned. I know Lady Marjen has been gone for some time," he said sadly. "Did you live in the castle before it was sacked, Mr....?"

"Pent. Adrian Pent is my name. And no, I'm not from the castle, we were just passing through."

"Two names? Where are you from then, Mr. Adrian Pent?"

"Just Pent, please. And explaining where I'm actually from is just about impossible. But Hanar is from a village to the east called Somerville—and that's where I live too." *I guess I used to live in Somerville in my world too. Yeah, impossible to explain...*

"Somerville. I am not familiar with it, but it has been a long time since I've traveled anywhere. Seward has served my needs well enough. There is a relative safety here. A safety that I hear is becoming more and more uncommon in the world, with the fall of Lord Yozer. If your village is far to the east, you must have encountered many dangers to make your way here."

"There's been a few close calls,"—*like bumbling bandits, murderous preteens, and giant monster-spiders*—"but we have to press on. Our village's children have gone missing, and my friend is an expert tracker. We've been searching for them, looking more and more west for answers." He flexed his arms, feeling the strain of his worn muscles, and wondered how long he would have to be confined to a bed. "What were you saying about safety?"

Darson walked to an end table and grabbed a pitcher that was resting there. He poured the steaming liquid into two glasses and handed one to Pent. "Tea. It should help calm your nerves some. I've noticed you keep straining those huge arms of yours."

"Sorry, I'm not used to feeling so beaten down. And I don't like sitting still either." He lifted the glass to his lips, smelling the aroma of mint. He sipped at it, burning his lips in his eagerness. "Not used to tea."

"It's somewhat medicinal, but also is a pleasure to drink," Darson said. He took a long sip, unfazed by the tea's scalding temperature. "Those dread spiders—looking upon them can be quite a horror. It is not often that one sees a spider able to carry away a man. A traveler once told me a tale of them. He claimed that they are the surviving offspring of the old Scourge, Urgonite, and that years upon years ago, sorcerers came and did battle in those hills, destroying that monster and ridding the world of its evil.

"But those spiders, whatever their origin is, still haunt these hills. I know not why, but they never cross the final row of hills or come this far south. Perhaps they fear the water. Whatever their reason, they serve as a natural barrier for us, to the dangerous elements of the world. Other monsters stay far away, and bandits are dragged off in the night. It is a blessing that you were seized so close to Seward. I can only imagine how many others are taken off in the dark and never seen again."

Pent tried not to think about where he and Hanar would be right now if someone hadn't come to help. "Yeah, that's some blessing. I gotta thank you for saving us, Chief Darson. We would have been done for without you."

"Just Darson, please. I'm not much for titles; they don't serve nobles, and they don't serve me." He took another sip of his tea. "And mine was not the hand that saved you. When you've had more rest, you can speak to the man who rescued you from your dire situation. For now, please finish your tea and take some rest."

CHAPTER TWENTY-TWO

Pent woke up several hours later. There were two grilled fish on the table beside the bed. Realizing how famished he was, Pent grabbed one, ripping it apart with his fingers and eating it piece by piece, then falling into a fit of coughing as he nearly swallowed a bone. *Careful, man. It would be a shame to choke to death after all that.*

After his meal, he tested himself by attempting to rise. His muscles were still tender, but he felt much better. He swung his legs over the edge of the bed and stood up. "Yeah, much better." Pent knew he had worked his body to the brink of exhaustion. By any estimation he had, it should have taken days to feel this good, but already his joints were loosening. *It's kind of like the cuts I got when I fought Gilbrand. I just... heal faster here.* He couldn't think of a better explanation than that. On his second step, he stumbled slightly. *A word of caution from my body to take it slow.* But slow was better than nothing, and he crossed the room to the straw door and pushed it open.

Faldo's map had illustrated that Seward was on a southern coast, but Pent hadn't realized how close it really was. A dozen of the round straw huts dotted the edge of the beach. The sand was soft to the touch and glimmered white in the sunlight. The waves pushed in and out gently. *It's like an east coast beach—none of those giant waves they have in California.*

It dawned on Pent that he hadn't seen the ocean of this world. In reality, he hadn't seen much of the world at all. "I haven't traveled that far, and yet already I've seen rolling hills, forests, and now a beach." It was as if he was in a model version of his real world—*like one of those model train sets or something*—and he found it eerie in a way he couldn't explain. He knew nothing of geology, but the layout of the land didn't make sense to him. "I guess there's nothing I can do but admire the view."

"Do you speak to yourself often, stranger? Or is this because you are in a new land?"

Pent turned in place and found himself face to face with a man as tall as him. *Speaking of California beaches...* The stranger had strong arms, thick legs, and wavy blond hair. He looked like he belonged on a beach more than anyone Pent had ever seen before.

"I guess I do sometimes, especially when I'm getting used to things I've never seen before. My name's Pent," he added, and the two men exchanged a firm handshake. "I thought the handshaking was a Vinalhaven thing. But you and the chief do it too."

The man frowned. "Darson hails from Vinalhaven, that I know. But as for me, well, I am not sure where I am from. My name is Clarence. I'm the one who fought those monsters off you."

"Thanks for that, man, I really owe you." Pent raised an eyebrow, unsure if his ears had failed him. "I'm sorry, did you say Clarence?"

"Yes, Clarence is my name." He patted at his head. "It is one of the few memories I've retained."

"Clarence. Like, Clarence?" Pent couldn't help but laugh. "My whole time here I've heard the craziest ass names that I could never come up with in a million years. Gordenthorpe and Yozer and Pohk and Faldo. I guess Ellie is kind of normal. But Clarence?"

"Are you insulting me?" The man narrowed his eyes. "I only came to give my greetings, but if you'll excuse me, I'll find kinder company to keep." Without waiting for Pent's reply, he stormed off, walking down the beach to the east.

"Ah, damn," Pent muttered. *Yeah, that was pretty rude. But Clarence? This place just keeps getting weirder and weirder.*

Pent made his way from hut to hut, poking his head into each in turn, until he found what he was looking for. Hanar was lying in bed, and Darson was standing over him.

"Hey Doc—or Chief. How is he doing?"

"Darson," the chief corrected. "And you're welcome to ask him yourself." Darson stepped aside, tending to some herbs he had laid out on the side table.

Hanar eased himself up in the bed, looking at Pent from across the room. "My friend, we meet again!"

Pent crossed the distance in an instant, moving faster than he ever had on the football field. He leaned over the bed, gripping Hanar in a tight embrace. "It's damn good to see you awake, Hanar."

"I wouldn't be, not without your efforts. I hope I was not too much of a burden for you. I will try and pull more of my own weight when our journey continues."

Pent rubbed at his shoulder, pressing the sore muscles through his tunic, but grinning, nonetheless. "Nah man, no burden at all. I'm just glad to see you're okay. I gotta be honest, I was kind of nervous there. That fever was no joke."

Hanar looked around the hut. "I have to confess, coming here was a bold decision."

"It was your idea," Pent laughed.

"And you took the advice of a feverish man at his wit's end?" Hanar scratched at his beard. *Same old Hanar.* "In truth, I don't even remember saying this to you. It must have been a desperate gamble for you to take."

"Well, yeah." Pent shrugged defensively. "What the hell else was I supposed to do? I'm in that castle, stranded. I could maybe make my way back, but couldn't be sure, you know? I don't know how to treat wounds. I don't know what kind of herbs you need. I don't know anything about this. You're damn right it was a gamble, but what was I supposed to do? I couldn't just let you rot in that castle."

Hanar smiled. "Don't mistake my words. I am grateful. It was through my own carelessness that I was wounded. And you shepherded me here. Thank you, Pent."

"You saved me in the forest, right? Let's call it even for now."

Darson cleared his throat, breaking up their cheery reunion. "You are welcome to continue your parlay in a moment, but now that I have you both together, I would like to formally introduce you to Seward. And..." He stalled, stumbling to find his words. "And I have a few questions, about your dealings with Gilbrand Castle."

Pent sat down on the bed and crossed his arms. *He's been nothing but kind to us, so I'd like to be as honest as I can. But who knows what his relationship with Gilbrand was?* He tried to wiggle into the subject as subtly as he could. "The castle was deserted when we got there. Was Gilbrand a friend of yours?"

"A friend? No, not exactly," Darson said. "Before Lord Yozer's fall, he controlled this area. He kept the path to the castle safe enough, or at least well-traveled enough to scare the spiders off." Darson shrugged noncommittally. "But he was a terse man, and a drunk. There was nothing noble about Lord Gilbrand. I suspect he met a fate that fit him.

"But his wife, the Lady Marjen—I was an acquaintance of hers. She came from Vinalhaven, the same as I, and she had a certain grace to her. How she came into Gilbrand's company, I'll never be able to guess."

Pent glanced at Hanar. "Well I didn't see a sign of her. Like I said, the place was deserted."

"Until we were attacked, of course," Hanar added.

"I know she was not there," Darson said. "She's dead. She died shortly after Lord Yozer passed. Fell to brigands and bandits, along with the castle and its inhabitants." He spoke bitterly, clicking his tongue in between sentences. "All of these desperate men, thinking they can swing a sword and take control of the world for themselves. Horrible death is wrought when fools lose sight of their place."

"But these fools—" Hanar started cautiously, "If they took the castle, why was it deserted? It looked ransacked, not lived in."

"They took what they wanted, and then marched north," Darson said bitterly. "I heard word that they crossed swords with other bandits up that way and were mostly scattered. In the months that followed... who knows? Some made their way back here and have been wallowing in their own failure since."

"Made their way back?" Pent asked. "They were from here initially?"

"Some, yes. I'll not speak their names, but some were."

"How can you house such men in your village?" Hanar asked. "Murderers and thieves? You seem so kind. Is Seward not the place I take it for?"

"You can take it as you may," Darson said, an edge in his tone. "I did not ask you to prove your virtue before admitting you to my home. I took you in as you were and cared for you both. You could have been killers in your own right. Honestly, I do not know if you are not."

"We're not," Pent assured him. "I've never killed—" He paused, catching himself on the word. *You have killed, Pent. You've killed men, and that's not something you could have said before you came to this world.* "I've never killed anyone who didn't try to kill me first." Pent nodded to himself.

"I take any in, killers and otherwise, even if I disapprove of their lifestyle," Darson said reverently. "Seward is a place to find healing and shelter, not judgment."

"That is of some comfort," Hanar said. "But how do you keep the peace, knowing you've made neighbors of thieves and killers?"

"Well, there are some few that have done ill deeds, that is true. But I may have overstated their presence; most of the villagers of Seward are kind folk, who have lived in these parts for a long time."

Darson gestured around at the straw hut. "There is nothing of consequence to take here, which may be our best defense. I provide aid to those who need, and my wife, she creates the only luxury we have."

"Which is?" Pent asked.

Darson jumped in place. "Surely you have seen them? Her art can be found everywhere you look in Seward!" He waved his arm out, pointing to several small statues in the hut. "The glass!"

Pent had noticed them in each hut he'd visited in his search for Hanar. *One person made all of those things?*

"Beautiful," Hanar said. "I've always held envy for those with skills in the arts."

"She's the treasure of the beach, my pearl in this endless expanse," Darson recited, as if he'd said the words many times before. He spoke more to himself than to the others, seeming to drift away for a moment, almost as if he were in a trance. "Unless pillagers want glass or fish, there's nothing of value to take. And as I said earlier, the spiders certainly help protect us. We've not been threatened by any of the wandering brigands."

"The same can't be said for every other place we've seen," Hanar said. "You are blessed to be here, apparently."

Darson nodded. "I shall go then, and leave you both with a moment of peace." He spared a glance at Pent before turning. "You seem to be on your feet and well enough. Another few days rest should serve you both." He nodded again and abruptly left the hut.

Pent studied the door as he left, waiting a few moments before speaking. "It's a lucky thing we made it here at all. You were knocked out, but you should have seen those spiders. I don't think I'll ever get over that."

"I owe you another favor then. How were you able to fend them off?"

"I wasn't. Have you seen that tall guy with the blond hair? He's the one who saved us."

"Yes. He was not very forthcoming with information. Just that he lived here, and his name. Clarence, I believe. He seemed a capable enough person."

"Clarence! Can you believe that? His name is Clarence. You don't think that's odd?"

Hanar scratched at his beard. "Odd?"

"Yeah. I mean, that name... isn't it, like, different from all the other names here?"

Hanar looked at Pent skeptically. "But all names are different, my friend. I've never met another man named Hanar."

"That isn't what I mean. All you guys have names that I've never heard before. But I've heard the name Clarence before. You don't think that's odd?"

"Well, you're the world traveler, Pent, but if that's an oddity, you're the only one who would notice it. I've never met another man named Pent either, or Clarence, or Faldo, or Cenk." He shook his head. "Sometimes a name is just a name. And names aside, we should handle the matter set in front of us, before we take on more burdens."

Pent stared at the woodsman for a moment, then sighed. "I guess you're right. One mystery at a time. That's how Sherlock Holmes would do it, right?"

"Sher...lock?"

"Sorry, he's a fictional detective from my world. Him and his boy, Watson."

"And are those normal names in your world, Pent?"

"Never mind, man."

Pent and Hanar spent the day recovering from their respective injuries. Before the day was done, they were both walking tall. They had both recovered remarkably well, but Darson had been clear about the danger Hanar was in. The wound had been infected and, without treatment, would have surely killed him. Even now he'd need to be careful to keep the wound clean and change the bandage regularly.

Pent considered asking him about the quick rate of healing he had observed in this world, but that would mean explaining where he had come from to begin with. Despite all the man's kindness and generosity, that seemed like a risk not worth taking to Pent. *He seems a bit torn about all this turmoil since Yozer's death. And that's all still my fault. I let him know one thing, it leads to another...* It seemed safer to keep the man at arm's length.

The two adventurers spent some time wandering through Seward. It did not take long to acquaint themselves with the entire village, which was made up of only a dozen or so simple huts dotted around the sand. Pent saw maybe twenty people, some weaving nets to cast into the water, others cutting fish to prepare for cooking. None of them moved with any kind of urgency.

"This place makes Somerville look like a bustling city," Pent said. "I never thought I'd see a place so sparse."

"Their sparseness seems another line of defense. It is as Darson said: who would attack a village such as this?" Hanar said. "There is nothing of consequence to take." Hanar plucked a fishing pole from a rack, which held several identical poles, and waved it toward Pent. "Just poles and nets and glass." Pent noticed that Hanar seemed to take comfort from the fishing pole, which he leaned on his shoulder as they continued their walk. Although there wasn't a tree in sight, Hanar seemed just as comfortable here as he had at the rivers surrounding Somerville.

They stopped at a grassy incline, a hill that overlooked the village and the beach. Atop the hill was a single hut, and right away Pent was reminded of Cenk's forge in Somerville. A small hole at the top of the hut emitted billowing white fumes, carrying with it the smell of something burning.

Pent pointed to the hut. "That's looking like the place. You sure you don't want to join me?"

Hanar shook his head. "Enough meetings with strangers for me, my friend. I need something familiar before we set out again." He wrapped his hand around the fishing pole. "And perhaps I can grab something from the stream, to help pay off our debt to these kind people." He walked off, past the hut to the narrow stream which fed into the ocean.

Pent watched him leave before approaching the hut. He knocked gently on the side of the wall, fearing that if he put too much effort into it the whole hut would come tumbling down. After a moment, a thin woman appeared from within. Her red hair was matted and frizzy, and when she raised her hand for Pent to take, he noticed the grime and sand in her untended fingernails. Her hand had many calluses, and, despite her thin frame, her grip was strong.

"You're the man my husband treated then?" she asked, sizing Pent up.

"His friend, actually. Pent, pleased to meet you."

"Verra," she said, pushing Pent forward. "And I've spent enough time inside for the day. Come, let us look out into the sea."

It was only a few yards to the edge of the hilltop. From this view, they could see the length of the beach running east to west. A few subtle streams and waterfalls dotted the beach line, leading the inland waterways and rivers into the ocean.

They sat on the sparse grass, both quiet for several minutes. Pent opened his mouth to break the silence a couple times, but Verra's stare was unflinching. She seemed like a statue, staring out into the infinite movement of the sea.

"We're indebted to you and your husband, for your kindness," Pent finally said.

Verra answered with silence.

"I saw some of your glass art, it's really amazing. Never seen anything like it."

More silence.

"Uh. Great weather we're having today. Wish I brought my surfboard."

She glared at him.

"Never mind."

"Do you always speak so frequently, Pent?" She hadn't taken her gaze from him. He suddenly wished she would look back at the water.

"Only when I'm feeling particularly awkward."

She nodded slightly and turned back to the water. "Darson talks when I fill the room with silence as well. Sometimes silence is what we need."

"Sure," Pent said. He wasn't sure what to make of this woman. He came up to the hilltop to thank her and compliment her on her glasswork, but now he wished he had joined Hanar on his fishing outing. "Your art is really beautiful though. I just thought you should know that."

"I already know it," she said, then raised her hand and pointed to the water.

Pent looked out where she was pointing. The waves swept gently in and out from the beach. He saw birds that could have been seagulls flying in a V formation, off in the distance to the west. The warm sun, the wind, the waves—the peace and quiet lay over him like a blanket, and he found it suddenly hard to concentrate.

"Do you see?" she asked.

Pent had closed his eyes, apparently missing what she was pointing at. He looked again. Far off in the distance he could barely glimpse something that seemed impossible. It looked like a snake, but as far as off as it was, it had to be gigantic. He squinted, imagining the creature vanishing like a mirage. But it continued to move through the water, undulating rhythmically before shooting upright, leaping out of the sea. The waves crashed when it plunged back down, and it showed itself no more.

"What in the world was that thing?" Pent asked, now fully awake.

Verra shrugged. "Monsters are not native only to the land. They roam the seas, and it is said that, ages ago, they roamed the skies as well. I make glass, based on what I see."

Pent nodded, realization dawning on him. *I remember seeing fish and sea creatures, but I figured they were normal sized. Not scaled down versions of sea serpents.* "Do they come close? That thing was huge—looked like a friggin' battleship or something."

"There is no purpose for a sea creature, here on the land. I've heard tales of those monsters waging war with humanity, though. Warriors with spears made of glass, fighting sea serpents commanded by skeletal sorcerers." She brushed her hand through her hair. "But those are old tales for children, stories to make them cower in the night."

Pent scoffed. *I don't think Lyle would appreciate her view of storytelling.* "I don't need the stories. That thing was scary enough as it is." He stood up. "I'll be fine if they stay that far away."

She nodded. "Perhaps I'll make something for you, if you ever come to Seward again."

"Hopefully I can make that happen." With a nod, he left her there, sitting in the grass and watching the waves for monsters.

Hanar believed he would find some peace by the small stream—a moment to gather his thoughts for the journey ahead of them. He paused when he saw a haggard man sitting down next to it. The man had already cast a fishing line and was sitting so still he could have been asleep.

"Ho there," Hanar called. "Do you mind some company? It's been some time since I've fished, and I would like to reenter the game, shake the dusts off."

The man turned to Hanar. He had a deep gash on his upper lip, splitting the top of his mouth in two. There were dark rings under his eyes, and he had the look of a man who hadn't been eating or sleeping right. He stared at Hanar before muttering, "What?"

"Erm. Pay me no mind," Hanar said. "Just a phrase I learned from a friend. I don't know if I'm saying it right..." He absentmindedly sat next to the man and began to unravel his line.

The man grunted. "We don't see many travelers here. Violent times and all."

"Indeed," Hanar said. "Only a day ago I was nearly the victim of such violence. Your chief nursed me back to health." He flicked the pole and his line drifted out over the stream, falling in with an inaudible splash. "Hanar," he said by way of introduction.

"Hubard," the man said. "You a fisherman too?"

"Me?" Hanar said. "No, no. Not by trade anyway. I have been known to cast a line—whatever I can do to find food for my people." He scratched at his beard. "It's odd, I have more success doing this than I do hunting or taming animals. Maybe I should reconsider my craft!"

Hubard grunted. "It's stale work if you ask me. Seward people have some nets they cast west of here, and they catch more doing that than you would ever dream of catching with a pole."

Hanar watched the water flowing gently past. *Not a lot of fish in this stream at all.* "If that's the truth, then why are you here with a line?"

"This is the only thing I can do right," Hubard said, shuffling in his spot a little.

Hanar looked around, studying the stream and the land next to it. *I don't see any catches. How long has he been out here?*

They sat in silence for some time, alone with their fishing poles and their thoughts. *That was a close call, back at the castle,* Hanar thought. *It's lucky for me that Pent was able to shoulder that burden. I don't know if I would have been able to do the same.* Not for lack of wanting, of course. Hanar would go to the edge of the world and back for Pent. *But I'm not sure if I could physically carry him...*

These were supposed to be dark times; Hanar had seen plenty of evidence of it already: attacked by monsters in Somerville, ambushed in the castle, nearly devoured by spiders. Before Yozer's fall, there was some turmoil, of course. Gilbrand had not treated them well, or fairly. But Hanar had never heard of spiders that were as tall as your knees before. Monsters were leaving their hidden haunts and traveling back into the world to wreak havoc. *And I should not forget the children, the only reason we entertained this notion of a journey in the first place.* Darson was kind, Somerville's people were kind, but they seemed only drops in the ocean. *Perhaps Yozer really was keeping the peace.* Hanar shook his head, trying to make sense of his thoughts. *But he was a profoundly evil man, from everything I've heard of him. What good is peace if it comes at the price of freedom? But then, is death better than slavery?*

"I used to be a lord, y'know," Hubard said, jostling Hanar from his thoughts. He had pulled his line back and was restringing the hook.

"A lord?" Hanar echoed. "Forgive me sir, but I am unfamiliar with the nobility of these parts."

"Ain't a lord anymore." He baited the hook and cast it out. "No, I went ahead and messed all that up. It was a short-lived reign." He looked at Hanar, then quickly back to the water. "Don't know why I'm telling you this. I guess I haven't had anyone to tell in a while."

"So, you're not from Seward then," Hanar said. He swore he felt a tug on his line, but when he pulled back, there was nothing on the end of the pole.

"No, I am," Hubard said. He tugged on his ponytail. "I been living here since I was a boy; been fishing that long too." He pointed at the cut in his lip. "Have this to show for it, and nothing else. Fishing accident. I caught a hook with my teeth. Lucky I still have a mouth after all that."

"Yes. Lucky," Hanar said. He wasn't sure how lucky the man felt, but it seemed appropriate to humor him.

Hubard cursed under his breath. He raised the pole over his head and threw it into the stream, line and rod together. "What a waste."

"The pole?" Hanar asked. "If you think so you shouldn't have thrown it." *That was a perfectly good fishing pole...*

"No, not the damned pole," Hubbard growled. "Damn the pole and damn all the fish in the ocean and all the fish in every river in this damned place." He wrung his hands as if they could crush the life from all the fish in the world. "I'm supposed to be destined for greater things than this, aren't I?"

Hanar shrugged. The question was clearly not directed to him, but he answered it regardless. "I find I'm learning more and more about destiny as I go on. You have to make your own destiny, my lord. Sometimes you are flung into a desperate situation and need to rise above. And sometimes you can choose to move calmly down the river or fight violently to move up stream." He felt a tug on the line but ignored it. "A friend of mine told me once that life is full of people who do the same thing, day in and day out. You can find contentment in doing this, or you can break free of it and do something else. You have to choose what kind of person you want to be." He scratched at his beard. "I think it was something like that."

Hubard blinked. "Make something of yourself or do the same thing." He stood up abruptly. "You making it to this village alive past those monsters is cause enough. I've had it with being a fisherman. Never again."

"Well, I'm sure we can find you a new fishing pole, my lord," Hanar said.

"I won't have it. The 'lord' or the pole." He scoffed. "I'm done with all this. I'll be traveling north, on to Vinalhaven. I'm sure I can make something of myself there. No more convincing farmers to turn away from their crops—that kind of person is like you described. No ambition and stuck in their day to day life. I can make a real start, in the greatest city in the world."

He began to march off to the north and over the hilltop. "Wait!" Hanar called to him. "What of your friends in Seward, don't you wish to say goodbye before you leave?"

Hubard spit on the ground. "Damn this place and all of them. I'll never return." He continued walking without looking back.

"What a strange man," Hanar muttered. He returned to his line and fished in peace.

Pent stood at the edge of Seward, his back towards the hills that protected the village on the beach. He had his pack filled with dried fish, his sword in his scabbard, cleaned and sharpened, and his friend flanking him, standing upright as if he had never caught fever at all.

"So then, you've had your fill of Seward?" Darson said. He had a vacant look on his face. "We have so few visitors, it's a shame to lose some who appear good of heart."

"It is as we told you," Hanar said. "We must return to our journey, to find the missing children of our village. Perhaps after we have them in hand, we can break bread again."

"Of course," Darson said. "Seward did not have any children to lose. I hope you find answers in your journey."

Pent nodded. He sized up Darson, his eyes lingering on the man's graying hair. "You're wasted out here." The chief looked at him in confusion. "I don't mean any disrespect. If you want to live out in the middle of nowhere, hey, that's your call. But you could do much better, help a lot more people, if you came back home with us."

Darson coughed into his hand. "We're safe as is, and Verra has a world of sand to turn into her glass creations here. Isn't that enough?"

Pent shrugged. "Like I said, your call. I just know someone back home who would love to meet you..." Pent trailed off, watching the large man with the blond, wavy hair named Clarence approach them. *Clarence, I still can't get over that.* He glared at Pent for a moment.

"I'm willing to escort you past the hills, but no farther. I won't stray far from home." His tone suggested any bartering would be futile.

"Sure. That's good enough for us," Pent said. "I figure we'll head back up to Gilbrand Castle, then head west from there."

Hanar nodded, referencing Faldo's map. "All we have to go by is 'west.' I mean to find some clue of the children's path along the way." His nose was buried in the crumpled piece of paper. "It won't be easy. We still don't have much else to go by."

"There are a few villages to the west," Darson said. "People tend to settle by water, so you'll find more who live along the western coasts, but there is one village of decent size inland. Their chief is a decent man, and he rules with a pleasant demeanor alongside his two children. But it's been some time since I've spoken with him. Raham was his name. His children should be adults grown by now." The old doctor seemed to drift off into thought as he continued speaking: "It is hard to account for all these villages. There are scarcely two dozen who live here, while Vinalhaven has thousands. It's hard to imagine so many people in one place."

Pent stifled a laugh. *Man, if you only knew.*

Hanar frowned. "Only two dozen, and less now that you've lost your man Hubard."

"We will manage well enough without the company of such brutes."

Hanar looked to Pent in bewilderment. "A brute? Wasn't he a lord?" Pent shrugged.

"We should be on our way then," Clarence cut in, "before we lose any more sun. The spiders are no trouble in the daylight, and I'll need light enough to make my way back to Seward."

With that, they embraced Darson, thanking him for all he had done, and followed their escort past the small borders of the tiny beachside village. A shiver ran down Pent's spine when he passed the familiar abandoned huts.

"All of these homes," Hanar said. "Were their inhabitants dragged off in the night?"

Clarence looked at the dilapidated huts; there were three of them here. "For these ones, I'm afraid so. Those monsters will take any unwitting soul they can get hold of. I'm not sure for the homes up ahead though. They very well could have moved on elsewhere."

Pent again pictured himself being dragged off by the spiders; whatever grim fate awaited him would surely have ended in his death. "Hey, just want to thank you again for saving us that night. And I'm sorry about the jokes on your name. It just took me by surprise is all."

Clarence stopped, sizing up Pent for a moment. "That's all right. You've surprised me as well, if I'm being honest. I've only lived on the shore, under Darson's care. He has been hoping to find some cure for my memory, but none has come."

"For how long have you suffered this ailment?" Hanar asked.

Clarence stared vacantly to the south toward Seward. "It's been... round about a year now. Maybe a little less. I washed up on the shore, not far from Seward. The people there brought me in, nursed me back to life. All I have is my name."

"Damn, talk about a fish out of water," Pent said. He glanced from man to man.

"I understand that one," Hanar said, smiling. "At least I think I do."

"Someone who is in a spot they aren't used to," Clarence said. "Considering my loss of memory, any place would be that for me." He was staring at his hands, as if trying to see an invisible thread woven between his fingers.

Pent studied his expression. *What is the deal with this guy? Is he deep in thought or is this the amnesia messing with his head?* He glanced at Hanar. *A mystery for another day, I guess.*

Clarence snapped out of his trance. "This is as far as I should go. You have plenty of daylight ahead of you. By the time the sun falls, you'll be far from the spiders' den. Travel in safety, my strange friends."

"And you as well," Hanar said. They watched him for a moment as he made his way back down the hillside in the direction of Seward.

"All right then," Pent said. "Let's get back on track."

"Indeed, we've lost more time than I would have wished. Let us march on! Surely answers lay to the west."

"Fingers crossed, buddy." Despite the loss of a few days due to their detour, Pent was hopeful about their chances of finding the children. They had come this far and survived, and the world wasn't solely populated with thieves and monsters. *We can do this. We can make this happen.*

CHAPTER TWENTY-THREE

Agme tugged at the reins and smiled as the horse responded instantly. "Very kind of Gilbrand to offer me such a fine steed." He mused over his good fortune, finding the horse right outside of Draemar castle, right before he had handled the matter of the hemites. It was malnourished and afraid, which served Agme well enough. "Much easier to control a beast when it's at its weakest."

The gathering of the hemites had been a simple task. They had been plentiful when Yozer's essence had arrived at the castle and given Agme his commands, but as the weeks passed, the hemites began to vanish. When Agme had approached his master regarding this strange phenomenon, Yozer had only said, "Gone to the sea, or perhaps back to the mountains. KILL PENT." Agme was happy to have an excuse to leave. His Master's demeanor had always been less than cheerful, but now it was exhausting to deal with. If anything, he had become very inconsistent in his new form. One moment he would demand the blood of the Scribes, the next he would demand a conquest against the Crusader. "I must have Pent's body! I must!"

. . .

Neither the blood of the Scribes or the body of a Crusader would be found at Draemar Castle. He was prepared to travel the length and breadth of Cinraia if necessary. *I could spend an eternity in Master Yozer's halls, studying tomes, discovering new secrets. But I don't have an eternity to spend. Not yet...* Master Yozer alone was the key to that elusive magic. *And all I'll need to do is take a few insignificant lives.*

As Agme road through the countryside, the evidence of Master Yozer's absence was all around him. The world needed a firm hand to guide it. The absence of order brought out the worst in men and beasts alike.

A sounder of wild minches had rushed him, threatening to knock him off his horse. He sent lightning and fire hurtling after them but, even after roasting two of them, they would not break away. "They're usually skittish, shying away at the mere sight of man," Agme told his horse, "but now they rush to their death, for nothing."

Treehoppers made the forest route treacherous, so Agme endeavored to cut north of Draemar castle before moving farther to the west. "No point in risking a confrontation with the brutes, eh Horse?"

He watched as men and women, simple villagers, took up arms and crossed swords in the ruins of Eccue tower. "And for what, Horse? There's nothing there but cracked gravestones and fetid corpses. A complete waste of life—people can be so fickle, willing to throw away everything they've been given, and for what, Horse? For nothing."

The further he traveled, the more clearly he saw the chaos. "Creatures of the old times, some of which even I've seen only in books, are leaving their ancient haunts and preying on the foolish and unprepared. Did you know that, Horse? The balance of life has shifted. All of Master Yozer's protections are fading away.

"Even the Scribes are active again; the seal is broken. I can feel their power. I'm sure many have already succumbed to their call. Soon enough, they will become a danger to the world," Agme said, continuing a lecture that he'd been giving for some time now. He'd found the horse, who he named Horse for expediency, to be a very good listener. "Their only remaining home is in a cave, far to the west. And as long as they are active, they will never rest. Master understands well enough. They will try and reclaim their powers. They will haunt the world."

And people would move against them. The Scribes were strong and horrifying, but in their desperation they would act foolishly. "Sometimes you must lie in wait—gather your power before you strike." Agme grinned. "When put into a position of weakness, those who were once strong act brashly."

Where the balance had turned to chaos, and where threatening forces acted in haste, opportunities would present themselves. Agme chuckled to himself as he went. "I've already claimed the hemite, the rest of the components of Master's return will come soon enough." He palmed his dagger, cupping the handle of the blade. "I will work with caution, and take Master's enemies at their weakest."

Only a fool would rush to their death.

CHAPTER TWENTY-FOUR

The journey north to Gilbrand Castle was much less tiresome than the trip south, and after leaving those damaged stone walls, Hanar and Pent turned to the west. It wasn't long before Hanar perked up as he caught sight of a trail. *I knew our labors would bring fruit eventually.*

"Here, and here," he said, pointing. "Signs of disturbed brush. People have traveled this way."

"But is it the kids? Or someone else entirely?" Pent asked. They had traded the grassy hills for forests again, and Pent did not seem happy with the change. *I can't blame him for being skittish. He can't navigate the forests like I can.*

"We shall see, my friend." Hanar pushed on, with Pent close behind.

They spent the next week weaving their way through the woods. On that seventh day, they decided to set up camp around noon in order to take stock of how far they had traveled and plan their next move. Pent glanced at Faldo's map. He had stopped referencing it after the first day. "Not much use to us now. I'm starting to question if there's anything out here. Aside from those weird rabbit-squirrel things. What did you call it again?"

"This is a kana," Hanar said, continuing to skin the creature. Their rations had run out three days ago, and they had only what Hanar could catch and what they had been able to forage to eat. Pent had described the woodland creature as a squirrel with floppy ears and a bunny's tail. *Curious, all of the divisions between us. To me it's always been a kana.*

"Well, at the very least, we can help Faldo finish his map when we return to Somerville."

"Sure. 'Hey Faldo, there's a ton of trees over here,' good luck!" Pent sank his teeth into one of the cooked kana. The nights of alternating watches, the diet of wild plants and kana, no further sign of the children —the last week had seemed to wear him down. He ate in a sullen silence.

Hanar finished skinning the kana and primed it for roasting on the spit. "We'll find them soon enough. I'm sure of it."

"I trust your judgment, buddy," Pent sighed. "I just wish we had more to show for it."

An hour later, they were on the move again. Before long, Hanar's optimism was proven well founded. The trees gave way to a sight for both of their sore eyes: a village in the middle of the forest.

Hanar chuckled to himself. "Up ahead my friend. It seems we have reached a village at last."

"I can see that," Pent said. "But it looks like they've seen better days..."

At a glance, Hanar could see small homes, made mostly of wood, set up in a several neat rows. Some were open to the elements, with wares on display ranging from cured meats to crafted goods. They were all pushed close together, the side of one connected to another, to the point where they all looked to be one giant house. *How many people live here? And who would want to live in such tight quarters?*

The houses very well could have been made in Somerville based on the construction. *Not much difference, one house from another.* But of these, many had been burnt or partially destroyed. Broken beams jutted from the sides of buildings, and roofs had been caved in. *This damage must be recent, why else would they still look this way?*

Men and women stared at them as they entered the village, curious and haggard looks on their faces. A few held chipped and worn weapons, and they all looked fatigued. They had clearly met with hardship. *Somerville seems blessed in this regard. It is like Aisa and her friends said; perhaps we were shielded, being so close to Yozer's castle.*

Hanar waved to the nearest villager, who approached cautiously. "Hello! Do you have accommodations for weary travelers? And what might the name of this village be?"

"This here is Tofac," was all the man would volunteer. He went silent after that, looking down the graveled village road. A group was approaching: an older man in front, with another man and a woman behind him. The younger two were carrying weapons.

Pent puffed out his chest, but Hanar gestured for him to relax. "We're visitors here, let's not spit on their hospitality before they grant it."

"Like all the hospitality you got at Gilbrand's castle, with your arm getting sliced up?" Pent said under his breath. "The old man's face doesn't scream hospitality to me. I'd rather be ready for a fight than not."

The old man stared at Pent as he approached them. He wore a light brown coat of leather, with matching leather boots. His short brown hair was thinning on the top—within a few years he would have nothing left. He stood up straight with his hands behind his back, his high cheekbones and severe brows giving his face an impression of intensity. "It's an odd sight," he said, "seeing a giant Freewalker in these parts. Do you have business in Tofac?"

"Not here, exactly," Pent said. "But we're searching for something we lost, and we've been traveling for days. And I'm not a Freewalker."

He hesitated for a moment. "But... I'm not really sure where I'm from. Uh, it's amnesia. I can't even remember."

Hanar nodded along to Pent's falsehoods. *Some inspiration from the man in Seward, I see.* "We hail from the east," Hanar said. "Far east."

At that, the man smiled. "I figured as much. I've traveled far in my day, and I've met many of those desert people. You don't share their jagged features. And I've never seen one as large, and as... filled out as you." He raised his arm in a greeting. "My name is Raham, and I'm the chief of Tofac." Waving his hand behind him, he introduced the others, "My daughter Gesta, and my son Tanan."

Hanar noted the family resemblance immediately. *Their cheekbones are all raised.* Tanan was the spitting image of his father, but with a full head of hair. His posture was just as stiff as Raham's. The daughter could have passed as another son in less light, her hair only slightly longer than the brother's. Gesta held a knife in her left hand and was picking at her nails with the edge of the blade. She seemed indifferent, while Tanan was staring daggers at Pent. *They could be near the same age as Pent and I.*

Raham continued, "I imagine you're weary from your journey. Let us sit in the shade, in my orchard." They followed him through the town. Hanar tried not to stare at the broken fences, the overturned piles of dirt. They continued through what could only be Tofac's village center; a circle of wooden planks surrounded a tall, narrow rectangular object, which was itself obscured by a leather covering. *I wonder what is hidden under there.*

They walked past the circle, and Raham led them into a home. It was shabby, with a large hole in the side of the wall. *Not even their chief has escaped all of this chaos.*

The comforts of Raham's home caused Hanar to long for his own house in Somerville. Containers made of glass adorned the table, leather hides were strewn about the floor in place of rugs, and, although the furnishings were markedly different from anything to be found in Somerville, the home was lived in. Except for the hole in the wall, it seemed a pleasant place to spend your days.

Pent glanced at the hole for a moment before speaking. "This is a real nice place, very cozy, Chief."

The old man gestured toward a piece of art on the opposite wall. It was a blown glass sculpture, in the shape of a large, snake like creature with legs. "A beautiful work, from a genius in the south," he said, shaking his head. "Please, call me Raham. I apologize for the earlier interrogation. We're a peaceful people, and seeing two men approach with such weapons, it's not a normal occurrence." He led them out the back, making no mention of the damage to his home.

Behind Raham's home was a fenced off orchard of trees set in neat rows. The old man approached the nearest, reached up, and plucked an apple from the lowest hanging branch. He rubbed the apple on his coat, and then tossed it to his daughter. Gesta leaned against the side of the house and began to slice the apple with her knife. "Or it wasn't normal," she said, "before the Master died. The times of peace are all but done."

"Easy now, sister, we don't know what the future will hold," Tanan said. He grabbed a piece of apple from Gesta and bit into it, then gestured to Pent and Hanar. "May we treat you with something? We have fine drink here in Tofac. The envy of all Cinraia."

"I wouldn't mind a drink. Whatever you have would suit me fine," Pent said.

Raham glanced into the tree, looking for another apple to pluck. He rubbed at his temples as if the decision was incredibly taxing to him. "Amnesia then, that is a rough lot in life. It might be difficult to explain where you're from, but I'd like to hear what you do remember. You said you traveled far, and you're from the east?" He chuckled to himself, still looking through the branches for the perfect fruit. "I was a bit of a traveler in my day. But I'm an old man now, and those days are long past."

Pent shot a glance at Hanar and cleared his throat. "Well... It's a painful past to talk about. I remember being orphaned as a child. I've just been wandering since then," Pent said.

Hanar scratched at his beard. *The lie seemed to come easily enough to him. Lies upon lies.* "He was picked up by my village chief, a long time ago. He's been one of us since," Hanar added.

"Orphaned as a child—so when did the amnesia start?" Tanan said, finishing his piece of apple and grabbing for another from Gesta.

Gesta handed him the rest of the apple, and then pushed him away. "Your childhood doesn't concern me. I'm more interested in the village of which you speak," she said.

Hanar juggled the question in his mind. *How much will the truth hurt us here?* "Far to the east, nearby to the coast. It's a small village, of little fame."

Tanan's eyes went wide at that, and he exchanged a glance with Gesta. It was only for a second, but Hanar didn't like what that glance suggested. He saw Pent shuffle in place. *Perhaps Pent noticed as well then.*

The only one who hadn't seemed to react was Raham. Tofac's chief smiled. "Tanan, could you get these men the drink we spoke about? I could use one as well." Tanan went back into the home and returned with three glasses. "Our finest brew," Raham said, gazing pridefully at the glasses. "We've spent a long time perfecting the formula."

Hanar raised the glass to his lips and was startled by the taste. *Alcohol.* It was like Lemen's liquor, but not nearly as strong, and with a sweetness reminiscent of apples. "A great taste."

"Damn, I'll say," Pent said. "Haven't had a beer this good in a long-ass time."

"A long time then?" Raham said. "You must be well traveled indeed. I wasn't aware of another village that even made a drink of this like. It's our greatest trade."

Pent stared at the chief and took another sip of the drink. "I... can't place it. I'm sure I've had something similar in the past. Don't really know where."

Raham nodded. "Hm, amnesia again, I suppose. What did you say the name of your village was?"

"What does that matter?" Hanar said. He glanced through the door of the chief's home, certain that he had seen movement. "Brighton is the name of it, if you must know." Pent shook his head at the mention of Aisa and her friend's village.

Raham glanced at his children. They began to spread out along the orchard, taking up a position on both sides of Pent. Gesta began twirling her dagger with one hand. Tanan had laced his hands behind his back.

"Brighton does lie in the east," Raham said, "you speak true. A fine place, it's been sometime since I've been that far. Like I said, my traveling days are past me now." He leaned upwards, grasping an apple, and ripping it free. "What's the name of your chief? He was a kind man, but I can't seem to remember."

"Why are you asking all these questions?" Hanar said. He did his best to sound insulted but was unsure if it came through. "Are we your guests, or aren't we? I thought the interrogation was over."

"The interrogation is never over, I'm afraid. You're all outsiders, and I trust no men who march in from the wilderness in these times. But I do apologize, I've been rude. Please enjoy your drinks in peace." He stepped forward and passed the apple in his hand to Pent. "I find the taste of these compliments the drink very well."

Pent took a bite from the apple and immediately had to spit it out. "Sorry. It's really tart. I wasn't expecting that. I don't think they're ripe enough yet."

Raham took the apple and looked at it cautiously. "Too sour for you then? Perhaps my judging eyes are failing me in my old age." He cocked his arm back and threw the apple over the top of his house, towards town. "I'll have to find you another."

They sipped their drinks in silence. The chief drained his beer, and then began to twirl the glass in his hand. "Everything was in order, just a few months ago," Raham said. "It's a shame what happened to the Master. Have you heard of these affairs where you're from?" He didn't look to see their response. "It matters not."

"Father held council with the Master himself, in days long ago," Tanan said. His arms were still pressed behind his back. Gesta stood to Hanar's side, acting as Tanan's mirror. She was staring at the back of Pent's head.

Raham laughed to himself. "Indeed. I was once a vassal of the Master. His word brought order and peace to the land. Unsettling company, to say the least." He shivered. "His disciple was as off-putting as he was, and he had an odd name. I suppose all sorcerers do, maybe it's a rite of passage for them. Most often, I did not meet with either man directly. His apprentice sent his shadow minions to speak with us. There are wonders large and small in this world, and I never sought to question that which kept us safe."

At the last word, Gesta and Tanan sprung forward, knives in their hands. As they closed in around Pent and Hanar, a group of men shuffled into the orchard from the inside of the house, weapons in their hands.

Hanar had rested a hand on his sword, while Pent raised his hands in a defeated gesture. "Getting really tired of having knives at my throat," he said. "Let's take it easy here."

"I mean to keep us safe. You're a pack of liars, and I don't trust liars." The chief pointed an accusatory finger towards Hanar. "Brighton's chief was a woman, and the last I'd heard it was burned to the ground. This was months ago, so I think you live farther east than that."

His son grabbed at Hanar's pack and began to rummage through it. He withdrew the map and handed it to Raham. "Somerville is more on the mark, Father."

The chief held the map with a trembling hand, studied it for a moment, and then crumpled it. "You were foolish to come here, killers." Raham gestured to the villagers, who grabbed hold of the two men by their arms. "I don't have much trust in my heart for strangers. I felt sure you were liars from the start, and had my men waiting inside." He reached into the nearest tree and pulled another apple. He took a bite and smiled. "Order can have its benefits. Proper planning is the key to safety, my children."

"I see we've walked into a den of wolves," Hanar mumbled under his breath. "We have done nothing to you! Release us now!" He struggled with the assailants, but it was of no use.

"You're the reason Tofac has fallen into despair," Raham said, his voice rising. "You killed our Master, and you're the reason why our children are missing! Take them away!"

CHAPTER TWENTY-FIVE

"This is some cruel stuff we've gotten into here, buddy." Pent craned his neck to try and see Hanar. It was difficult, as his head was locked in a set of medieval stocks.

Their struggles against the people of Tofac had proven useless. They were disarmed completely and dragged to the center of town. The leather covering was removed, and the wooden stocks were revealed. Pent felt like he was in a play about witch trials, standing there helpless in the village square. They were both cuffed at the wrists and necks, while their knees dug painfully into the ground.

Raham had glowered over them, pointing and gesturing to them and to the growing crowd. "You will stay here as long as we deem fit. And if you do not produce our missing children, you shall meet a fate worse than death."

After their capture, Pent and Hanar had tried to explain that their village had encountered the same problem, and that was the only reason they had come to this part of the world. The chief ignored their explanation, waving it off as another one of their lies.

. . .

So, the two men waited there, counting the minutes to what could only be their damnation. Pent had grown tired of counting the houses in front of his face. *About twenty. It's eighteen really, but I can't tell if there's another one or two beyond that one.* He had grown tired of staring at the faces of the villagers who had come to gawk. *They could be the same people from Somerville, honestly. Their hair seems lighter here though. Maybe it's just my situation, but they seem uglier too. Damn, I miss El. I miss Somerville.*

Pent laughed grimly to himself. "Man, I've got pretty bad luck when it comes to first impressions with village chiefs."

"Ha, that is right! Chief Pohk was very much the same way. I suppose we'll be joining him soon."

"Wherever he is. Damn, the least they could do is scratch my back for me." Pent rattled in place, unable to break out of the stocks. "This itch is killing me."

"If I could help you with that I would, my friend." Hanar turned sullen for a moment. "Oh, damn it all. They should have sent someone with a silver tongue. I'm miserable at selling a lie."

"Don't kick yourself about it, man. You did what you could. This is, what, the third time we've gotten ambushed on this journey?"

Hanar paused, thinking the question over. "Third? Or fourth? The travelers from Brighton, the little girl, the spiders…" He shook in place, rattling the stocks. "And this, of course."

"Oh right, the spiders." Pent shivered in place. "I can't believe I forgot about those." He sighed. "Why can't everyone be like Darson? Only place we've gotten a happy welcome is at Seward."

Pent glanced around. The chief's children were standing guard, staring at them as they spoke. Some of the villagers who hadn't been involved were gaping at them, muttering amongst themselves. "They had our number as soon as we stepped into town."

"And we'll have your heads, if you don't stop talking," Gesta barked. She twirled her dagger in her hand. "Unless you have something else to share about our missing children."

"Nothing you haven't heard already, or are you deaf as well as stupid?" Pent shot back. He glared at the girl, and, despite his pathetic state, she stepped back in surprise. "You're making a mistake, locking us up like this."

Gesta and Tanan looked at each other pensively. "What if he's right?" Tanan asked.

"Father seems sure he's a liar, and a killer besides," Gesta answered. She eyed Pent cautiously.

"Killer, killer. What an evil man!" Pent said. He spat on the ground. "I'm so tired of all this. I didn't kill a single person who didn't deserve it. You want to hear about killing so badly? Yeah, I killed Yozer! My name is Adrian Pent, and I'm the one who killed Yozer!"

"He admits it!" Gesta said.

Hanar laughed loudly. "I only wish I had been there to see the glory of it when it happened! All I've had to satisfy me is tales of the battle. Yozer was a demon and a worker of evil magic. Pent rid the world of its worst on that fateful day."

"I never tried to do a thing but protect people I cared about," Pent went on, working himself into a frenzy. "It wasn't about the world; it was about destroying a monster. He came to Somerville, shooting off lightning and leading an army of dozens of men. Would you stand aside and let a man like that kill you and your family, just because he threw a 'Master' in the front of his name?"

Tanan and Gesta looked at each other. They whispered amongst themselves and then took off.

"Well, at least I got to speak my mind," Pent said. He sighed and hung his head. From beside him he heard Hanar laughing louder than before. "What's so funny?"

"Look over there, off and to the right some," Hanar said. "Or do my eyes deceive me?"

Pent glanced to the right. He focused past a fence, and after a moment realized what Hanar was speaking of. He began to laugh as well. A half dozen cattle were grazing in a fenced-off field, munching happily on the grass, oblivious to the world around them.

"That explains all of the leather. Can't believe I didn't notice them before. At least we know they have milk here."

"Indeed! The first goal has been accomplished. We have secured the milk."

Pent frowned. "It's a shame we're not gonna get a chance to get word back to Lyle. I wonder if they'll even send someone else. I didn't think all this Crusading would end like this."

They sat in the stocks, stomachs growling, knees and backs aching. They passed the time reminiscing about the times they had shared together. They spoke and kept each other occupied, often joking about their imprisonment, but inside Pent mostly felt a bitter resignation regarding their fate. They had failed.

Pent had begun to doze when he was roused from his slumber. There were shouts coming from the entrance to town.

"What's going on? What's all that noise?" Pent asked.

Hanar's eyes strained forward. He was studying their surroundings deliberately. "I'm not sure. There was a yell earlier, and some earth-shattering sounds. It seems the village is doing battle with some kind of beast." He paused for a moment. "It must be very big indeed, to wake you from your slumber."

Pent glared towards the noise. Windows shattered and buildings crumbled in the distance. *Something big is right, but what?*

Then the monster stomped into his line of sight. "Good God almighty!" he yelled. Hanar gasped in surprise and fear.

What is it called? He had seen it in old picture books and cartoon shows: a giant, demonic beast with twisted horns. It stood upright and was twice the size of the biggest man you could imagine. *Like a bull with hands.* "Minotaur," Pent said as realization dawned on him. It was something out of a twisted fantasy. The beast was covered in red fur, but there was a bizarre shimmer surrounding it. He could see every color of the rainbow in the outline of the monster. Pent felt his stomach twist as he stared at the minotaur; he held back bile in his throat.

Men and women alike from the village had assembled and were striking it from all angles with worn swords and arrows. But the wounds carved into its flesh faded nearly as soon as they appeared. A skilled archer put an arrow into the monster's eye, only for it to pop out moments later. The eye was unscathed. The beast tore through the village, ripping doors and roofs from homes, and limbs from the men who got too close.

Tanan ran close by, his face flushed red and dripping wet. Pent couldn't tell if it was from sweat or tears. "Hey! Hey! Let us out!" Pent called. "We can help you fight that thing."

Tanan stared at Pent, seemingly staring through him, as if his mind had been lost to the horror. "It matters not, all is lost besides," he muttered to himself. He walked slowly to the stocks and released them from its locks. "If you speak truly of killing Yozer, prove your valor now."

Pent rose slowly, easing out of the cramped position he'd been forced into. He cracked his knuckles and rubbed at his neck. "I'll give it a try. I'm gonna need my sword though, if you want me to play the matador."

Hanar sprinted to him, holding out some familiar-looking gear. "They had our things displayed as well, like some kind of trophy. Make haste my friend, don your armor."

As fast as he was able, Pent pulled on the chest plate and cinched up the various straps that kept it in place. By the time he was finished, Hanar had buckled on his sword belt and had his short sword drawn. Pent ripped his own sword from the sheath, and together, they stepped toward the monster.

"Ok, starting to regret this decision," Pent said as they approached the beast. From a distance it seemed as big as two men. It had to be over fifteen feet tall. *I've got my sword, Hanar has his stuff. We could just run off right now. What do we really owe these fools anyway? Girl had a knife to my throat less than twenty minutes ago.*

Pent turned around and glanced at the stocks that held them moments before. He groaned. *I promised Lyle and El that I would bring those kids back. And I promised the chief's son I would fight this thing.* Pent couldn't back down, not now. Not after what he said to Tanan, and not after watching Tofac's bravest men and women launch themselves at the creature.

"Kind of wish I still had my gun for this. But if I'm gonna catch heat everywhere I go for destroying Yozer, I guess I need to show them what being a Crusader means." Pent raised his sword; it blazed to life like a beacon as the sun caught its edge. "You got my back, right?"

Hanar had pulled up beside him, an arrow nocked and ready. "Always. Let me see what Yozer's killer can do."

Pent charged forward. The minotaur was turned away from him, occupied with another villager. It grabbed hold of the frightened man with both huge hands and began to squeeze; it was going to crush him like an aluminum can. Pent, taking advantage of the situation, rushed in, and slashed down the length of the Minotaur's leg. From thigh to shin, the beast was torn through.

An agonized howl rent the air as the minotaur dropped its victim. It swiveled in a rage, swiping down with one arm. Pent met its hand in flight and knocked it to the side with his sword. His legs nearly buckled as he was pressed down by the might of the blow. *It's slow, but damn it's strong.*

"Pent! Look out!" Hanar called. He fired two arrows, and each found its mark in the minotaur's eyes. Pent had been staggered by the blow; he nearly fell backwards to get out of the way of the beast's other arm. It howled again, a sound like an injured bull mixed with a freight train.

Gesta had run up next to Hanar. "You're warriors true, to defeat that beast!"

Hanar narrowed his eyes. "It does not seem that simple." He began to nock another arrow. "Look at it now."

The silhouette they had noticed before began to shimmer. It glowed in every color of the rainbow, and all at once the fresh wounds began to fade. Pent hacked at the leg again, but no sooner had he stuck than the wound began to vanish.

It's not like the cuts on my leg and shoulder though. The wounds didn't scab up or heal. *They just... vanished.*

The minotaur had fully recovered now, and its attention was solely directed towards Pent. It planted both hands firmly in the dirt and kicked up dust with its hind legs.

"Oh boy." Pent backed up, clutching his sword with both hands. It was clear that the monster was about the charge, and he scrambled to think of a way to—

Pent smirked. He sheathed his sword and pulled his cloak off to the side. *It's green, not red. But it'll have to do.* He backed up a step and swung the cloak around him, twirling it with bravado.

"Pent, what in the world are you doing?" Hanar stared at his friend with his mouth agape, thinking that he had lost his mind. He launched another arrow at the beast, trying to attract its attention.

"Toro! Toro!" Pent shouted. The minotaur lurched forward, barreling towards him at full speed. Pent stepped to the left at the last moment, flourishing his cloak to disguise his true shape and location, just like he'd seen in bull fights on TV. He cleared the minotaur's horns, but at the last moment the beast lashed his arm out, clipping Pent on the side. He rolled across the ground, clutching at his ribs.

Pent groaned in pain from the flat of his back. "All right, not my best idea." The bull-like creature had recovered and was stomping towards him. Hanar launched another arrow, but just as before, it had no effect. "Hanar, this is hopeless!" He shook his head and leapt to his feet. *I'm not waiting for this thing to make its move.* He charged ahead, ducking under a club-like hand, and swinging as hard as he could at the beast's leg, just below the knee.

This time he cut completely through the leg. But instead of being severed from the rest of the beast's body, the cut was sewn shut before Pent's eyes. His charge had carried him past the minotaur, and he was momentarily out of its reach as the lumbering beast turned to find him.

There was something off about the minotaur. It wasn't the bizarre, multi-colored outline, although that was odd. And it wasn't the never-ending healing, even though that was odd too. *There's something else.* It didn't feel like flesh he was cutting into with his sword. It was almost as if the monster was made of... *Paper.*

Pent dodged to the left then to the right. He was a step too slow on the last; the minotaur cut him off. It clawed at his face; Pent could only raise his arm and block the blow. He felt his entire body quake as he left the ground and went sailing through the air. He landed on his back, gasping for breath.

While he reeled on the ground and tried to get to his feet, the rest of the villagers had rejoined the fray. They launched attack after attack, but to no effect.

Gesta ran up to Pent and helped him to his feet. "Can you stand? You have amazing resilience; I thought it had killed you!"

Pent spoke hurriedly between gasps. "The—Scribes. Paper—blood—milk."

"What? What are you speaking of?"

Pent frowned, grabbing Gesta by the collar. "Milk! Get me milk!"

She freed herself and ran away in a fright. Moments later, she returned with a glass jar full of white liquid. She handed it to Pent, her confusion and fear worn plainly on her face.

Pent caught his breath and stood upright. He palmed the jar and chuckled lightly to himself. "I have no idea how this is supposed to work." Removing the lid, he poured the milk over the length of his sword. "Give the rest to Hanar. And wish me luck."

She started to speak, to ask him a question, but Pent did not hear it as he charged again. He yelled at the top of his lungs, trying to shout courage into his body. The minotaur swiveled and Pent leaped in the air.

He thrust his sword into the beast, dragging a cut from the monster's chest, all the way down to its leg. It began to shimmer again, but this time the cut didn't vanish. It oozed a black, tar-like substance.

"Blood?" Pent said. He swung twice more, slicing the beast's other leg like a sausage. It howled as the leg fell free of the body completely. Pent stared at the black tar, which ran freely from the wounds now. "No... it's ink." He turned to Hanar and howled. "It's ink! Use the milk!"

Hanar nodded with grim determination. He chucked the glass in the air, and then deftly fired an arrow into it. A white shower rained down onto the monster. As it was coated in milk, all of the villager's blows began to have an effect. The blood-like ink flowed like a river from the minotaur's many wounds.

The villagers ripped the beast apart, slicing it into several pieces. It howled, the ear-piercing sounds ringing unceasingly through the air. Even as it was chopped to pieces, it wriggled in torment. Pent and the others watched as it writhed, and then went inert. Moments after, it began to fade away.

Pent sheathed his sword. He ran a hand along his ribs, relieved that none of them had been broken. The villagers looked upon him reverently.

"You—you've saved us!" a man carrying a broken sword said.

"Saved us, and you've killed that monster!" a woman said, her eyes misty.

Another man fell to his knees and began to weep openly. "We've lost so much, yet within the course of a day you've shown us that hope still exists."

The crowd dropped their weapons and let out a shout of approval. Cries and chants of "We're saved!" and "Bless the outsiders!" rang out.

Pent looked through the crowd, spotting Hanar in the group. The woodsman worked his way free of the knot of people, joining Pent and slapping him on the shoulder. "This is more a reception to my liking!" he said.

"Damn right." Pent grabbed Hanar's hand and raised it in the sky. "We did it, man, we took that thing out! Nice moves with that bow."

Hanar laughed aloud. "And you as well! Except for that bizarre lapse of judgment with your cloak. You'll have to explain that to me."

"Don't worry about it, man," Pent said, laughing.

The village chief appeared in the crowd, pushing his way through the mass of people. He was flanked by Gesta and Tanan; they all had remorseful looks on their faces. Raham studied Pent, his arms pressed behind his back. His posture was still firm, but his voice was less sure. He had to shout over the crowd to be heard. "We—we need to speak."

CHAPTER TWENTY-SIX

The chief escorted Pent and Hanar back to his home for the second time. They sat at his table, Raham at one end, his children flanking him. Pent was across from him, Hanar seated by his side. They both crossed their arms and stared at Raham's family. Tanan was looking away, examining the glass serpent on the wall as if he had never seen it before. Gesta was twirling her dagger but kept fumbling it, nearly cutting herself in the process. The chief was wringing his hands at the head of the table. His eyes were misty, and he couldn't sit still.

Pent hadn't had much time to admire the glasswork when they were first here, being much more focused on the chief. *Has to be Verra's handiwork. It's just like one of those monsters we saw out at sea.*

Tanan broke the silence, his eyes still fixed on the serpent. "You saved us all." He glanced at Pent, probing him with his eyes. "I never would have imagined it, but you saved us from that horrible monster."

Pent nodded slowly, leaning back in his seat. "Looks like it. From wooden torture devices to gold medals. Some benefit of the doubt would have been nice." He checked his fingernails on one hand and sighed. "Some kind of hospitality you guys gave us. I've had way too many knives to my throat for my liking. How many travelers have you detained who might have saved you? If it wasn't for us, you'd all be dead."

The words hung in the air. Pent opened his mouth to speak again, but the chief raised a hand to silence him. "Words fail me, sir." He stood up slowly from his seat. His arms crossed behind his back, he began to pace back and forth. "I've acted shamefully. But not without warrant, you may soon learn."

"What's he talking about?" Pent asked. He stared from Gesta to Tanan and back. "I'm tired of playing this guessing game. Just share the whole truth this time, all right?"

"This is not the first time we've been attacked," Gesta, now very still, said with a glance at her father. "Monsters have come before. Different creatures, but with that same bizarre glow."

Pent pictured the beast again. It was something straight out of myth and legend. *That bizarre glow...* It had shimmered and glowed, looking like light through a prism. "That glow—it has to be the work of the Scribes," Pent said, more to Hanar than anyone else. "Gordenthorpe said something like that, right? Something about them writing things into existence—blood to power their creations... The minotaur wasn't really there."

"It was real enough to destroy our village and kill our people!" Tanan said.

Pent rubbed on his ribs. *Felt real enough to me too...* "Yeah I get that. But I meant more like, it wasn't a real animal."

"That's why our blows did nothing to the creature," Hanar said. "I had several clear shots, but none harmed it until the milk was drawn."

"I don't understand. What's all this business with milk?" Gesta asked.

Pent and Hanar glanced at each other, shrugging simultaneously. "I just went toe to toe with something straight from *Dungeons and Dragons*. All bets are off. Let me tell you the whole story..."

They took turns telling Raham and his kin their tale. They spoke of Somerville, of the battle with Gilbrand, and then Yozer. They spoke of Gordenthorpe and his information regarding the dangerous Scribes. And they spoke of their own problem with the missing children.

"I see," Raham said. He was nodding his head as he pondered their words thoughtfully. "I see. So, you came all this way on a hunch and little else. In search of your children." He hung his head in his hands.

His son patted him on the shoulder. "You must not be so harsh towards Father. Perhaps we took things a touch too far with the stocks, but we wouldn't have taken your lives."

"This village has reached the end of its life," Gesta said. "When we saw the two of you approach, we were desperate for answers. We've had so many questions, but no answers. Many of our people have already deserted us; they believed that their children were lost forever. Most disappear in the middle of the night, fleeing Tofac under the cover of darkness. Some have surely gone northeast to Vinalhaven. Perhaps some have even joined the mad cultists of Nenahnezad, to the northwest." She huffed, a bitter and defeated sound. "We didn't act fast enough. In the confusion, there was much time spent deciding where to shift the blame, and none on finding solutions."

Pent frowned. *Gotta give Lyle credit—at least she's solution oriented. And she gives people a chance before assuming they'll do her wrong.*

Hanar scratched at his beard. "But what of the monsters? You've said they have attacked before. How have you survived them, if you weren't aware of their weakness?"

"We have just barely survived, but it hasn't been because of any action on our part," the chief said. His eyes were shut tightly. "They come in many forms, destroy what they will, and leave. Why, we have never been able to ascertain. The beasts seem mindless— are not open to pleading or negotiation." His shoulders slumped. "Tofac has been on the verge for some time. We used to be ten times the size we are now, but we have dwindled in these dark days. I fear that this is our end."

To Pent, Hanar said, "If this has been happening for some time, what could their purpose possibly be?"

"If it's really the Scribes doing it, maybe they're just flexing their strength. Gordenthorpe said they had been sealed away. If they've been cooped up somewhere this whole time... maybe it's just their way of exercising?"

"A blade grows dull if not whet," Hanar said.

"Yeah, exactly," Pent nodded excitedly, glad to have an answer to a question, even if it brought them no closer to their final goal. "But who knows. Just based on the monsters they're sending out I don't think we'll get a chance to ask them. Yozer wasn't really that open to having a sit-down conversation when he finally showed his face at Somerville."

At the mention of Yozer's name, the chief's face flushed red. "That's another matter entirely. You admit to it willingly; you struck down Master Yozer. Under his rule, none of these horrible things happened." He trembled as he spoke. "I'm indebted to you for what you've done today, but you've still ruined us."

Pent dug his fingers into the table. It took all of his will to not turn around and heave his chair at the old man. "Look, I don't know how else to say it. Your so called 'Master' was a monster, no better than that thing we just killed in your village square. He kept everyone in the world afraid, and he came to destroy my home, to kill my friends. I defended myself." Pent raised his hands, palms out. "I'm sorry for all that's happened. But I can't change the past. All I can do now is try to help find these children."

Raham gave Pent a long, searching look, then sighed wearily. "Master Yozer, he was an eerie man, but he always treated us fairly. And he kept us safe." He ran a hand along the top of his balding head. "But I can't wave away what you've done for us today. Perhaps you've spoken true, and I need to look beyond the past. I've been relying on the name of Mas—of Yozer for too long and have lost the faith of my people through my inaction. We need heroes of the now, not of the long ago."

They continued to speak through the day. The chief offered to let them stay the night, which they willingly accepted. Pent was thankful for the night to rest his wounds. He hadn't broken anything, but his stomach was tender and sore.

The following day, Pent and Hanar were escorted to the edge of town. There were groups of people out repairing damage to their homes, but Pent saw even more people gathering their belongings and taking their leave of Tofac. Half the homes he looked at were abandoned now, but only a few of them had been destroyed by the monster.

"You see?" the chief said. "Even after the events of yesterday, their faith has shattered. Where else could they possibly go? What safety is there out in the wild?"

"Some do better when they take their chances," Hanar said. He clutched at the milk bottle on his belt. "Are you certain three bottles is all you can manage?"

"We need to consider the safety of our people as well, in case more of those monsters come to harass us," Tanan said. "Besides, our cattle have not given us a great yield this season. It's an unfortunate weakness, milk. We'll have to use it sparingly."

"Gordenthorpe spoke of another weakness too," Pent said. "But I've seen the milk work, so we'll stick with that." He palmed his own milk bottle. "The three you've given us will have to be enough."

"And where will you go now?" Gesta asked. "I fear you're leaving us too soon; we've done little to reward your bravery."

"If the monsters we've seen are any hint of what awaits you, I fear there will be worse horrors ahead," Raham said.

"Horrors perhaps, and hopefully the missing children," Hanar replied. "The trails are confused; too many people have walked through these lands." He pointed through the forest. Pent could not tell the difference from one direction to the other. "But I believe our hope lies in this direction. South and east—there are more tracks heading that way than any other, with no regard for thorns or brush. We'll try that way and hopefully find something of note."

"I can only hope that there's still a village for you to come back to," the chief said. "Go, and good luck."

CHAPTER TWENTY-SEVEN

Catherine had been taught the basics of tracking in her old life. It was not the typical route for a noble's daughter, but Gilbrand believed in preparing his children for whatever harsh fates the world had in store for them.

She had taken to the lessons well enough, but living in the wild, surviving on those skills, was entirely different than creeping through the halls of the castle, trying to sneak up on her brother in the dark. There were many things she did now which she had never imagined she would do in life. *Like eating bugs and frogs. That's something I would not have imagined.*

But she did what she had to do to survive as she hunted for her brother. Despite her long days scouring the forests, however, she saw no sign of him. Near and far she had searched, calling out his name into the dense woods and over open plains, always hoping to hear his small voice come back to her. But there was never a response.

Her travels had taken her far from Gilbrand Castle. Truthfully, she had begun to give up hope; she despaired in failing her mother's last wishes. *I never should have left him alone. Oh Peter...*

Despite her failures, she often reminded herself that all was not without hope. If she had survived out in the wild without her mother or father to guide her, then perhaps her brother had as well. *I've learned how to hunt, how to lay traps for beasts, and he had the same training.* She could only hope her brother had listened to their parents' lessons as she had.

The forests she had been roaming most recently were much less dense than what she was used to. She had picked up two trails of note. There were horse tracks in the dirt. *Someone lost out here, who happens to be on horseback? Or something else entirely?* The tracks where closely spaced, indicating the horse was not dashing to or away from anything. But she had been unable track them to their end.

The other set of tracks made her shiver to think of them. The tracks of that... *thing. Because it wasn't a person.* She had seen monsters and killers, but she had never seen anything like that before. She had followed it to a cave, and the horrors of that cold, dark tomb were unspeakable. She shook her head to dislodge the memory of it, regretting thinking about the cave again.

After that, she started to plant more traps in the area. Whatever that *thing* was, it walked on two feet, and it would fall into a hole just as well as anything else.

A rustling in the distance grabbed her attention. She glanced out from her hiding place behind a tree. *Two men.* Perfect. Maybe she could get some food off them.

She hurried along to the nearest clearing, hoping the men would join her soon enough.

CHAPTER TWENTY-EIGHT

Pent couldn't tell one forest from another, and the prospect of following Hanar into the thick of one again was not pleasant. The high from their victory in Tofac had already begun to wear off. They had managed to walk away from two desperate situations: fighting a minotaur and making their way out of the stocks. *Being locked up in the town center certainly hadn't been what I was expecting when we found that town. 'Course, I hadn't been expecting to fight some mythical creature, either.*

Hanar had been adamant that these trails were more promising than any he had seen to this point. He had excitedly told Pent how these forests were less dense than those near Somerville, and the ground softer to show their quarry's passage. *One group of trees or the other, I've had enough stomping through the forests for a lifetime.* After the third tree branch slapped him in the face, he began reminiscing over his time in Seward. *A cold drink and a day on the beach—I'd take that happily.*

"In every one of these stories, the heroes are always on horseback," Pent grumbled. "I've got sores on every inch of both of my feet. So tired of all this walking."

"Oh?" Hanar said. He pretended to look through his pack, rummaging through his milk bottles and Faldo's crumpled map. "Well, I don't happen to have a horse in my pack, so I suppose we should keep walking. Or perhaps we should go back to Tofac and ask for two mighty cows to carry us into battle."

"Hilarious. I get it—you've lived in a tree longer than you've spent under a roof, man."

Hanar frowned. "Does everyone from your world complain as much as you?"

Pent felt his blood pressure rise, but then considered the question for a moment. "Yeah, that's pretty much the case, actually."

"Hm. I don't see how you miss it, my friend," Hanar said. "Whether you speak or don't, you need to walk all the same."

"Oh, I see, so I should just shut up then," Pent said. He brushed past Hanar and walked ahead of him. "All right then, just try and keep up with me. Fake-ass Bear Grylls-looking—"

Pent continued to grumble as he led them into a clearing. Suddenly, he was being shoved to the side; Hanar had slammed into him, knocking him onto his back. He swore loudly.

"Yo, what the hell—" he started before realizing Hanar was gone. "Hanar? Quit playing around, where are you?"

Pent heard a groan from below. He crawled a few feet toward the sound and found himself at the edge of a pit.

"My leg!" Hanar gasped. "I've twisted it. Pent! I've fallen into some kind of trap!"

Pent leaned over the edge of the hole. *Really sloppy work too. I should have seen this a mile away.* He cursed again. Hanar had seen it; he had been keeping an eye out for threats, even in the middle of their argument. "My bad man, let me get you out of there."

"Pent! Look alive! Whatever dug this might be close by!"

Pent swiveled in place, drawing his sword and he glared out into the trees. The clearing was circular in shape and clear of obstructions. A short figure stood at the other end of the field, staring at Pent. "No kidding," Pent said to Hanar. "Looks like trouble." Pent studied their stalker; she was a small, familiar girl, with long dark-blonde hair. *She's the one who attacked us.* She glared at Pent, disbelief and anger clear on her face. "That explains the child's tracks you found Hanar," Pent called down the pit. "We've got company—that girl from Gilbrand Castle."

"You!" she yelled. "How can it be you? Of all the people to encounter..." She breathed in slowly. "The world is smaller than I thought. Perhaps I can accomplish this at least." She drew her thin sword. Despite its size, Pent knew well enough how dangerous it could be. In her hands, it was deadly.

Pent took a few steps away from the hole. "Listen, we don't have to do this. We can just talk about this. I don't want to hurt you."

"You've hurt me enough already!" she yelled fiercely, beginning to walk forward, the tip of her blade drawing a line in the dirt beside her.

"You, and everyone else in the world, apparently," Pent sighed, his sword gripped tightly in both hands.

She entered a fighting stance as she approached slowly. "Your name. Your name is Pent, right?"

He glanced at the hole Hanar was stuck in. "Yeah, you got it."

"Then there's nothing else to discuss!" She charged him, her eyes blazing and sword slashing across Pent's body. He was more prepared this time and knew not to underestimate this girl half his size. He parried each strike, waiting for an opening, and then swung hard with the flat of his blade. She blocked it but was sent sprawling across the field.

She's tired, Pent thought. *There are bags under her eyes, and she's breathing heavy.* "Just stay down!" he shouted, towering over her.

She growled like a rabid dog and charged again. She stayed low to the ground this time, cutting at Pent's legs. *She tried that move at the castle too.* He stepped backwards, keeping at a safe distance while knocking away her blows.

Tired—and thinner, too. She hadn't been eating well. *I'm stronger, sure, but I'm moving faster than her now too. And my sword's bigger than she is*. The reach advantage hadn't felt so certain back in the castle, but now Pent felt like he was doing a great job of just keeping her back.

He stuck his blade out to ward her off but panicked when she nearly ran herself into it. He pulled back at the last minute, desperate not to impale her through the chest. She didn't seem to have this same worry regarding him; the point of her sword shot toward the gap in his chest plate under his left arm, but she mistimed the blow and it glanced harmlessly off the armor.

Pent reached out and cuffed her across the shoulder, knocking her to the ground. If looks could kill, the murderous glare she gave him then would have done the job her sword couldn't. She hissed like a wildcat and fled into the trees.

"Come on, this is pointless!" Pent yelled after her. He saw her figure dart from behind one tree to another. "You can't beat me; we both know it."

He stood in silence, his sword in one hand, waiting for her reply. A stone came hurtling towards his head from behind one of the trees. He blocked it with his forearm. As soon as he lowered his hand, another rock followed.

"Damn you!" she yelled from behind the trees as she sent another stone at Pent's face. "You killer!"

"Bah," Pent said, swatting away rock after rock. "So, what's your problem, huh? What did you lose when I killed Yozer?" Pent shouted into the forest. "Poor old Yozer—what a sad, lovely old man. How dare big, black Pent pick on him?" He jammed his sword into the ground. "That insane bastard left me no choice! What do you people want from me?"

He listened for the girl, trying to pinpoint which tree she was hiding behind. She was panting and gasping in bursts. "My affair is not with Yozer," she growled. "You murdered my father!"

"I haven't killed anyone who didn't try to kill me first. They don't have self-defense in this screwed up world?" He raised his arm to deflect another projectile, but it exploded on impact with his arm, spraying dirt into his eyes. *Damn dirt clod—I can't see.* He furiously wiped at his face, trying to clear his vision.

"Nothing is sacred to liars and killers!" She poked her head out from behind a tree directly across from Pent. "My name is Catherine, and I'll avenge my father's death at your hands. I'll avenge the great Lord Gilbrand!"

"Oh, crap." Pent yanked his sword from the ground and looked around through squinted, watery eyes. He narrowly deflected her strike at the last moment. "You've got it all wrong. I didn't kill him!"

She swung at his neck, missing by a hair. "Don't lie to me! I know the truth. I heard it from Master Yozer himself."

Pent's sword clanged against Catherine's. "He's the liar, damn it! You're listening to stories, told by the man who did your father in himself."

Tears poured from her eyes as she swung desperately. "Don't lie to me! I'll have your head! For you, Father!"

Seeing Pent half-blinded seemed to have renewed Catherine's strength, even though he was so sure that she was at the end of her rope. *All this passion, and she spends it trying to kill me.* Pent fought defensively, pushing away her blade and trying to find a moment to disarm her. He glanced over to the pit that Hanar had fallen into, but it didn't seem like any help was coming from there.

Catherine took advantage of his brief distraction by lunging in under his guard and striking Pent across the hip, drawing blood. He grunted in pain and stumbled back, clutching the wound. In a flash of rage, Pent drove his own sword down on her, smashing the flat of his blade against her shoulder. She cried out as she fell, the small sword tumbling from her hands.

"That's enough!" he shouted at her. She set her hand atop her sword but didn't get up. Pent stared down at her. "Believe what you want, I don't care anymore." He pointed the tip of his sword at her face. "But I'm not going to let you get in the way of me finding those missing kids."

She looked up at him and blinked. "What?"

"I made a promise, and I'm going to see it through." He kicked the sword out of her hand, sending it hurtling into the woods. "You got it?"

He stood over her for another moment, until he was certain she wasn't going to charge at him again, and then went to attend to Hanar.

"What do you mean by missing kids? Wh... which missing kids?" She mumbled the words, staring at Pent with eyes as wide as saucers.

Pent reached into the hole, giving his arm to Hanar, and heaving the thin man free of the pit. "How's the leg?"

Hanar grimaced, but then smiled. "I'll hobble for some time, but I'll survive. Nothing broken."

"Would be nice to have Ellie to take a look at it though," Pent said. Hanar's ankle was already swelling up. "Damn, done in by a freaking hole."

"What do you mean missing kids!" Catherine shouted. They both turned and looked at her. She was crawling towards them, her eyes wide in shock. "Answer me!"

"Our village lies far in the east," Hanar said. "And the youths of our town have wandered off in the middle of night. We were sent to track them down."

"You don't have to be so open to someone who just tried to kill me," Pent muttered.

Catherine wiped at her eyes. "But i... if... if you're looking for missing children," she tucked her head onto her knees, "If other children are missing... maybe..."

Pent looked on her with pity, stepping towards her. She recoiled in fear. With a single motion, he yanked off his sword belt and flung the blade to the ground. "I don't know what all this new drama with you is about, but what do you say? Truce?" He stuck his hand out to her.

"Trust in you?" She glanced at the ground. "I'm not sure if I can."

Pent nodded slowly. "I get that. But how do you think I feel? I don't want you lurking around if you're gonna try and slit my throat when I'm asleep." He shrugged. "These are dark days, right? Dark times make people do things they regret. I'm not asking you to be my friend. Just stop trying to stab me, okay?" He slowly offered his hand to her.

She looked at him uncertainly. "This is a Vinalhaven greeting..." After a moment's pause, Catherine took his hand and shook. "All right. I can do that. Until you give me a reason to stab you."

"Fair enough." Pent sat down across from her, leaning back on one hand. "So, let's talk—at least while my friend is figuring out how to walk again." He glanced at Hanar, who was limping toward them. "I guess we already got introduced, but my name is Pent, this is Hanar. And you're... Catherine, right?"

She nodded in affirmation, glancing from man to man. "You said you're from the east, but that greeting is from my mother's homeland. I know no one else who uses it this far south."

"Yeah, we're from the east," Pent said. "Sort of. It's hard to explain."

Groaning like an old man, Hanar sat down next to Pent. "Perhaps we should settle on a story for the next adventure we go on. To save on the pain of explaining it to every new person we meet." Hanar smiled at the youth. "And Pent was not lying about your father. He bested him in single combat, but Lord Gilbrand left our town very much alive afterwards."

"You defeated my father in a sword fight? You?" Catherine narrowed her eyes at Pent. "I find that very hard to believe. You're a complete mess with a blade. I've never seen a sloppier sword hand."

Hanar scratched his beard. "Come to think of it, I don't believe I was around for either of your incredible victories. Come now, Pent, do you send me off before the battle begins because you're embarrassed?"

"I grew up watching TV and playing football. Give me a break." He smacked Hanar on the shoulder. "Besides, you just saw me fight that bull monster yesterday."

"You attempted to dazzle it with your cloak and were sent hurtling through the air for your troubles. That was an odd choice."

Pent rubbed his forehead and sighed. "It was something I saw on TV once. Never mind, man."

Catherine looked from one man to the other, blinking rapidly. "You speak very oddly. What village did you say you were from?"

"Girl, you have no idea."

Hanar had doubled over in laughter. "In time, you become used to his mannerisms. But it is still a touch odd!"

Pent ignored him. "I beat your dad because of my strength, not skill. He wasn't ready for someone bigger than him." He paused, studying Catherine's face. "Look, I didn't kill him myself, but I know that fight helped lead to his death. I'm sorry you lost your dad. Killing me won't bring him back, but..." He fumbled with the words. *Who am I to tell her how to think or feel? My dad left when I was a kid, but he wasn't murdered by some crazy wizard.* "I don't know. You can give it another shot if you still hate me. But only after we find these children." He raised a hand towards her. "It seems like you have some investment in these children, too."

She nodded slowly. "My little brother, Peter. He's been missing for a long time now. I thought he just wandered off by himself and was... was killed by who knows what. But it made no sense to me. He would never do something like that."

"Neither would any of these kids." Pent gestured through the forest behind them. "And that village back there, Tofac. All their kids are gone too."

"Do you—" Catherine started, rubbing at her eyes. "Do you believe that Peter could be with the rest of these children?"

Pent stared at her. She had a tired, defeated expression on her face. Pent couldn't have imagined her looking so vulnerable only a few minutes before. *Damn. Dead mom, dead dad—and now her brother is missing too? That's one hell of a life, and I sure didn't help things. At least not for her.*

"Well, wherever the children are, I don't see why he couldn't be there too," Pent said. "It seems too crazy for this all to be a coincidence."

"We won't know until we find the Scribes, regardless," Hanar added.

"Scribes?"

"An ancient race of people, or so we've been told. They are seemingly responsible for all this trouble—the children and monsters both."

"We don't have much to go on," Pent said. "I saw a drawing of one of them in Gordenthorpe's book. Guy looked really thin, malnourished even. Weirdest thing was the ears: long and pointy, but it almost looked like there was no rim to them..." Pent thought for a moment, then went on. "They do this thing in my world with dogs, I don't know why. But they, like, cut the edge of the ear. That's what this guy looked like: a tall elf with cropped dog ears." He shook his head. *I swear, I've seen someone like that before...*

Catherine's face went pale. She trembled and hugged her shoulders. "An emaciated giant with ruined ears." She closed her eyes and struggled to speak. "I think I know where you need to go."

CHAPTER TWENTY-NINE

Catherine led them through the western forest at a steady march. Pent gave Hanar a shoulder to lean on, trying to take some of the pressure off his injured leg. *That trap worked pretty well.* She smiled, despite her current circumstances. *We might be allies now, but if this giant can't help me, he might find himself and his friend in another hole.*

"I'm telling you, you should just head on north to Tofac," Pent said to Catherine. "This isn't on you—it's our quest. And I don't want to be responsible for a little girl—I've already got gimpy here."

"You couldn't force me to head back if you tried," she shot back. "You might need someone who can actually handle a sword." She gripped at the hilt of her blade. *Let's see him argue with that. I'll bet I can take him now.*

Unexpectedly, he nodded. "The odds are better with three of us for... whatever we're up against," Pent said. "And maybe this makes more sense—three bottles of milk, three people."

"I... have some bad news, my friend," Hanar said, casting a guilty look toward Pent. They came to a stop while Hanar rummaged through his pack. His hand came back wet with milk.

"What the hell?" Pent shouted. "The glasses broke? When were you gonna say something?"

"Right now, if you could imagine." Hanar sighed. "In our haste to keep moving I could not decide when was appropriate. One glass broke when I fell in the hole." He nodded to Catherine. "Thank you for that by the way. I'll have to teach you how to dig a proper trap."

She scoffed. "Worked on you well enough."

"I happened to see it from scores away," Hanar said. "Our fearless leader on the other hand—"

"Okay, okay. Enough bickering—damn. We've got two glasses then, and Raham wasn't willing to give us more." He gestured for them to move forward. "It'll have to be enough."

As they marched, Catherine told them of her travels, how they had been slow and harrowing, and had yielded minimal results. At first, she had circled around Gilbrand Castle, hoping Peter would have made his way back home somehow. After that, she had discovered the odd tracks, which didn't match any animal or person she had seen and had led her all the way to a cave.

"It was... eerie," Catherine said. "I don't know if I can explain this, but the cave felt... wrong. It looked like a normal cave, but when I stared at it," she trembled all over, "I felt as if I was frozen solid. Looking on the entrance chilled me to the bone. It felt like the cave would swallow me up."

"So, then you turned back," Pent said.

"No," she said sternly. "I went inside. I'm no coward." She stood up, straightening her posture. "Peter would never go into a place like that, if he had been this far. But I had to be sure, so I crept in."

A scream in the darkness. Her brother's scream, echoing against the shadows.

They both stared at her, waiting for her to catch her breath and finish the tale. Tentatively, Hanar asked, "Surely there was more to the cave than just a sore feeling?"

"Of course there was. But I had no torch, and the cave was black as night—and cold," she said. "Colder than you can imagine. Then something happened. I began—to see things. Things that could not be there."

Her mother, cut down by bandits, drenched in blood, howling in agony. Her father, picked apart piece by piece by a giant stranger.

Pent frowned. "That doesn't sound very good. It does kind of go with the minotaur thing, though." He glanced at Hanar, gauging his reaction. "They seem pretty good at making things appear that aren't really there."

"It felt so real. I—I'm not a coward, I promise you!" She stopped and glared at them. "I'm not! I would do anything for my brother. But I ran out of the cave then—it was too much. When the light of the world shined on me, I felt the heat of the sun restoring my body. I felt safe again.

"But one of those cropped-eared monsters had followed me out of the cave." She studied Pent. "I don't know what you saw in your book, but just thinking of that—that thing... It makes me sick. Pale, sickly skin, like it was diseased; tall, slender limbs; fingers as thin as a thread with black sharp nails at the tip—and it was tall. As tall as you, Pent, maybe even taller." She shuddered and began to march towards the cave. "I'm not thrilled to go back there."

"Odd, that it would let you escape," Hanar said.

"I stabbed at it once with my sword in a blind fury, but following that, I turned and ran." She shook her head. "I ran as far and as hard as I could. It didn't pursue me, but..."

"But?" both men asked in unison.

"But maybe it just wanted me to go. Maybe it wanted me to leave and come back with others."

CHAPTER THIRTY

"Up there, do you see it?" Catherine whispered, pointing at the cave at the base of a dead hill. The grass surrounding the field was vibrant and thriving, but on the hill, it was as if all the moisture had been pulled from the earth, or if the ground itself was poison. It was a grim contrast.

As Pent stared at the hill, he felt a sense of dread grip his heart. He gasped, suddenly short of breath, and tore his eyes from the scene, looking instead back to the path they had walked. A shiver ran through his entire body. *Like getting stabbed in the chest with an icicle.* He found that Hanar and Catherine had joined him.

"Man, what the hell was that?" he said, his hand to his chest.

Hanar seemed at a loss. "Catherine, you spoke true. It's cold."

As cold as a winter night. Pent spared another glance at the mouth of the cave. An icy stream ran down his back as every nerve in his body tensed up. *It's just a damn cave.* But something about it was horribly unnerving. All at once, Pent found a new respect for Catherine. *She's got some guts, going in there alone.*

Whatever bravery had compelled her to storm into the cave before had all but gone now. All the red had drained from her cheeks.

She shook her head back and forth, and her eyes began to mist over with tears. She whispered to herself quietly, but Pent couldn't make out what she was saying.

Pent focused on the entrance to the cave. A man had appeared, or something that was designed in mockery of a man.

"That wizard's book didn't do it justice," Pent said. The others glanced at the mouth of the cave and Pent heard their breath catch. Finally, what could only be one of the Scribes had appeared. It shambled into the open; it looked like a corpse that had been left out in the sun. The skin was deathly white, as Catherine had said, but she hadn't described the ruffles in the skin. Rolls and flaps of skin covered the hairless body. *Rolls—that make no sense.* If the creature was fat, Pent would have understood. *But it's thin as a rail.*

A black cloak was draped from the creature's shoulders; it's only covering. Its rolling, folded flesh was bared to them, and, despite himself, Pent noticed that it lacked any features to distinguish it as a male or female. *Looks like a bare-assed Dracula out here, but damn that thing is gross.* Its wrists were as thin as twigs, and the long fingers ended with sharp, black nails. That was the only notable feature aside from its eyes, and its ears.

"It has no mouth," Pent said. He squinted to make out more detail. There was a thin line across the bottom of its head where a mouth should be. "Or if it does, it has the smallest mouth I've ever seen." The ears were jagged and looked mutilated, and its eyes were midnight black orbs set in the colorless face.

Those dark, inhuman eyes locked onto them. The Scribe raised its hand, palm out, and an image began to appear. The air rippled before them like heat rising from desert sand, and a book fell from the open air, into the Scribe's waiting hand.

It began to write in the book with its fingers. As it wrote, a creature faded into existence, just like the book moments before it.

"Oh no," Pent moaned. He leaped out into the clearing, trying to rush the Scribe before it could finish summoning its creation, but he was a step too late. He skidded to a stop, now staring at several ugly monsters, which had just been conjured from thin air. The closest creature—a gray thing, as big as a man, with two spiked horns growing from its head and bat-like wings sprouting from its back—twirled its trident, staring at Pent menacingly.

Pent gripped his sword, staring at the group of gray monsters. "Gargoyles..." *How is this even real?*

Six gargoyles, each one as ugly as the next, stood between Pent and the Scribe. Each one held a jagged trident, a spear with three points on one end and a curved hook on the other.

They leapt forward, flying through the air, dipping and darting sporadically, and rapidly clearing the distance to Pent. They held their tridents like lances, ready to drive them into Pent's flesh.

"What—what are those things!" Catherine shouted. She clutched her sword like a security blanket, eyes wide with fear.

"Stone monsters of some kind," Hanar grumbled. "They're just as real as that bull-demon." He nocked an arrow and let fly at the nearest gargoyle. Just as with the minotaur, the arrow made contact, and then fell away impotently.

"They've got the strength in numbers this time." Pent backed away from the approaching group and parried a trident thrust, the clang of steel on steel ringing through the clearing. It snapped its jaws at him, spewing spittle into Pent's face. "This is too many for me to handle, man."

"Make that five," Hanar hollered. Another arrow, this one drenched in milk, sailed through the air and pierced the gargoyle in front of Pent. The arrow smashed the creature's head, and the rest of the body began to shake and crumble. "I'll handle these in short order."

No sooner had he spoken, the rest of the gargoyles flew towards him in an angry rush. Hanar ducked behind a tree, pulling his sword, and fending them off as best he could. They snapped and snarled, their tridents thrusting and stabbing wildly. "Some help would be appreciated!" Hanar shouted as he narrowly avoided a piercing jab meant for his throat.

They're so fast, and they can fly too. Pent charged back towards the forest but had to dodge to the side to avoid a flying trident. Off balance and distracted, Pent had no time to maneuver as the gargoyle dived toward him, tackling him horns first. The impact knocked the wind from his chest, but his armor was strong enough to save him from being skewered.

Pent lifted his left hand and hammered the monster on the side of the head. It stumbled and fluttered its wings, leaping several feet away and recovering its footing. The gargoyle lifted something from the ground where it had landed: the thrown trident. Pent frantically withdrew his milk and poured some down the length of his sword. Leaping after the gargoyle, Pent swung down and caught it across the shoulder. The monster howled as the blade passed through it, tearing it in two as if it were a sheet of paper. Ink-like blood flowed from the wound, splattering Pent and soaking the ground.

He moved to join Hanar at the forest but halted when he saw Catherine. She was staring, bug-eyed, at the Scribe. The Scribe was glaring at her, and its dark eyes were glowing.

She shook her head and seemed to break free of whatever trance she had experienced. "No. No! You won't take me!" Catherine readied her blade, falling into the fighting stance Pent had seen her use before. "Is that what happened to Peter? Did you do that to my brother? Give him back you freak!" She charged at the Scribe.

"Wait!" Pent called. "Don't go after it alone!"

The Scribe stepped back, opening its book.

Pent dashed after her, but two of the gargoyles blocked his path. "Damn it!" he yelled. Unable to continue forward, he could only watch as Catherine sped on a collision course with the hideous Scribe.

Milk running in rivulets down the edge of his sword, Pent lashed out, knocking aside a trident and cutting cleanly through the gargoyle's wrists. The second stabbed at him, but he sidestepped it and hacked its head off in a single quick strike. *Just like the Minotaur—like I'm chopping through paper.*

He glanced over his shoulder to see Hanar struggling with the last two. *Really wish I had my gun right about now.* Pent stood irresolute for an instant, torn between helping Hanar and chasing after Catherine. Luckily, Hanar answered the question for him.

Hanar chose that moment to break free of his melee with the gargoyles and sprint back out into the open field towards Pent. The gargoyles were after him in a second. Pent stood ready as Hanar led the monsters straight to him, but they did not close the distance, instead darting in and out of striking range of their swords. One snapped its jaws like a nutcracker, the other ran a lumpy tongue along the length of its trident. They stabbed and thrust towards Pent and Hanar but did not get within distance for the pair to strike back. *They're just trying to keep us occupied, distracted.*

Pent deflected a blow aimed at his head. He continued to struggle with the stone soldiers as Catherine made her way to the Scribe.

The Scribe moved, expressionless, completely focused on the girl. It struck out with its left hand, moving slowly but deliberately, grabbing Catherine by her sword arm, and lifting her effortlessly into the air.

"Wha—let me go!" She twisted and turned, trying to rip herself free of its grasp, then kicked at the ghoulish creature, but to no avail.

"Pent, look out!" Hanar shouted from beside him. Pent had grown distracted by the Scribe. He clashed with one of the gargoyles, locking his sword into the prongs of its trident. He dragged the weapon down, forcing it into the dirt and pinning it. His arms shook with the effort; the creature was starting to break free—

Hanar turned and swung wildly with his short sword, clipping one of its wings off. It fell desperately to the ground. Pent leapt on top of it, shouting like a Viking berserker and stabbing down into it to finish it off. *I feel like Conan the Barbarian out here. This is wild stuff!*

As he pulled his sword out of the earth, he glanced over to Catherine.

"What the hell?" he muttered aloud. His mind fought to make

sense of the strange, almost cartoonish image; all he could see of Catherine were her legs, sticking out of the pages of the Scribe's book.

Pent and Hanar lunged at the last gargoyle together, hacking at its trident with their swords until it fell to pieces. Their blades both pierced the monster at the same time, shredding it into an unrecognizable lump. It dissolved into nothingness before their eyes.

Pent turned and pointed to the Scribe, and the two hurried after it. They had cleared only half the distance of the field, though, before the Scribe closed the book shut and shambled backwards into the mouth of the cave, vanishing into the darkness.

Pent stopped at the mouth of the cave and kicked at the dirt. "Damn it!"

Hanar howled impotently into the cave, "Catherine! Catherine!"

CHAPTER THIRTY-ONE

Pent tried to catch his breath as he sheathed his sword. He felt the chill of the cave radiating outward as they approached. He pushed the feeling away, trying to maintain control of himself. "Damn it, we have to go after that... thing. It took Catherine."

Hanar nodded confidently. "There's no question there. This is a bizarre power we're up against." He turned to Pent, nervously scratching his beard. "My friend, in two days we've had two encounters with creatures the likes of which I've never seen before—but you seemed to recognize them. You mentioned them by name."

"So, you've never heard of them before?" Pent looked to Hanar, glad for a reason to turn away from the mouth of the cave. "This is all so crazy. But what else is new in this world? It's not like half the other things I've seen here aren't also completely absurd."

"You're speaking of the stone beasts then?"

"Yeah. Gargoyles. The other one was called a minotaur." He raised his hands in exasperation. "This is screwed up. Of all the people to have to explain this... I don't really know what they're for, but in my world, mostly in Europe I think, people would build these really creepy statues and put them on the sides of castles. Maybe just because they looked cool.

"But those statues are also in all kinds of stories, books, and video games, stuff like that. They're usually set up to be spooky, demon kind of things—monsters with horns and wings. The trident is a nice touch, and so was the snarling." He trembled. Thinking of the monsters this close to the mouth of the cave was too much.

"I see," Hanar said. "So, they are not living creatures from your world, but some kind of element of fantasy. And the bull-monster?"

Pent nodded. "The minotaur is the same kind of thing. A fantasy creature from old stories. Really old stuff—I think some Greek story about a big maze, and a hero is trapped in it—has to fight his way out." He shrugged. "I read that in high school, so it's been awhile. But then you see the minotaur in other stuff too. There's a lot of monsters like that in my world."

In my world... The chance of any of that being a coincidence just seemed impossible. Two instances of creatures from his world, popping up in this one? *Maybe it's just because of Hanar? Lyle has all of those stories in her head, maybe she has one with the minotaur too.* But Catherine hadn't recognized the creatures either.

"A bunch of stuff that feels like it got dropped here, straight out of my world," Pent said. He pictured the pale figure of the Scribe in his mind. The rolls in his skin, his thin line for a mouth, his cropped ears... *Cropped ears.* "Cropped ears... I think I know where I saw that thing before." He shook his head slowly, his brow furrowed in thought. "Yeah. I didn't get a good look at him, but outside the library—"

"You're mumbling to yourself, Pent," Hanar said, a look of concern on his face.

"Sorry man, just trying to figure this all out. I had just made my way to the front of the library, I think; there was a homeless man. I gave him my tip for the day, just dropped it down in his cup. He was bundled up, and he smelled horrible, worse than Arnold Schwarzenegger's gym bag. I remember noticing his ears, and thinking they looked so odd—like they looked like the cropped ears of a dog."

Hanar was staring intently. "Did this man have long, black nails on each of his fingers?"

"See, I didn't really get a good look. He was bundled up, and I wasn't about to jostle him awake." Pent cast a sidelong glance at Hanar. "It's messed up, but people in my world kind of... ignore homeless people. We see them suffering, we feel bad for a moment, and we just walk right on by. I gave him some money, but I know I'm not much better.

"But then, right after I left the homeless man, I went into the library. And right after I opened up that book, I landed here. Hurtling through the sky, out of my world and into this one." Pent looked back at the cave entrance. "That homeless man—maybe he's the reason I'm here in the first place."

"But Pent, how could that man be one of the Scribes?" Hanar asked in bewilderment. "How would he reach your world from this one?"

"I... I don't know," Pent said. "And I don't think they're really interested in answering questions. He seemed much more interested in snatching up children and retreating into that cave of nightmares."

Hanar frowned. "Did you notice, it was almost as if that creature dismissed us entirely after taking Catherine. Why not wipe us out while it was here?"

"Who knows, maybe it got what it came for." Pent stared into the fathomless void of the cave. The darkness gave his mind endless room to imagine terrors waiting for them. "Or maybe it didn't think we were a threat." He was gripping his sword so tightly his knuckles went white.

"Pent..." Hanar said. He pointed to Pent's belt.

Pent looked down and groaned. His milk bottle had been shattered, and he hadn't even noticed. Most of the contents had leaked out; the bottle itself was a useless ruin. "From bad, to worse. It must have happened when we were fighting those gargoyles." He chucked the broken bottle away in a rage. "How much do you have left?"

Hanar looked grim. "Only the one bottle remains, and half of the contents at that." He tied it gingerly on his belt loop. "We could journey back to Tofac, but I fear there is no time. We can't abandon her now; we need to rescue Catherine and the other children. Pent, if they've taken Catherine into this lair, the rest of the children must be here too!"

Pent tried to steady his nerves, but it was difficult to control the fear this close to the cave. *Yeah, it's easy enough to say, "let's storm the cave, save these kids, and come home to the cheers of the world."* He rested his hand on his sword hilt and grimaced. *Just me and Hanar, this sword, and a bottle of milk? I could still turn and run right now. I bet I could convince Hanar easily enough; he usually goes along with what I say.*

Pent glanced at the edge of the clearing, to the path they had come from, and let loose a weary sigh that sounded dramatic even to his own ears. *Who am I fooling? There's no turning back from this. All those promises... if I was gonna back down, I should have done it a long time ago.*

"All right then, I can't stall forever." Pent grabbed the thickest branch he could find and wrapped it with a piece of his tunic. He set the makeshift torch ablaze with his lighter. "Enough of this sitting around, if we're gonna die in this dark cave, we're gonna die trying to save these kids." He gestured to Hanar. "You've got the milk, so I'll take point. You cover my back with those arrows."

CHAPTER THIRTY-TWO

They marched cautiously through the cave. Pent had never been in a place so dark before. He was in a black hole, all of the light that ever could be had been sucked out of every corner of the cave. Even with the torch in his hands he couldn't see the ground in front of his feet.

"This darkness is unsettling," Hanar said, echoing Pent's thoughts. He was standing uncomfortably close to Pent, but in the oppressive darkness, he welcomed the outdoorsman's closeness. His breath warming the back of Pent's neck was a reminder that he was still alive. "As if we've stepped into nothingness itself."

"Yeah, well. We haven't," Pent said, more for his own comfort than his friend's. "Just keep your eyes on the torch, and let's keep moving." Their voices carried along the cave walls and reverberated all around them. Pent spared a glance backwards, but aside from Hanar's nervous eyes, there was nothing to tell them where they'd come from, not even a glimmer from the cave entrance.

They could only have been walking for a few minutes, but it felt like an eternity. They marched on, every footstep sounding like a rock cast into a well. Pent brought the torch closer and closer to him to fight away the cold that was gripping his heart.

He began to wonder what had brought them to the cave to begin with. *I've gotta be out of my mind, coming in here.* Many times, he paused, grappling with the question. When Hanar bumped into him, asking him why he had halted, all he could offer was his internal struggle.

"We should head back—ah, no—damn it, we need to save Catherine!" Pent said. He shook his head in frustration as they pressed on.

The torch dwindled, burning lower and lower. There were no sounds to tell them they were not alone, no signs of life at all, not the Scribes, not the children.

"This cold, it cuts deep into the skin. Let me carry the torch for a time," Hanar said, his voice pleading.

"Screw that," Pent said, and his voice echoed angrily through the dark. "You've got the milk remember? What happened to watching my back?"

"Do not be selfish, *outsider*," Hanar spat. "Would you have me freeze to death on your behalf?"

"Outsider? Who the hell do you think you're talking to?" Pent turned around suddenly. He squared up to Hanar and stared him in the face. A shudder ran through him as he saw the face of his closest friend staring back at him. The rage, which had arrived like a rogue wave, passed as quickly.

Hanar looked remorseful. "I... I am sorry." His teeth clattered in the darkness.

"Yeah, me too. Me too."

"D... damn this place!" Hanar burst out. "This is madness. The dark is endless, the cold is piercing to the bone. I feel my thoughts twisting in my mind, my own voice a perversion within me. I can't tell where I end and this darkness begins"

That wasn't how Pent would have phrased it, but he felt the same way. Through clenched teeth, he said, "Let's just keep moving, man. The sooner we're done with this and out of this cave, the better."

Pent pivoted away from Hanar. He stepped two feet at the most, and then caught his leg on something and fell to the ground, dropping the torch.

Cursing, Pent groped after the torch, reaching for it as if his very life was at stake. He felt the darkness swallowing him, flowing into every recess of his body and mind. As he crawled after the torch, it spun and rolled away as if it was mocking him.

"Just get back here! Get back here and stop messing with me!" Yet no matter how far he stretched his arm, the torch was just out of reach. He lowered his head, catching his breath for a moment.

"You need a hand, man?"

Pent glanced up. A familiar face was looking down on him and smiling, but not a face he expected to see.

"...Greg?"

CHAPTER THIRTY-THREE

"What about that drink you said you were gonna get me?" Greg laughed. He flashed a cocky grin. "You didn't forget, did you, homes?"

"No. No I didn't... It's just that—" Pent glanced over his shoulder. He was back in Nelly's bar. The pub had a sickly odor to it: dust mingled with spilled beer. The light in the corner of the room flickered and buzzed, a mainstay that brought character to the place. A few dead-eyed regulars occupied the tables. Pent's head swiveled around, glancing at them each in turn.

"Yo man, you all right?" Greg shook him on the shoulder. "You look *beyond* out of it—and you always give me hell for driving buzzed. You've gotta be twisted."

Pent forced a half-hearted chuckle. "Twisted—only a goof like you would say that. I don't drive drunk, man, that ain't a good look." Pent frowned. *Drive drunk? I haven't been behind the wheel in six months.* He reached into the pocket of his jeans. His keys jingled. *Was all of that a dream?* He patted himself down. His jeans were a bit more tattered than he would have liked. His jacket clung tightly to his shoulders; he was too big for it now. He fished out his phone. *No new messages, no new calls.* That was what he expected, really. Nothing ever happened in this town.

"Did you lie about Fortune Five Hundred giving you that cash?" Greg asked between laughs. "Don't keep Polly waiting!"

"Sure man, sure." Pent took his standard seat at the bar.

Polly sidled up. She was drying a glass and casting a familiar eye towards Pent. "Hey Adrian, pint of Coors?"

"Two pints sounds about right." Greg nudged Pent on the shoulder. "Polly, you know he's got my drinks tonight, yeah? Three-dollar pints, all on Pent!"

Polly raised an eyebrow. "What's he on about?"

"Yeah... Got a tip today. I was bagging groceries. This guy came in and he gave me a hundred-dollar bill." Pent clenched his fist. "Dude was talking about how he was some big shot. How he watched me play ball in high school, and he wondered why I hadn't gone anywhere."

Polly shifted in place. She leaned over to Greg. "Is he all right?"

"Beats me. All I know is he's got my drinks for tonight." He paused for a moment, considering his friend. "I think he's okay, Polly. Just had a rough day."

Pent studied the bar top with his hands and his eyes. "A rough day. Right." He glanced up at Polly. "Yeah, I've got the drinks; just put it on my tab if you could. Two pints. The regular."

"Sure," Polly said. She retreated to the tap, then returned with two glasses, filled to the brim with beer. "You enjoy yourselves now," she said as she left to serve the other patrons.

"Enjoy myself." He scoffed. "How am I supposed to enjoy myself in this deadbeat-ass town?"

Pent stared at the glass of beer. It was cold to the touch. He brought the glass to his lips and sipped slowly. The brew was cold going down and radiated a cool, relaxed feeling throughout his body. "Damn, that's good."

He turned and saw Greg had already drained half his glass. "Even better when it's free." Greg chuckled to himself as he downed the rest of the glass, he immediately called for another.

Pent laughed too. "Easy, man. Little dude like you? You gotta pace yourself."

"Yeah, yeah. So, what about that Wesley dude, huh? Putting you on for another shift like that."

"That's right..." Pent's mind was in a haze. *And I know it's not just the booze. One beer ain't enough to do me in.* "Yeah, he said Steve called out sick... I had to cover for his dumb ass."

"Sick, yeah right," Greg laughed. He did air quotes as he said the word sick. "I saw him on the way over here. Fool is walking around Chapel Street, blazed out of his mind, drunk or something. Asked me if he could bum a cigarette." He grabbed his second beer from Polly and drank from it greedily. She rolled her eyes and smiled at Pent, and then turned away as a man down the bar waved for her attention.

"Unbelievable," Pent said. "Some people are just completely worthless. What a bunch of nonsense." He was staring at his own glass; it was just about empty.

"What can you do, man?" Greg said. "Some people just want to take advantage of others." He smiled and slurped at his beer.

Pent grinned. "Maybe you should practice what you preach, man. What are you doing right now? It looks like plenty of advantage to me."

"Hey now, can a man enjoy a drink on a Friday night? No work on the horizon for us."

Greg had gotten halfway through his second beer. Pent rested his hand on his friend's wrist. "Yo, maybe you should ease up a bit. You can't plan on driving home like that."

Greg kept going. When he had finished the glass, he turned and smiled. "It'll be fine. These things have a way of working themselves out."

Pent glared at his friend. He lowered his glass slowly and shook his head. "Yeah... They do. I mean things do work out sometimes."

What the hell is going on? His head jerked up. "They worked out for you, 'cause I grabbed your car keys."

Greg frowned. "What you talking about, man?" He pulled out his keys and dangled them in front of Pent's face. "Got my keys right here."

"No. No, I took them later. And then I—" He saw flashes of things that couldn't have happened: A knight on horseback with a sword, a pale-faced wizard conjuring lightning, a smiling, red-bearded man... "And then I gave my last chunk of cash to that crop-eared homeless dude. Crop-eared..."

"Yo, you okay, man? You starting to look real pale for a black dude." Greg turned and gestured to Polly.

Pent grabbed at Greg's arm and yanked it down. "This isn't right. I'm not supposed to be here." All throughout his adult life he had been told that he had great potential, and that he was squandering it. He had waited around for something to happen in this deadbeat town, *and then something did.* "I'm supposed to be in Somerville."

Greg laughed. "You're drunk as hell. This is Somerville."

"Not this one though. The other one!" Pent clutched the sides of his head. He reached down and felt his gun in its holster. *I gave this away. This isn't right.* He got up abruptly and shuffled away from the bar. He stood for a moment, irresolute, and then reached for his money. His pocket was suddenly empty.

"What's going on?" Polly asked. "You're planning on running out on your tab, Pent?"

"I thought you said that business guy had you flush with cash," Greg said sympathetically.

"It's not that—I've gotta go—I've gotta get the hell out of here." Pent turned and walked towards the door.

"I don't like people leaving without paying for their drinks," Polly said. The bar had become silent and all the other patrons glanced towards him; Pent felt as if he was on a stage.

"Just put it on my tab then." Pent caught an earthen smell mingling with the dust and spilled beer, a smell foreign to the bar but somehow familiar. *This isn't right at all.* Shadows crept across the faces of all the bar goers, obscuring their features, and the overhead lights began to sway from side to side.

"You don't have a tab here, Pent," she snapped, speaking through gritted teeth. "You need to pay in cash." Polly dragged her hand along the length of the bar, scratching a line into the wood with her fingernails.

Pent's face flushed red as he turned away from the bar. "All right, I'm walking out of here. You want to stop me; you go ahead and try." He puffed his chest out, daring anyone to step to him. *I've been off the football field for a while, but I can still body any of these jokers.*

Greg hopped off his stool and walked up to Pent. "That's a typical move for you, isn't it?"

Pent backed up against the door. "I'm supposed to listen to a sermon from a drunk now?"

"Drunk, yeah. But right too." Greg's eyes darkened, and his drunken wobble faded away as he approached. In an instant, he seemed sober, standing tall, and eyeing Pent with dislike. *Since when was Greg as tall as me?* "You know I'm right. This is what you're best at, Adrian Pent—abandoning people."

Pent felt the blood drain from his face. "What did you say?"

"You heard me just fine. Or are you going to try and pretend about that, too? You're just a coward; all those muscles can't cover that up. Pent is just a coward everybody!" Greg raised his arms to a growing crowd of bar patrons. Everyone in the bar had turned to watch the spectacle unfold, but their eyes seemed empty and glazed over. "Someone who can't own up to anything. You would abandon everyone and everything you've known just for the chance at making your life better." He poked Pent in the chest, grinding and twisting his finger into Pent's skin. "You don't care about anyone."

"Th... that's not true." Pent swatted Greg's hand away. His hand felt cold and clammy to the touch.

"You only care about yourself."

"That's not true!" Pent cocked back and swung on Greg, hitting him square in the jaw. Greg tumbled onto his back. Pent towered over his friend, his fist clenched. "I'm out of here!"

No one else intervened as he stormed across the bar, kicked the door open, and marched through.

"Adrian Pent, don't you come in here tracking all that gunk on your shoes," his mother said severely.

"Momma, how?" Pent twisted around in place. The smell of cigarette smoke filled the air. He almost tripped over the clutter in his living room as he walked towards his mother.

"You carrying a lot with you. On your shoes and on your shoulders. Why don't you come and rest awhile?" she said.

Pent glanced at her and shook his head. "You're supposed to tell me to leave, to try and make things happen—and that I can't just wait around for things to happen to me." He looked around the room. The walls were slanted and warped. Their TV was playing static, but his mother was still enjoying it for some reason. "This ain't right."

"So, what you plan on doing? You gonna walk out on me then?" she said. She rose slowly, dropping her lit cigarette on the carpet. The carpet smoldered and began to catch fire, but Pent's mom walked over it as if she hadn't noticed. "You're just like him."

"Momma, the carpet. Let me get the carpet before this whole place goes up."

"You're just like your father."

Pent stared at her. He opened his mouth to speak, but she silenced him with a glance. "He abandoned this family, 'cause he was only interested in serving himself. And you're the same way. You're just like him."

"That ain't right, momma," Pent said, a note of panic creeping into his voice. He stared at the smoldering ground. The chiding made him feel like a child again, but the rising flames were igniting something deep within him that he couldn't fully comprehend.

"Oh no? Why don't you take a look?" She pointed behind Pent.

He turned. Everything was darkness. He was consumed by the void in every direction except one.

In front of him, a mirror rested against the wall of shadow. He walked slowly up to it.

The face of an old white man looked back at him. His hair was dark, straight, and graying on the edges. His face was set with wrinkles; his eyes filled with sadness. He wore a tan suit, frayed around the edges from constant wear. "Dad..."

The reflection simply stared back at him. Pent's heart went cold. He had done what they accused him of: He left his family, his friends —after a lifetime of condemning his father for doing the same thing. He had been his mother's support system, and he walked away. He left Somerville to rot; he had wished his whole life for something better for himself. He looked into his father's eyes and saw himself there.

No... No! Pent stepped closer to the mirror, his fists clenched. "I'm nothing like you! And I don't know what kind of nonsense you punk-ass Scribes are up to, but you're gonna have to do better than this." The image of his father looked concerned, and then enraged. It reached out through the mirror, its hands grasping for Pent.

Pent batted the hands away, and a burning fury flared within him. "My father was a loser; he couldn't handle the responsibilities he grew into. He left me and my mom, for God knows what. A better life on the west coast, somewhere he wouldn't have to worry about a thing, I guess."

Pent reached down to his belt and felt the ornate hilt of his sword. In a single motion he drew the sword and raised it into the air. "I'm nothing like him. I'm not about to back down from anything, not without a fight." He pointed the tip of the sword into the mirror. His father's reflection backed away nervously. "And I swear to you, I will never abandon anyone in my life who's important to me. I'll return for you all someday, I'll make everything right!"

His voice echoed through the darkness. Time and light stood still, and then the reflection that had horrified him so much began to shift. It was Pent—Pent as he was now—outfitted in his green cloak and plate armor, with a short beard and hair that could use a trim. Pent with a medieval sword in his hand, standing tall and proud.

The mirror shimmered, and then shattered into a million pieces. The darkness began to fade, and Pent found a familiar wooden stick at his feet. He sheathed his sword and picked up the burned-out torch. He lit it again with his lighter and swung it around in a circle.

"It felt so real," he said aloud. "It felt like I was really back there. Even the beer tasted real." He smiled grimly. "Nothing like Lemen's swill... I'm gonna miss those Coors the most."

He turned and, with a jolt, realized Hanar wasn't with him. *Damn, how long was I out for?* He rushed forward, searching the cave walls desperately. It didn't take him long to find Hanar; he was only a few feet away.

Hanar's body was huddled against the wall. Pent turned him over and moved the torch close to his eyes. His eyes were glazed over. They looked like the eyes of a dead man.

CHAPTER THIRTY-FOUR

"Hm. This does not seem right."

Hanar looked over the rim of the cliff. He breathed in the fresh, cool air; it was far better than a damp, claustrophobic cave. *Why has my mind wandered to caves?*

Caves made little sense to Hanar. He enjoyed spending his time in the open air, under the sun and stars. Nothing made him feel more at peace. Yet there was no peace here, despite the wonderful view. Something crucial was missing. This was the overlook that perched above the village of Somerville.

But Somerville was nowhere to be seen.

Hanar walked around the edge of the cliff until he reached the point in the river where Faldo's bridge should have allowed him to cross, but the bridge was missing with the rest of the village. Hanar began to ford the river. Within seconds, his teeth started to chatter. The water was beyond freezing; the current seemed to pull not only at his physical body, but at his energy, his vitality, and he felt himself grow stiff, slow, and clumsy.

He began to sink into the river, his slow clawing at the water no longer keeping him afloat. Frost burst from his lungs with each labored gasp as he flailed, panic momentarily burning away the fatigue. Hanar kicked out with everything he had. It wasn't enough. He felt the darkness close in, as he drifted beneath the surface of the water. He sank, and he kept sinking, down far deeper than the river should have been.

He could not move his arms or legs. His eyes closed in despair.

A warm hand grasped onto him from above, and an arm pulled him free of the water.

A thin man dragged him to the edge of the river. Hanar retched out water and gasped for air. Between coughs, through chattering teeth and lips blue with cold, he fumbled out his appreciation. "Th... thank you. Th... the water was c... colder than I w... would have th... thought."

"Think nothing of it, Hanar. You've always been so competent. I don't recall you ever needing anything from me before. I'm glad to be of service."

Hanar glared at the man and forced himself to his feet. The man's face was tan, and his hair was rustled and trimmed short. It was a face Hanar knew well. "Lemen? This cannot be. You are—"

"Dead," Lemen finished for him. Hanar studied Lemen closely. He was firm, standing tall and proud, like when they had been young. "It's regrettable, yes. But there's a peace in it."

"Indeed. You seem at peace." Hanar looked around. "How... how can this be? If you are dead—" He scratched at his beard. "This is most unfortunate. If this is not a dream, then I am dead as well." He tried to remember where he was when he died, but his mind drew a cloudy blank. *A cloud of cold and darkness.* "Lyle always said I would let my feet march ahead of me and walk into some trouble I couldn't walk out of..." He slowly shook his head. "Where are we, Lemen?"

Lemen smiled, turning away from the river, and beginning to walk. Hanar hurried after him.

They walked at a deliberate pace, stopping shortly after where

Somerville's entrance should have been. It was eerie, being in this plot of land without the buildings or people anywhere to be seen. Hanar trembled nervously. "I don't like this, Lemen. The afterlife can't be so lonely."

He hadn't noticed how quiet it was until then. Normally the air was filled with the sounds of birds, of the rustling of branches and trees. *And of course, the people.* But it was as if he had been struck deaf. There was no evidence of a soul in this place.

"I fell here," Lemen said. He shifted in place, kicking the dirt up. It would have been around where the first fortifications were placed. *That's right. Pent said that he fell against the captain of Gilbrand's guard.*

The thought tore something open in Hanar's mind. "Pent!" He said the name aloud and pondered it for a moment. *How could I have forgotten him?* Where could Pent have been when he died? How did it happen? The questions rang out in his mind like a bell. "Lemen, why have you brought me here?"

"There's no alcohol here," he said, continuing the haunting tour of this otherworldly Somerville that was not Somerville. He kept speaking as if he hadn't heard Hanar's question. "But that's all right. I have them, at least."

Hanar looked to where he was gesturing. A young woman and a small girl were off in the distance, close to the cliff walls where Somerville mined its ore. He recognized the woman at once. "Your wife. I see. So, this really is the valley of the dead." He had imagined the afterlife many times before, but it was never anything like this. "This was not the end I expected, but... at least I have friends to bide this time with. Are you here to guide me then?"

Lemen turned and smiled. "There's no one here for you," he said. "I have to go now, to be with my family." He walked on towards the ore wall in silence.

Hanar felt his heart thump with panic. "Wait!" he yelled. "You can't leave me here alone!" He ran after Lemen. He ran and ran, pushing his legs to their limit. But no matter how far or how fast he ran, he could not catch up. Lemen glided forward, just out of reach, until he caught up with his family. They all waved to Hanar a single time, and then faded away.

Hanar leapt after them, falling through their fading forms and crashing into the ground. He lay there for a moment, gasping, and shaking violently.

When he finally rose, he shambled away from the wall like a corpse. He shuffled around the town. He could see the forests above the outcropping, but their appeal was lost on him.

"I can't be the only person here, I just can't," he said hopelessly to himself. He stopped where Cenk's hut should have been. As he thought about the short man, tinkering away at his anvil endlessly, a sad smile curved his lips—and before his eyes, the conical hut began to appear. Though surprised, the familiar shape of it brought comfort as well, and he felt some of the hopeless, dreadful loneliness fall from him as stepped inside. He batted the smoke out of his eyes and called out for the blacksmith. "Cenk!"

When there was no response, he called again. "Cenk! Are you here?" He looked around, and the flame in the hut began to die down. He turned to call again, but something stopped him.

Who...? Who lived here?

He was sure there was a man—a man smaller than most—who lived here. He did something involving flames. But even that vision began to fade. Soon the man himself was gone from Hanar's mind, and the hut began to fade as well.

He shuffled back into the village square. His mind rolled over, and he fell to his knees. He retched again, vomiting onto the ground. There he stayed for a great while, eyes closed, mind a slow tumult of dreary emotion. Finally, Hanar wiped his mouth clean and stood, a half-formed thought pulling him toward a certain spot in town. He stopped at the outline of his sister's home. *Lyle. Mother Lyle. Chief Lyle.*

His sister had always supported him, even though she was so different from him. *She was never alone, always surrounded by friends and those she had impressed. While all I had was her.* She was always the leader: always in charge, never the outsider. The house appeared before his eyes and he rushed in, calling out her name.

"Lyle! Lyle, please!"

His sister appeared. Hanar wiped roughly at his eyes as he looked at her.

"Brother, are you minding yourself? Are you being careful?"

He burst into tears. "I don't know the means, but it seems I have perished. Have you died as well? Is this the end for us?"

She regarded him sadly and rested her hand on his shoulder. "When I pass, it will be in the company of others. My time has not yet come," she said.

Hanar let out a pained groan. "You've always been by my side. You would never abandon me. It cannot be so!" He rubbed at his eyes, wiping away his tears. When he opened them, Lyle had faded away, and her home along with it.

He charged back into the village square, yelling aloud. His screams tore into the soundless void like lightning in the dark. *What of—what of Pent? My friend... my closest friend.* Hanar had felt so alone, so much like an outsider until Pent had arrived. "We went on adventures together." But even those words were losing their meaning to him. He could not remember what they had done, where they had been, and, as he walked, even the image of his odd-looking friend faded.

He shambled towards the river, his mind a blank slate, filled with nothing but dread and despair. All the memories of his friends and family were gone. Before him, the river flowed past, fast and silent. *Endless, dark, cold.* He closed his eyes and plunged in.

The cold was crushing, asphyxiating, and it stole the life from his limbs in mere moments. As his head plunged underwater, he felt the darkness swarming in. He didn't fight it. He was fully resigned. He was completely alone.

His body shook, but he could hardly feel it. The only sensation was a warmth that gripped his arm. That warmth tingled in his consciousness, but the darkness was all encompassing, leaving room in his mind for nothing but itself.

It's so dark. It's so cold and so dark.

CHAPTER THIRTY-FIVE

Pent shook Hanar's body vigorously. "Hanar! Come on, man! Wake up!" he shouted in his friend's face. Pent pulled his eyelids back; Hanar's stare had gone beyond a thousand yards.

Pent reached for a pulse; Hanar's heart was still beating. *But way too slowly. What the hell am I supposed to do?* For all the man's cowardice, he wished Gordenthorpe was here—or Ellie, or Lyle. "Or someone who knows CPR. Come on, Hanar, wake up! Wake up, Hanar! Wake up!"

Pent's eyes fell on the torch. He grabbed it with a shaky hand and hesitated. "Sorry in advance for this."

He prodded Hanar's chest with the tip of the torch. The smell of burnt flesh rose into the air, and Hanar yelled out. Pent pulled the torch away and dropped it back to the ground.

Hanar shot upright. He clutched at his chest, gasping. "You burned me! You burned me with that torch! How could you do such a thing?"

"Do such a thing? You were a half step away from being a dead man. Almost no pulse, your eyes rolled back in your head—you should be thanking me!"

"Thanking you!" Hanar rubbed at his chest and frowned. "If I'm to thank you for burning me, I'd hate to see what your bad deeds look like."

Pent swept the torch up, desperate to keep his hands on it. "Whatever man, you have no idea what I just went through." He heard a sob in the darkness. Raising the torch up, Pent got a good look at Hanar's face.

Hanar was holding his head in his hands, weeping openly. "Ah, this despair is worse than hell. This is a dreadful place, Pent. I wish I hadn't come here." He sniffled, wiping his eyes on his cloak. "I spoke rashly and in pain. I am truly grateful."

Pent shrugged and began to turn away. "Don't mention it. You would have done the same for me."

"I give thanks for that." He wiped at his eyes again. "But even more, I give thanks for your place by my side. I pray that when I do pass, it won't be a lonely death. Having someone to banter with, to travel with... we must hold onto these moments forever."

"I take it you were going through a Scribe acid trip too?" Pent asked. He hugged Hanar with his free arm, and then waved his torch to the direction ahead.

"I understand your meaning. These Scribes are a loathsome people. Such horrible powers..." Hanar shivered. "They make Yozer seem like a gentle lamb."

"Tell me about it." Pent gestured forward again, the torch leaving an orange trail in the dark as he waved it. "Let's get this done. I'm tired of playing games with these fools."

They began to move, walking cautiously. Hanar rubbed his chest. "What inspired you to burn me with the torch?"

"Uh, picked it up from a movie I saw. *Temple of Doom*."

"That sounds ominous. Is there a movie called the Cave of Doom?"

"Well if there is, I'm hoping it has a happy ending."

CHAPTER THIRTY-SIX

They pressed on and on. As they moved forward, the cave began to widen.

"Pent, I'm not sure if my eyes are deceiving me, but does the darkness not seem as... horrible as before?"

The brightness of the torch seemed to reach out farther than before, illuminating the rough texture of the cave walls around them. "I can actually see my damn feet for once."

The features of the cave were becoming clearer. The floor, they noticed, was not of natural design. The pathway at their feet was covered with a mix of paved stone and loose rock. The walls also seemed a blend of natural cave stone and carved stone blocks. What appeared to be the roots of trees jutted in and out, zigzagging across the walls. *Roots? We're in a cave though. There's no way there's a tree on top of all this.*

Pent reached forward and touched one of the roots. It throbbed as if the cave itself had a pulse and he'd just set his hand to a vein. He drew back in surprise. "Can't it just be a normal cave? I don't think I'm asking for a lot."

"These Scribes—it must be their influence again," Hanar said, "their warped imagination. It can disfigure nature in such a way." He couldn't hide his disgust.

"You would think the forced nightmares were bad enough," Pent grumbled.

"If their power grows as Gordenthorpe said it would, who knows what will become of the world?"

"I'm not planning on finding out."

As the walls spread out and became wider, the path began to branch off in different directions. Hanar pointed off to the side. "There's a room there, and one there as well." He scratched at his beard. "I'm not sure which way to go. But I would advise not splitting up."

"To hell with that," Pent said at once. After the horrors they both experienced, he wasn't about to chance splitting up in the dark hallways of the cave. "More I think about it, that dark haze that made us trip out? Had to be some kind of trap. Catherine said something about hallucinating too."

"So, you believe the worst is behind us?"

"I don't believe anything anymore, but maybe. Who can tell with these freaks?" Pent waved the torch from right to left, illuminating the paths before them. "Let's just stick together and stay alert until we find the kids."

They chose the room to the left. Pent poked his head in first, waving the torch around carefully. He realized the purpose of the room immediately. "Books," he said aloud. Books were stacked haphazardly on crooked shelves, lining every wall. It made Pent think of a storage unit: not a single article of furniture for comfort in sight.

Together, they entered the room, feeling somewhat less intimidated now that they knew what it was. Hanar thumbed through the volumes that filled the entire room. "There are more tomes here than I have ever seen in my life. This would be the envy of any scholar." He pulled one out and flipped through the pages. "Do you recall of what the travelers from Brighton said to us?

Something of a great library at the base of Eccue's tower? I wonder if it was anything as grand as this."

"It makes sense." Pent carefully passed the torch over the volumes, scanning the spines. Most of them were in a language he had never seen before, and he could not make out what they said. "The Scribes. They write, they read. Man, I bet Gordenthorpe would kill to get his hands on these." After all he had said about making everything weird, this room was the most familiar thing he had seen. It reminded him of Somerville's library, the one from his own world.

Hanar let out a barely audible gasp. When Pent peered over, Hanar was holding a thick book in his hand. "My friend. This is perhaps worth your attention."

Pent strolled over. The light was dim in the room, but there had been enough from the torch to see the titles of the books. He handed the torch over to Hanar and held the book in his hands. He flipped the book over.

"America?" He read the word on the cover out loud again, in complete disbelief. "America." *How in the hell...*

"You've mentioned the name to me before. Is the tome familiar to you?"

"Familiar—of course it is." Pent ran his fingers across the cover. An outline of the United States was imprinted on the front of the book. "What in the hell is this?" *I picked up a book just like this one, with the same ornate lettering, back in that library on Maple Street. That one said Cinraia on it though.*

"That tall homeless man with the cropped ears. Here's the connection right here. Hanar, this—this could be my ticket home. Maybe it's like the one from my world, some kind of gateway back!" Pent said excitedly. He flipped open the book, then slammed it shut in frustration. "It's all in their screwed-up language. I can't read it."

"Perhaps Gordenthorpe would be able to," Hanar said. His eyes were as wide as an owl's. "He's the only one I can think of."

"Maybe. Damn, this is too crazy." Pent ran his fingers over the cover again. *There could be some kind of explanation in this book about how I landed here—maybe some kind of way for me to get home. All this time here, and I couldn't find a clue. But this could be it. I could go back to my old life, and everything I've left behind!*

He thought back to his march through the cave and the nightmares he had been trapped in. *Unless it's just another trap.* Knowing he would have to risk it to find out more, Pent took the book and slipped it into his belt loop. "Whatever's in here, it's wasting our time right now. We're not going to find the kids in this library. Let's keep moving."

The rooms adjacent to the hallway were filled with various structures and equipment with no obvious purpose, and each room more bizarre than the last. "It looks like that library was the only normal place in this whole cave," Pent said.

One of the rooms reminded Pent of a hospital. Long tables with straps and buckles were lined up neatly in the center of the room. The walls were obscured by various weapons—swords and spears, mostly—all of which were bent and deformed. Hanar spent a moment investigating the collection but found nothing he felt confident in taking with him. "I do not understand. These are as light as paper." He lifted a massive shield up, holding it with one finger. "Did the Scribes create these too? Did they create them already tarnished and mangled?"

Pent reached through a pile of misshapen daggers, all with dull blades. Next to them was a strip of what seemed to be a giant animal's intestines. "I'm not sure if I'm supposed to be disgusted or impressed by all this creativity," he said.

"Disgusted," Hanar said definitively. "And I see no trace of the children here either. Let us return to the hallway."

They walked on, leaving the bizarre rooms behind. The hall began to twist, turn, and narrow as they went on. It inclined slightly, forming a hill that obscured their view forward.

Hanar grabbed at Pent's shoulder, pulling him down. He

whispered into Pent's ear, his breath sending shivers down Pent's spine. "There's something wrong up ahead."

"What do you mean?"

Hanar shook his head. "Just believe in me; wait here a moment."

Hanar stepped deftly ahead, his footsteps were silent. Pent watched as his friend neared the top of the incline. Hanar glanced over the lip of the rise, studied something unseen to Pent, and then scrambled back down.

"Well?"

Hanar gestured to the torch. "You should put that out. There's light above. Light—and much more besides."

Pent stamped out the torch and left it on the ground. He followed Hanar slowly to the top of the incline. There was a small raised wall made of deformed stone blocks, just high enough for them both to duck behind. Hanar glanced over it, and Pent joined him.

It was as if they had stepped into hell.

CHAPTER THIRTY-SEVEN

Pent stared, scanning from one side of the circular room to the other. He picked out the source of light immediately. Hexagonal shaped crystals adorned the ceiling and the walls. They emitted a dull, blue light, and had the same otherworldly shimmer that the minotaur and gargoyles had. They were just about the only thing in the room that was not entirely unsettling.

Tapestries of cloth covered the walls. The images depicted horrible scenes of violence and warfare. Pent studied the closest one, and after a moment, he realized the tapestry was showing some kind of war against the Scribes. Men and women encased in armor put the Scribes to the sword. *The history of the Scribes?*

The tall figures of the Scribes cast their hands out in a field of black. Mountains and rivers appeared over a flat landscape. The sun and the moon rose to pierce through the darkness.

Then there were monsters as well as men, many scenes of death and horror, and rivers running red with blood. The entire length of the room was covered; the brutal imagery twisted Pent's stomach.

Two men with robes were surrounded by men and women in tunics with swords and axes. The men and women were of every shape and size, some with pale skin and some darkened by the sun. The picture painted them as villains, but Pent felt a kindred spirit with them somehow. *Is this the Age of Crusaders?*

The entire history of the war seemed to be on display, highlighting the battles between the monsters and men, the rise of small villages, and the Scribes' flight from the open land to the dank caves. On the right, near the start of the story, dozens of the grotesque figures stood together, but as the tale moved to the left, the figures dwindled away until there appeared to be only five remaining. *So, they were all killed off in the fighting?*

Pent's eyes were drawn to a scene towards the center of the tapestry. The five Scribes stood in a circle, creating some kind of portal. *Looks like a black hole.* In the adjacent scene, one of the five fell into the hole. The last four fled from the encroaching warriors and settled in a cave.

The two robed men held large staves and encircled the cave: one frail-looking, bald, and short, wearing robes as dark as the night; the other tall, taller than any man had a right to be, with thin limbs and long jet black hair that flowed below his shoulders. The taller man's robes were a lighter color; they could have been white, or a light gray. Together, they raised their staves, and the front of the cave was obscured.

The imagery stopped there. Pent closed his gaping mouth, shocked as he was. *I've never been to an art gallery before, but I imagine they're not so... violent?* The scenes of death were unlike any war movie Pent had seen and reminded him more of a book he read in high school. *Dante's Inferno—was that it? This is some grim stuff.*

Hanar pressed against his shoulder, jostling him out of his daydreaming and pointing downward toward the center of the chamber. Pent had been so taken with the gallery of tapestries that he had failed to mark the presence of multiple figures within the room below. Three of the Scribes encircled a stone fountain and were shuffling around it slowly.

Whispering so softly that Pent had to lean in to hear it, Hanar said, "That's the one we saw outside."

Pent nodded. The Scribes seemed to be almost identical in appearance, but it was clear which one they had fought. *He's the only one wearing anything.* His black cloak swayed lazily as the three Scribes continued their slow circle around the fountain. They each had a thick book in their hands. "So then, Catherine must still be in that one's book," Pent said. "We need to get our hands on that book."

"And more than that," Hanar whispered. He pointed to one corner of the room. Children, many children, were lying about haphazardly, like toys that had been cast aside and forgotten by a careless child.

"Are they...?"

Hanar frowned, knowing what Pent meant without finishing the thought. "I cannot tell from here. I can only hope they're all right." He leaned over the wall to get just a little closer, squinting. "Some of the children are moving. But not all."

Hanar ducked down, and Pent followed him. There was movement in the circle of Scribes. The one with the cloak went to the huddle of children. It raised its hands, and as they rose a child began to float in the air, drifting back to the other Scribes. Pent and Hanar stared in horror as the child hovered over the stone fountain.

"That's Tash—she's one of the kids from Somerville..." Pent whispered. He clenched his fist in impotent rage.

The Scribes all emitted a low, droning noise as they spread their arms around Tash. One of them dragged its finger along the child's belly; a thin line of blood seeped from the wound and dripped into the fountain, which already contained some kind of liquid. Though it was difficult to see from where they hid, it looked like the contents of the bowl turned a thick, black color when the blood was added. The cloaked Scribe drew a nail along its own wrist and added its own blood to the fountain. There was a multi-colored shimmer as the liquid settled.

The Scribes placed the child back in the pile of children. Faintly,

Pent heard Tash groan miserably. Once that was settled, the three monstrous creatures placed their hands in the fountain itself. An inhuman noise of ecstasy burbled through the chamber; so intense was their pleasure that Pent could feel it like a static charge in the air, and it made his stomach churn.

"They're not dead, they can't all be dead," Pent said. "They're holding them here, using them as batteries. The blood of the Scribes—that's how they use their powers."

Hanar nodded. "It's their ink. And they need the children to fuel their evil fountain."

"They must pull enough blood for what they need, and then they put the kids to the side," Pent said. "Probably so they can get more later." He looked all over the room, hoping to find some hint, some vital piece of information that would help him save the children and defeat the Scribes. The three Scribes were back to staring at the fountain, deeply trapped in their own thoughts.

"Pent, I have no inkling of a plan here. We know where Catherine is, and the children," he rummaged through his pack, "and I have the one glass of milk. We have an understanding of the situation, now we need a plan."

"Well damn, the milk is our ace in the hole. We've got them in our sights, and that's where we need to strike," he said, pointing. "The fountain is where they draw their power from. So, we'll poison the well."

Hanar clutched the milk bottle. "That's sure enough. But I don't trust my throwing arm that much. We can't risk throwing this bottle—if we had more than one perhaps—but if we miss with this..." He shook his head. "We cannot miss with this."

"No, we can't. So, you're gonna sneak around to the side. Wait for your moment, and then drain the bottle into the fountain."

Hanar stared at him. "Me? And what about you?"

Pent rested his hand on the hilt of his sword. "I'll distract them. Give me a minute to get their attention, and then you move as swift as you can."

"Have you lost your mind?" Hanar said, his voice rising above a whisper for a moment. He glanced in the direction of the Scribes to see if they had noticed, but they hadn't moved from their positions around the fountain. "That's a suicide mission; you can't face them alone."

"We don't have a choice. You've got those light steps—no way my huge lumbering self is sneaking over there unnoticed. We could barely handle the one of them outside together. Against three of them we would lose, and then that's the end of everything." Pent shook his head. "This is the only way I can figure we make it happen. I'll give you an in, and then you use the milk to take the fountain out. Hopefully that's enough."

"You don't even know if that will stop them."

"It worked on the minotaur and the gargoyles. And damn, man, we're fresh out of options here." Hanar stared at him accusingly, but Pent just rested his hand on his friend's shoulder. "Just trust me."

Hanar nodded. "Fine. Fine. I'll have to pass the children to reach the fountain."

"Sure, but don't spend too much time there," Pent said. "Check them out, and then get to the fountain as soon as you can."

"This plan still does not sit well with me. Dare I even ask you to try and not be so reckless?"

Pent smiled. "Nah, that's not gonna happen. I'm going wild on these creeps. They won't even see this coming."

CHAPTER THIRTY-EIGHT

Pent watched as Hanar snuck off, hugging the wall. The woodsman was poised and ready to spring forward.

Pent took a deep breath. Whatever they had been through, it all came down to this. He rubbed the book on his belt, feeling the indentations of his home imprinted on the cover. *If I die here, well, there goes my shot at seeing momma again.*

The thought made him smile, and he nearly burst out laughing, but he held it back, desperate not to give away his position. He recalled the football field. *Everything always goes back to that damn football field.* But he couldn't help it. He had never felt so many eyes on him until the first time he stepped out on that green grass. The pressure was unreal. It was smothering. And then, only a few months ago, he'd felt that pressure again. He'd had the weight of people's lives on his shoulders, as he brought Somerville to arms against the powerful Yozer.

He swallowed past the lump in his throat. *But I had a team with me on the field—and I had a town with me against Yozer.* He was all alone here. Hanar was his only backup, and he had sent the man away. He would have to stand alone against these horrible terrors, creatures capable of wielding powers he could barely understand.

He had promised himself he wouldn't be the kind of man his father was. *Lord knows I could turn and run out the damn cave right now.* He could come up with some kind of lie: He could tell Lyle he tried his best, but in the end, he couldn't save the children; he couldn't save Hanar either. Cinraia had become a chaotic mess, but he could find a quiet life here somehow. Or maybe he could search the world and find a way home. These thoughts flashed in his mind for a brief second, and then were wiped clear.

There wasn't a real choice, as far as Pent was concerned. *Step after step, I've had the chance to turn tail and run. The time for backing out is long gone.*

He dug his hands into the stones by his knees; one of them was loose enough to jostle free. He yanked it out, clutching it in his right hand. He took his time, cradled it, lacing his fingers up like it was a football. *I don't think I would have made quarterback, but let's see if my aim is still on.*

He rose slowly and observed the full length of the room. The weight of everything in front of him was heavy on his shoulders. He stepped over the wall, one leg after the other, and stepped down softly on the other side. The Scribes still hadn't noticed him. A metallic smell drifted in the air, tickling his nose and throat; he stifled a cough. Pent cocked his arm back.

He launched the stone block at the nearest Scribe, and his aim was true. The creature hissed and reeled backwards. In the dim blue light, Pent spotted a black trickle falling from its forehead. *Looks like I don't need milk to draw blood against these guys.* The three Scribes all turned towards him. They hissed in unison.

"You like to make people bleed, huh? Well how do you like that?" Pent raised his arms, taunting them from across the room. "Come on then, you think I'm afraid?" He flipped off the nearest one, wondering if they would even understand the gesture. Their hissing ceased. "Just a bunch of freaks, picking on children. Why don't you try someone your own size, you bastards?"

They began to approach. They hovered above the ground, gliding smoothly but slowly towards Pent. *So, they can fly too? Terrific.* The one with the fresh head wound and the one with the cloak floated in front. The third had larger ears than the others, and they appeared to be hooked forward slightly. It maintained a safe distance behind. The Scribes moved with confidence and determination. Pent waited for just the right moment.

When the cloaked Scribe came close enough, Pent unsheathed his sword in a single motion and struck out. Its eyes went wide as the blade flashed in the blue light. It raised its arm, book in hand, only to have the limb lopped off entirely. The ghastly severed arm fell at Pent's feet and, on instinct, he kicked it across the room. It landed near the far wall by the children, still clutching the book.

Pent turned and stabbed forward, narrowly missing the Scribe with the head wound. It darted back; its book was open, and it was already conjuring something from its depths. Pent cursed under his breath, wishing that he had doused his sword in milk before sending Hanar on his way. *A lot of good it does, thinking of that now. Damn it.*

The cloaked one was on its knees, whimpering, holding the stump of its arm. The Scribe with the hooked ears stood over it, its own book out. Pent could make out the blood from the fountain slithering through the air and surrounding the severed stump. It shimmered, and then all at once its arm had returned. *Terrific.*

He slashed across the chest of the closest Scribe, leaving a savage gash in its pale, folded flesh. It backed up against the wall, and then pushed the book towards Pent. *I can't let him work that magic!* He lunged desperately at the book, aiming to cleave it in two, but his sword struck only air as it missed the target by inches. Pent gasped in awe as he saw what was being conjured from the book: Small, dark-winged creatures took flight all at once, filling the air with ear-piercing screeches. *Bats. This just gets better and better.*

Pent swatted at the creatures as they swooped and clawed at him.

His strikes were of little use; when he managed to hit something, the bats would fall to the ground, shimmer, and then take flight again. He barreled through the swarm and found himself face to face with the three Scribes.

He stabbed wildly at them, but this time the three all backed up in unison. *Looks like they're ready for me now.* Though he'd cleared the swarm of bats for an instant, they coalesced around him once more and started diving for his eyes, forcing him to close them and hide his face. *They're trying to blind me.* Swinging blindly with his sword, Pent felt a sharp pain on his wrist. An impossibly strong grip attempted to tug him forward, but he yanked his hand away violently, managing to free himself.

As he did, he felt the hilt of his sword slip free from his grasp, and heard it clang to the ground underfoot. Pent cursed and opened his eyes as he stepped back to give himself space to look. The Scribes had walked in front of it. A shiver ran down his spine. "Is this it then?" The bats began to fade away, but without his weapon, he was all but defenseless against the Scribes.

He ran his hand over the wall and dragged his feet across the floor, feeling for loose stones. He found a few and, after quickly pulling them free, launched them desperately. Some landed, impacting solidly against their targets, but the Scribes were ignoring the wounds now; their rage had boiled over. Pent felt on his belt for anything to use. He flung the first thing he laid his hand on, and then cursed again when he realized it was the book labeled "America." *Well, I guess it doesn't matter now.*

He felt the butt of his folding knife and drew it from his belt. He flicked it open as the Scribes formed a circle around him. "It's just me and you, boys," Pent shouted at the approaching fiends. "And I'll promise you this. You're gonna have to work for it!"

CHAPTER THIRTY-NINE

It took all the willpower Hanar could muster to not abandon his mission in order to assist his friend. From a distance, it seemed that Pent was finding success at first, but the mysterious powers of the Scribes quickly turned the tide. Hanar heard Pent's sword clatter onto the ground and turned, expecting to see the worst. His friend had been pushed back to the edge of the room, and the Scribes made a tight circle around him.

Hanar bit his lip. He reached for an arrow but pulled his arm back without drawing from the quiver. *I cannot waste this moment. I must act now!* He tiptoed through the shadows until he came upon the children.

His hopes were colored by a cascade of emotions. *Some are still alive. But some... some have perished.* He recognized few among the dead. *These others must be from Tofac, or other nearby villages. The Scribes use them until they are depleted, and don't even have the decency to bury them.* He clenched his fists against the rage that boiled within him, and he made himself move on.

His eyes halted at the cold body of a boy he recognized, and he felt his burning anger doused by icy dread. Hanar let out a pained moan as he checked the child for a pulse. "Bart..." The boy was dead. He leaned forward and closed the boy's eyelids. *Marall's son. Oh, this is a misery. We delayed for too long, and that blame—it rests on my shoulders. If only I hadn't fallen ill, Marall. I'm so sorry.*

He glanced over to the war Pent was waging with the Scribes. *We must defeat them, to protect the world—and to free those who've survived.* A new vigor welling up inside, Hanar crawled over to the fountain. He rose next to it, looking down into the well of black liquid. "It's time to put an end to this madness," he whispered to himself.

He pulled the milk bottle out of his pack and wrenched the cork free. *This has to work, please let this work.* He raised the container high in the air—

The bottle leapt from his hand and smashed against the wall behind him, a shimmering spear sticking through what remained.

CHAPTER FORTY

"No!" Pent shouted in horror. From the corner of his eye, he saw the milk bottle smash into a thousand pieces. Their only hope was soaked up by the tapestries on the wall.

A fourth Scribe had appeared from the shadows, this one much larger than the others, standing a full two feet taller than Pent. From its book, it had conjured a spear that shot across the room as if fired from a harpoon gun.

"Damn it. Damn it!" Pent howled. He swung outwards with his knife and struck the nearest Scribe. It fell back, clearly surprised by his renewed attack. The two others still stood in front of him, blocking him from his sword.

Pent ducked down for a second, and then charged forward, barreling into the cloaked Scribe. It hissed into his ear as he felt its chest cave in under the force of his metallic shoulder pads. The one with the hooked ears grabbed at him, but he smashed it in the neck with a backhand. It went tumbling into the wall and shook as it struggled back to its feet.

He had made it to the sword, but before he could grab it, an inhumanly strong hand clasped him on the wrist. The largest Scribe towered over him, leaning down with its impossibly long fingers and clenching his arm tightly. He struggled with everything he had but could not break free. *How is this frail-looking thing this strong?*

It slowly straightened, dragging Pent with it. He tried smashing the giant in the face, as he had with the other Scribe, but it caught his fist mid swing and pulled his arm to the side. His muscles bulged as he tried to break free, but the Scribe's grip was unshakeable. It stared at him inquisitively, like someone who has found an unusual bug crawling across their floor, and Pent was lifted off the ground, held in the air like a cross.

He kicked out instead, driving his boots into the Scribe's stomach, but after a moment's struggle, he felt his feet bound by more strong hands. The hook-eared Scribe held his feet together, leaving Pent entirely unable to move.

The Scribe with the head wound glanced at Hanar, and the cloaked one drew next to Pent. Mechanically, the monstrosity began to disassemble Pent's plate armor, ripping it free from his body with its bare hands. When that was done, it ripped the tunic down, and then pointed a single black nail at Pent's face.

Pent howled in agony as it stabbed into his chest with its nail. He flailed, attempting to break free, but to no avail; he could scarcely move an inch. The Scribe dragged its fingernail along the length of Pent's chest.

The pain was beyond anything he had ever felt before. As he felt the sharpness peak, he looked down. Something inside of him had begun to stir. *My blood.* He felt the blood inside of him move. As he watched, a thin streak began to rise from the line the Scribe had drawn into him. *They're taking... my blood...*

CHAPTER FORTY-ONE

"Pent!" Hanar screamed, horror raising gooseflesh on his arms and neck as he watched his friend's crucifixion. He nocked arrows one after the other, desperately loosing them at the larger Scribe. If he could kill that single Scribe, he knew he could release his friend.

But the Scribe with the oozing head wound was already aware of Hanar's intentions. From its book it had conjured a shimmering shield of light, and the arrows rebounded off harmlessly. Hanar looked around in desperation. The Scribe was drawing in closer, and he had quickly been pressed back against a wall.

He brushed up against the hilt of his sword but felt only grim pessimism at the thought of using it. *If Pent couldn't manage with his sword, what hope do I have?* He fell in despair against the wall, looking up at the milk splattered on the tapestry across from him. *If only we had more milk—or something else entirely.*

His eyes went wide. *Gordenthorpe spoke of another weakness.* But it was already so late in their quest, and he had nothing else he could think to use. He could try to dash along the length of the room to get to the milk puddle on the floor—

He shook his head. *They already knew enough about it to prevent me from using it the first time.* The Scribe was staring at him intently. It moved slowly, but not slow enough; Hanar knew that he wouldn't have another chance with the milk.

Another weakness, another weakness... What was it that Gordenthorpe had said? *Something about life... The foundation of life? The essence of life? The forge of life?* Hanar's head was a cascade of tumbling, half-formed thoughts. He fumbled at his quiver, cursing when he realized he had only a single arrow left. "Ah, good, another obstacle. I was starting to feel as if this would be too easy!"

Another weakness—something to do with life. *What can create life? Milk doesn't create life, only support it...* He felt a chill run through his spine as the Scribe drew closer.

Hanar gasped.

A chill. What can beat back a chill? What can you use to support life? These monsters, they live in the freezing cold and the endless darkness.

He glanced around, taking in the scene, bathed in blue light. *Those crystals, it's like we're coated in frost. Why not just use torches?*

It came to him in a flash. *Fire—the forge of life. That must be it!* It was his only chance. He clawed through his pack, his shaking hand clutching his flint. He had done this a thousand times, but never in such a situation. *Tinder, tinder, what can I use?* He sucked in air through his teeth as he whipped his cloak around in front of him. *This will have to do.* He struck the end of his flint with his knife. A small spark shot out. The Scribe was close.

He struck again—another small spark, but no flame. The Scribe was mere feet away. It stared at him, an inquisitive look on its horrible face.

He struck a third time. *Fire!* A wispy trail of smoke curled up from a fold in the cloak where the spark had caught. Hanar blew gently across the smoldering fabric and a flame burst to life, dancing quickly along the dry wool.

The Scribe hissed and recoiled. The three who had attended to Pent all shuddered and began to screech and squawk in a horrifying, high-pitched bugle like that of an elk. They dropped Pent to the ground—his body fell limp—and they all began to glide towards Hanar.

In a single swift motion, Hanar ripped a piece off of his burning cloak. He tied it to his last arrow and pulled back on his bow, his hands throbbing from the angry red burns he'd suffered.

The closest Scribe, still bleeding from a knock to the head courtesy of Pent, had recovered from its earlier fear and was advancing toward Hanar once again, its long, clawed fingers curled as if they'd already wrapped around his neck.

He met the creature's eye and aimed as true as he had ever known. A moment before he felt the hands grip his neck, he shouted out. "BURN!"

The flaming arrow arced through the air; it landed dead center in the fountain. After a moment of confused silence, the haunted well of blood and ink erupted into a raging inferno.

CHAPTER FORTY-TWO

Hanar felt the hands release from his throat. He watched as the four Scribes converged on the fountain. They all hissed, gesturing in horror, and attempting to pat down and douse the flames. Their clumsy, panicked efforts did little to quell the inferno, but in their flailing, one of the Scribes, Hanar couldn't tell which, burst into flames. The creature burbled and screamed as it stumbled blindly about the chamber. In its last moments, the Scribe seemed to sense Hanar, and it threw itself at him, using its own dying body as a weapon. Hanar shoved it away, sending it tumbling to the ground, where it fell still. The smell of burning meat filled the cave as the remains continue to smolder, but Hanar hardly noticed. The flesh of his fingers and hands had burst open upon contact with the burning Scribe, and the dead skin fell away in clumps. Though the pain was unlike anything he had known before, he could not succumb to it; they were not yet done here.

The three remaining Scribes shouted in hate and fear. They raised their books, but either the magic had left them, or their resolve had. They seemed unable to create anything from their canvas of dread powers. The fountain of fire was becoming more dangerous by the moment, and the Scribes fell back in fright as liquid droplets of fire began erupting from the fountain, many landing on the tapestries that had adorned the wall. One after another, they were engulfed in flame. Soon the dull blue light that had suffused the room was snuffed out, and Hanar began to feel like he was in the center of a bonfire.

He dashed across the length of the room and fell to his knees next to Pent. He jostled his friend.

"Pent! Pent! Now is not the time for your heavy sleep!"

Much to his delight, Pent groaned. "Feel like I got hit by a Mack truck." He rolled over, and Hanar recoiled at the sight of his bloody chest. "I'm so tired."

"You've been grievously wounded," Hanar said. He patted at the wound, only to jerk back from the pain. He looked at his burned hands, having completely forgotten them in his haste. "As have I. But so have our enemies, and we need to press this advantage!"

Pent's head swung around. "Jesus, this whole place is going up. This isn't another hallucination, right?" Hanar shook his head. Pent squinted, looking across the flames. "Looks like you figured out a Plan B."

"Indeed," Hanar said. The larger Scribe plunged its hands into the flaming fountain, and like its predecessor, was immediately cloaked in a raging flame. It was quickly reduced to a pile of ash on the floor.

The last two Scribes shrieked in horror. They turned and fled from the cave, floating easily over the wall of stone blocks, and drifting out of sight down the inclined hallway.

"I'm so woozy," Pent said, grappling with his head as if he was afraid it would roll off. His eyes snapped open. "The kids!" he shouted, struggling to stand. "Hanar, this place is going to hell. We need to make like those freaks and get out of here while we still can. We need to get the kids!"

They rushed over to the pile of children and began shaking them awake. Those for whom they had not been too late started to wake, shaking their heads, and standing groggily.

"Mr. Pent! Mr. Hanar!" A few of them recognized the duo immediately, wiping their hazy eyes. When they realized where they were, with flames lapping at their faces, they began to scream in panic.

"Children, to us now!" Hanar said. He winced as his hands brushed against their heads. "This is no dream. We must escape from this place!" He pried the cloaked Scribe's book from its dead hand, briefly considered Catherine's fate in all of this, and dropped it in his pack. "Help us, shake the rest awake!"

One by one, they revived each of the unconscious children. Pent had to pull one little girl away from the body of another as she shook and shook, trying in vain to wake the girl. Several children screamed and cried then, as they realized some of the small forms would never wake again.

Pent shook his head in despair. "We were too late, man. We couldn't save them all." He leaned down and shook Bart's body. "Not you too—oh god," he cried out loud. "I swore to Marall I would return his son, but I couldn't even manage that." He began to lift Bart's body, but his legs gave out and he nearly crashed to the floor.

"Pent, you're still too weak!" Hanar ushered the remaining children along. He batted at his teary eyes. "I know it's harsh, but we must attend to those who still need us!"

"But I couldn't save him," Pent wept, cradling the boy in his arms. "I promised him, man, and I couldn't save his son. We failed. I've failed."

"We'll have saved none, if we don't leave now!" Hanar replied. "Let us hurry, lest our journey have an even more tragic end."

They wrangled the survivors, over thirty of them in total. Four children had fallen into their eternal slumber. Hanar led them out, hurrying them along and away from the scorching fountain and burning tapestries. Pent fetched his sword and took up position in the rear.

They vaulted the stone wall and made their way down the incline. Even here the flames were burning, clinging to the walls and ceiling somehow. *As if the entire cave is coated with their dread ink.* Hanar shook his head in disgust and wiped sweat away from his brow. His hands throbbed with every step he took; he ignored the pain and pushed forward.

"Wait!" Pent said. Hanar glanced over his shoulder. Pent was walking away from them, back towards the fountain room. "The book!"

"Pent, don't be a fool!" Hanar fished through his bag and withdrew the Scribe's tome. "The one that monster used to imprison Catherine—I have it here."

"No, not that one," Pent called back. "The one that said America on it!"

Already the flames had formed into a wall of death, blocking their entrance to the fountain chamber. As they argued, the killing heat pushed closer and closer, and the children cried out in terror, begging to be led away from the monstrous place. "Pent, please! It is lost to us now!"

"That might have been my one chance at going home," Pent groaned. He inched closer to the flames. "I can't lose that too."

"And it's your one chance at a swift death now. It is gone, as we will be too!" Hanar begged his friend. "Please! I need your help. I can't finish this journey alone!"

Pent stared into Hanar's eyes. His doubt hardened into resolve, and he jogged back down the incline. "No tragic endings, got it." He urged the children forward. "You take the back Hanar, I'll take the front."

As they were crossing paths, Pent slapped Hanar on the shoulder. His eyes were red from tears, but a small grin had formed at the edge of his mouth. "Hard to make jokes at a time like this, but you're channeling the wrong Indiana Jones movie. That's from *The Last Crusade.*"

Hanar raised a confused eyebrow, and then laughed. It was the most humor he had felt since Catherine had led them to the cave. "*The Last Crusade?* Aptly named, Mr. Crusader."

"Yeah, but let's make sure this isn't the last one."

They ran through the caves at a fevered pace, Pent constantly urging the children on. They stopped briefly outside of the library, but the flames had already spread, annihilating any chance Pent had of finding answers here. He cursed under his breath as they moved on, avoiding the flames pouring from the library entrance.

Though the impossible darkness was pushed back by the inferno, their escape from the cave system was still dangerous. The fire was spreading at an unbelievable rate, and it threatened to overtake them as they ran. The children struggled to keep up, and several times the group had to halt so Pent or Hanar could pick up a fallen child. Hanar groaned every time he needed to use his burned hands. *They're all tired and beaten. We just need to reach the end of this cave.*

There was no time to coddle the children. "If we stop, we're dead," Pent said. "Haul ass, guys, I'm not ready to be cremated yet."

When the light of the cave exit became visible, everyone let out a cheer. It renewed their drive, and they all pushed forward.

The group tumbled out of the cave and into the open field. The children hugged the ground, coughing and gasping for air. Hanar rested his hands on his knees and yelped in pain. He glanced up to see Pent, straight and tall, with his sword out and ready.

Pent mumbled something under his breath and scanned from one end of the clearing to the next.

Hanar forced himself to take the few steps required to reach Pent. He tried to draw his own sword, gritting his teeth through the pain until he managed to pull the blade free of its scabbard. "We seem to be alone," he finally said.

"Yeah. Seem to be." Pent slowly sheathed his sword and breathed a sigh of relief. "Weird, I would have thought those two Scribes would be here, waiting for us. One last fight to close this out. But they're not here."

"In a day short of blessings, I'll take what's given."

"Can't disagree with that." Pent turned to the kids. He stood tall and tried to mask the pain in his voice. Hanar looked at him with pride at the way he was maintaining his dignity and composure. *Surely, this is the courage of a hero—of a Crusader.* He did not believe he could have done as well in the face of such loss.

"All right, y'all," Pent began. The children all stared at him, weariness and fear in their eyes. "This... this isn't how a fairy tale is supposed to go. We left Somerville with almost nothing to go on. Just our swords and the hope that we would find our children. And for all that effort—" He cut off, shaking his head. "I know this doesn't help any of you at all, but I don't know what else to say. You've been through a living nightmare, and some of those who were taken didn't make it all the way." He glanced at the mouth of the cave; smoke still billowed out of it.

"But we're here now—me and Hanar—and we'll keep you safe the rest of the way. That's a promise I aim to keep." The children seemed at a loss, some staring up at Pent in awe, others weeping silently, though most simply sat and tried to catch their breaths. "Let's take a moment, relax here for a bit, and then we have to get moving on to Tofac. We need to get you all back home."

"Well said, my friend," Hanar added. "I think a moment of rest is well called for."

Pent sat on the ground, joining the children. "And while we breathe, let's remember those who stayed behind. We'll pray for them here, and we'll promise to never forget them. We've lost one boy from Somerville, Bart, but I don't know the names of the others."

"Mina," a girl said, clutching her knees. It was the little girl Pent had pulled from the body of her friend. "My neighbor's daughter. We're both from Tofac." She choked on her words. "We played together, every day."

"Tamash," the boy next to her said. "I don't know where he was from, but he was one of the first snatched up. He was older and stood up to those... things. He protected us."

"F'alk," a girl, who couldn't have been older than eight, said in a tiny voice. "My brother." She wept into the shoulder of another child as the two kids flanking her hugged her tightly.

Hanar glanced at the children, at their sullen faces. *What was the name of Catherine's brother? Peter? He is not among the dead then.* He tapped his wounded hands together and grimaced at the pain. *There will be time yet to ask. Let them rest for now.*

"Bart," Pent added grimly. "Bart. We won't forget you, buddy."

CHAPTER FORTY-THREE

As they neared the town of Tofac, Pent breathed a sigh of relief. He had been on edge the entire walk through the forests, sure that the Scribes would come and attack them again. They had to be desperate after losing their fountain, the source of all their power. When he saw the town, he finally relaxed.

"Oh, oh!" A man turned from repairing a hole in the side of his home and shouted as they approached. "Those men who were sent off, they've returned! They've returned with the children!" he shouted down the dirt road. Villagers ran from their homes, their dreary looks brightening as they saw the children. They swarmed Pent and Hanar and surrounded the kids.

Children were hefted onto parents' shoulders, and the group let out a wild cheer. The kids had been fatigued and desperate, but now they laughed with the adults. Pent smiled, watching them celebrate. *They look like kids again.*

"You've done it then." Chief Raham approached, sifting his way through the crowd, along with the rest of his family. Tears fell from the stoic man's eyes. He fell to his knees in reverence before Pent.

"Father!" Gesta said. She and her brother Tanan were taken aback by their father's reaction.

"You—you have..." he blubbered out between sobs. "In this age of darkness, how could this be? A hero has emerged at last. You have returned with the children!"

"Not—not all of them," Pent said. As if to illustrate the point, a woman cried out, yelling for her daughter, Mina. Many of those not already occupied caring for the children rushed to support her, and there was an outpouring of sympathy for her loss. "We couldn't save all of them," Pent said, his shoulders slouched as he observed the mother's pain.

Chief Raham wiped at his eyes and slowly rose to his feet. He moved his arms behind his back, taking on a familiar posture as he took stock of the children that had crowded around Pent. "Many of these children I do not recognize," he said at last.

"Many are from Somerville," Hanar said. "By the time we arrived, some few had already perished—and some is already too many. I won't speak of the horrors we bore witness to, but the Scribes were using them for their own ends."

"It's the chief's fault, it is!" one of the villagers cried out. "Blessings to the hero, Pent!"

Pent looked around nervously. "And Hanar," he added. "It wasn't a solo act." Hanar had a wounded look on his face. *Probably those messed up hands again—need to get a doctor to look at them.*

A stout woman with broad shoulders jammed an accusatory finger at the chief. "You wasted your time, wallowing pitifully in your orchard as our children were taken away!" The crowd let out a shout of agreement to her accusations.

The chief hung his head. "Had we acted sooner, we could have saved them all. I was too indecisive." He trembled slightly. "I've lived in Master Yozer's shadow for too long and lost the skill to act on my own."

"You can't just blame yourself," Pent said, to the chief and the restless crowd alike. "I know all about that; it gets you nowhere. Sometimes you just need to pick up the pieces and move forward."

"A man of principles and bold actions," Tanan said. "We are indebted to you."

"More than we can repay," Gesta said.

Pent and Hanar glanced at each other. "Some time to rest, to tend our wounds," Hanar said. "That would be most appreciated."

"Of course, of course!" Chief Raham said immediately. "Let us accommodate you in any way we can." He gestured towards one of the abandoned homes. "Please, allow us to let you rest here."

"We've been on our feet for long enough," Pent said. "And I know the kids need some time too. We've got a long trip back to Somerville."

The children were allowed to share the beds in several of the households, spending the night with the families of Tofac. Space was abundant, as many of Tofac's people had already abandoned their homes, and many more had been killed in the repeated fighting with the Scribe's conjured monsters. It was a somber victory; already their people had lost so much.

Tanan had offered Pent and Hanar his own home. He called it the smallest luxury he could offer to a true hero. And after their cuts and scrapes were tended to, the dirt, ash, and blood rinsed from their aching bodies, and soft beds found, the two heroes still lay awake in the middle of night.

Pent watched as Hanar turned his hands over. They were wrapped with cloth bandages from his fingertips to the middle of his arms. But Pent had seen his wounds before the wrappings, and he admired the brave face Hanar was putting on. His hands had been mutilated by the inferno in the cave. "How's the burns?"

Hanar frowned, pressing his hands together and looking grim. "Tofac's doctor seems skilled. But some things are beyond the skill of any medical worker." He yanked his hands back; they were clearly still sensitive to the touch. "I know not what I can do now, Pent, besides wait and see what will become of them. I—I cannot imagine a life without my hands. What good can I provide anyone, if I cannot use my hands?" He closed his eyes in despair. "At least I walked away with my life. At least that."

Pent nodded, unsure how to answer his friend. He traced a finger along the scar that ran the length of his chest. "I think I came out better off than you did."

Hanar grunted. "Some hero's reward this is." He laughed to himself. "Not that I've made much of an impression! That crowd and Tanan alike spoke as if I did not help at all, and that you were the only hero living."

"We both know that's not true," Pent said. "You've saved me more times than I remember now, and I'd be dead in that cave if it wasn't for you." He propped himself up on one arm to look over at Hanar. "That was a clutch move back there, by the way."

"Clutch, indeed," Hanar said. He laid his hands by his sides. "One would wonder how Gordenthorpe remembered milk but forgot fire. But it explains why they had no torches in their cave. Paper burns, books burn—the seat of the Scribes' power is laced in darkness and blood, in death. Fire brings life."

"Glad you managed to figure that out. I was too busy bleeding out on the floor." Pent shook his head. "Gonna have nightmares about this for the rest of my life." He leaned over, resting his hand on the flat of his sword. It was propped up against the wall next to Hanar's bow. The quiver and bow strings had been burnt up. *Just like his hands*. Pent could only hope that he would recover. *I'm sure he's thinking the same thing.*

"I had no illusions of basking in glory at the start of this all," Hanar said at last. "Most of the children were saved, but for the families who lost someone..." He shook his head.

"Poor Marall." Pent thought back to the day when they had left.

He had promised Marall he would do everything he could to bring his son Bart back. *And I did. I did everything I could.* But when they returned to Somerville, they would be walking into town without him. "Damn it all, I can still hardly believe anything that's happened. What the hell am I even gonna say to Marall when we get back?" He gestured to the Scribe's book they had recovered. "What about Catherine?"

"We'll have to cross both bridges in Somerville, for Marall and Catherine. Our only hope is that Gordenthorpe can do something for her. He removed the trance from Fen, after all." Hanar frowned. "If she is all right, she'll be less than happy about the results."

He was speaking of Catherine's brother. They had learned that the children had spent most of their hours locked in a trance, not unlike Fen's. But sometimes the Scribes' spell would falter, and in those times, they spoke among themselves, commiserating and becoming friends. When Hanar had questioned the children on their journey to Tofac, he asked if there was a boy named Peter among them. The kids all knew each other at that point, and none could remember a boy named Peter.

"We don't know for sure if he was one of the Scribes' prisoners," Pent said. "Maybe he was captured by the trance but didn't make it all the way to the cave. He could have fallen into any kind of trouble out in the forest. She's not going to be happy to hear that."

"No, she will not," Hanar said glumly. "And what of the Scribes themselves? The two that escaped, will we need to hunt them down? They were without their books, and their fountain has been destroyed. It seemed that den held great power, beyond anything an individual Scribe could manage."

"I guess when kids start going missing again, we'll know what's going on." Pent thought of the Scribes fleeing in terror from the fountain chamber. "I have a good feeling though. I think they got the picture. They know what'll happen if they mess with us again." He paused before lying back down on the bed. "I hope so anyway."

. . .

When they arose the next day, Gesta was waiting for them. "My father would like to speak to you," she said, her eyes focused on Pent. She hurriedly looked to Hanar and added, "To both of you."

They passed through the town square. Many of the villagers saw them approach and swarmed them, cheering, and patting them all over.

"To the hero, Pent!"

"The savior of the world!"

"The Crusader reborn!"

The chants came from all around. Gesta tried to shove the crowd back, but they hardly seemed to notice her. Pent was thankful that she had pocketed her dagger for once. He waved his hands, trying to silence the crowd.

"Calm down, calm down!" He felt like he needed a PR person for this kind of thing. "I did what anyone would have done."

"That's false!" one of the women in the crowd yelled out. *That's Mina's mother, the one who didn't make it.* "Our coward of a chief sat around, twiddling his thumbs, while our children were left to rot. To hell with him!"

Several in the crowd yelled their agreement. Gesta's eyes darted from person to person. She stepped back, looking defensive at the remark.

"The chief is doing his best. Try and put yourself in his shoes," Pent said. "It's hard to lead a village, especially with all this madness everywhere you look. Who could have predicted some weird elf creatures conjuring monsters to attack your village?"

The crowd listened at first in silence, and then began cheering his name again. Pent shook his head in frustration. He raised Hanar's hand into the air. "And what about my boy? I didn't do this alone; we'd all be dead if it wasn't for Hanar."

They paused for a moment, and then continued their cheering. Only now, they had added Hanar's name to the chant. Hanar grimaced at the hold Pent had on his hand, gently pulling himself free and looking bashfully at the villagers. He waved to them and smiled.

"Pent and Hanar! Pent and Hanar! The heroes have arrived! Crusaders reborn!"

Pent sighed and shoved Gesta through the crowd. "Let's just get out of here." They walked to the chief's home, followed by many villagers, who crowded around the door and tried to peer through the windows after their heroes. Pent did his best to ignore them.

Chief Raham offered them both seats at the table. He seemed to have aged considerably in the short time they had known him. He had a large stain on his leather coat and appeared not to have noticed. "Thank you both, for all you've done."

"I appreciate the sentiment," Pent said, "and the opportunity to rest. But we really need to be on our way." The chief passed a tired look to Tanan and then Gesta, before returning to Pent. "No disrespect meant, but we've got a lot of kids that need to get home."

The chief nodded. "The children from Tofac have reunited with their families. We're working to send the others home as well. You may leave whenever you choose," he glanced towards Tanan, "but—"

"But you're not going alone," Tanan said, his arms crossed. "You're a man of principles and courage, and I would join you, to see how your ilk lives on the east coast of the world. If you would have us, that is."

Hanar looked quizzically at the chief. "Us? What does he mean?"

"Many people here have lost faith in my father's ability to lead," Gesta answered, "my brother principle among them." She was passing her dagger from hand to hand again and gripped it tightly after mentioning her brother.

"Father has made a real mess of things," Tanan said, speaking as if the chief wasn't sitting a foot away from him. "He's proven that he's a weak-willed man, propped up by Yozer, and with no real ability to lead." He pointed at Pent. "Meanwhile, an outsider, a man we have never met before, who we condemned to the stocks mere moments after meeting, is our salvation. A day after visiting us, you rescued all the children and stopped the approach of those wicked monsters. Say what you will about the villagers' chanting: you're a hero."

"Whatever," Pent said, rubbing at his weary eyes. "Over the course of a week I've heard it all. I'm the reason for everyone's hardship, the reason the world has fallen to crap. I'm a killer, a coward, someone who runs from their problems. Now I'm a hero." He shook his head. "I'll tell you what I really am: tired. So, say your piece already, so I can get these kids home."

"I want to go with you," Tanan repeated. "I've spoken with several of the families, and they would feel safer living closer to you both." He folded his arms behind his back. "But we can't impose on you; we'll only join you if you allow it."

Pent looked at Hanar, who shrugged. "My sister is the chief of Somerville. I imagine when we return with the children, she'll be willing to accept anyone else along with us. And I don't mind the company."

"You have to go where you want to go," Pent said. "Here or there—I can't tell you how to live your lives."

"But what of this village, your home?" Hanar asked. "You've already spoken of all you've lost. The battle of the Scribes has certainly taken its toll on Tofac."

Gesta spoke, stroking her dagger slowly. "Many of the villagers will go with you, and many others have spoken of their urge to travel. To travel far away from here and try their luck in the outside world." She flipped the dagger from one hand to the other. "But Tofac is strong, and there are still some with a hint of loyalty."

"Gesta, please." The chief raised his hand. "There is no need to be bitter—and would you put that damn knife away? Fondling it like some toy... This is a different world than before, and new hearts and minds will need to lead it. Your brother has my blessing to leave, as do any who wish to travel with him." He turned to Tanan. "Go with safety and speed, my son. And do not let your ambition blind you to new viewpoints."

Tanan scoffed. "Ambition is where you have failed father, by hiding behind a dead sorcerer's skirts, tending to your apples, and nothing else. I'll live my life as I choose, if that pleases you." He rose and brushed past his sister in a hurry to leave the room.

The chief sighed and beckoned for Pent and Hanar to leave the room as well. They shared a glance and left without another word.

CHAPTER FORTY-FOUR

Pent and Hanar left Tofac, leading a much larger group than they had expected. Pent appreciate having all the extra company; he had not been looking forward to marching a pack of children through the forest, defending, and feeding them the whole way. The other villagers looked to Pent and Hanar as if they were above normal men and happily did whatever Pent or Hanar asked of them. *They have no idea how helpful they are.*

It was not an easy journey, and the children were on edge the whole way. Their voices shook and they trembled at every noise in the forest. They had been through hell and just wanted to be back with their families.

Tanan sought out Pent's company often as they made their way from Tofac to Somerville. He marched with his hands behind his back, looking much like his father. "Tell me of your life when you are not adventuring, Pent. Surely this hasn't been a normal day for you."

"There's not much to me. Me and Hanar, we like to go out hunting and fishing. I help out in town where I can. There's been a lot to do as of late, between the fall of Yozer and the missing kids. I've stayed busy."

Tanan frowned, looking disappointed at the answer. Pent wondered if he expected him to disagree, to tell him that he did spend most of his time adventuring. *I can't lie to him now though.* "I hope I didn't shatter your expectations of life in Somerville."

"No, I suppose it's not so different from life in Tofac then." He sighed. "And what of this leader of yours?"

"Lyle? She's great." Pent paused. "Great doesn't really describe it. She helped lead us to victory against Yozer, after all, and she's been keeping everything together in Somerville since then."

"She must be bold, to stand against Master Yozer," he said, his tone reverent. "Not since the Age of Crusaders has anyone opposed him openly. I look forward to meeting with her."

"Sure thing," Pent said. He walked a step faster, putting space between the two of them. "I'm sure she'll be happy to meet you, too." *What is this guy's obsession with boldness?* Pent shook his head, leaving Tanan behind, and joined ranks with Hanar.

After days of travel, they saw Gilbrand Castle on the horizon. Hanar lifted his hand, urging Pent to halt. "Someone has set up a campsite outside of the castle walls."

Pent only noticed the tents after Hanar pointed them out. *How did I not see those before?* Two tents, conical and made of straw, cut off their route to Gilbrand Castle. Pent gripped the handle of his blade. He heard the men behind him mumble nervously. "Could be nothing, but it could be trouble too. Hanar and I will check it out, you all wait here a moment."

Hanar grumbled his disagreement, but he followed behind Pent anyway. As they drew near the tents, a thin man with graying hair approached. "Pent and Hanar," he said in his high-pitched voice.

"Darson!" Pent said. He lifted his hand from his sword hilt. "I knew those tents looked familiar."

Hanar smiled at the chief of Seward. "What good fortune, to meet you here! I feared more trials before we reached home, but this is a pleasant surprise." He glanced from the tent back to Darson and raised his burnt hands slowly. "I have a matter that I would appreciate your help with. But first, what brings you this far north?"

Darson crossed his arms. "I've been considering what you said to me, Pent—a long time after you left—about how I'm wasted in Seward."

"So, you've decided to join the rest of us in civilization, huh?" Pent said. *Or whatever counts as civilization in this world.*

"In a sense," Darson said. "My home still lies in the south. But you mentioned living in the east and passing through Gilbrand Castle before you met us. I suspected you would come back this way after venturing west." He glanced at Pent's group of people, and then at Hanar's hands. "And that you would have need for medical care. It seems you were successful in your quest?"

"More or less," Pent said. The travelers who had joined them from Tofac closed the distance, hovering behind Pent and listening to his every word. "I don't want to dwell on the pain they've all gone through, and everyone here is in good health. But you're welcome to take a look as we stop for rest."

Hanar brushed against Pent's shoulder. "Two tents won't suffice for this group. The castle would be a great place to rest. However…"

Darson nodded, a grim look on his face. "We've only just arrived a day before, but I believe I understand what you're thinking. The grounds are littered with bodies of the fallen."

"The children have suffered enough," Hanar said quietly. "I'd not have them spend the night among corpses."

Pent studied the outskirts of the castle and the tents they had set up. He glanced into Hanar's pack, staring at the Scribe's book. *I'm sure it's painful for Catherine to see her home in such rough shape.* "When I was searching the castle before, there were still all kinds of equipment and tools. Is that still the case?"

Darson hesitated. "I believe so. There were various tools, hoes, and shovels for farming mostly. It seems that most of the valuables of the castle were plundered some time ago." He clapped his hands together. "Ah, I understand your intent. We have some able-bodied men with us."

"All right." Pent turned to the crowd. "Listen up. I need every adult who can handle a shovel to come with me. We're gonna scope out that castle. All the kids are gonna stay here with Hanar."

Hanar raised an eyebrow. "What are you up to, my friend?"

Pent smiled. "Don't want to make you dig with those messed up hands of yours. Keep your ears open. We're gonna clean up the place a bit before we stay for the night." Hanar looked at his useless hands and grimaced.

"How many holes do you think shall do?" Darson asked. "There were many dead in the castle. You're speaking of many graves to dig."

"Um, I'm thinking we just do one of those funeral pyres," Pent said awkwardly. "I've kind of got a thing against graveyards. You never know when the dead will rise up out of them." He studied Darson's face. The chief wore a skeptical expression. "Just trust me on this one."

It was nighttime before all the corpses had been retrieved. Pent had led the group in digging a large hole in the center of the castle grounds. All of the bodies were laid out on a foundation of sticks and cloth, and then the pyre was set alight.

This isn't even the first funeral pyre I've been to, Pent thought as he watched the bodies burn. It was a grotesque image, and the smell made his stomach turn. But this was the humane thing to do, grim as it was. They all would be able to rest easy tonight, and with time, the castle would be habitable for people again.

Hanar's hands ached as he looked upon the flames, and he was forced to turn away. Pent felt sympathy for the man. The throbbing pain had subsided, but he hadn't gained complete control of his hands yet. Unfortunately, Darson hadn't been able to do any more than the doctor in Tofac.

The three men stood side by side as the fire raged on. Darson cleared his throat. "I'm not the only doctor in the world," he said, patting Hanar on the shoulder. "There might be other solutions to your plight, but none of my herbs or medicines will treat those burns."

"Perhaps there are answers elsewhere," Hanar said, staring off into the distance. "Staring at this flame is turning my insides out. I shall attend to the children. That, at least, I can manage."

Pent watched as he walked off, holding his tongue until Hanar was out of earshot. "He's not usually so serious. I'm really feeling for him. I can't imagine what he's going through."

"He seems like a man who makes constant use of his hands," Darson observed. "Without those, he feels lost."

"Yeah, but come on. He'll bounce back," Pent said, forcing a chuckle. *I mean, he has to.* "So. what about you, Darson? You've left Seward with at least half your people. You sure you don't want to join us?"

"No," he said promptly. "I've left matters in Seward in Verra's competent hands. With Clarence supporting her, I'm sure they're surviving well enough. But Seward is my home, and already I miss the crashing of the waves along the beach."

Pent nodded. *The glassmaker and the mysterious man with amnesia.* Pent wondered when he would meet them again. Before he could ask, Darson turned and left without another word. Pent stared at the flames and sighed. *Leave new mysteries for a new day. Let's just close this one out and get these kids home safe.*

CHAPTER FORTY-FIVE

"Here we go, folks," Pent said, staring at the entrance to Somerville. The two guard towers perched over Faldo's bridge were manned. They had passed several towers as they cut through the forest, but all were empty. *I guess things haven't been too rough for them if they're not manning the outer towers.* It was a good sign, Pent hoped.

The guards clenched their weapons nervously as the group of men, women, and children approached. "Halt!" one of them said. His voice was shaking as he tried to look more intimidating than he was. "Speak your business with Somerville or turn and leave! We don't want trouble!"

Pent smiled when he recognized the man. "Monty! You're really gonna give your old drill instructor the business like that?"

The thin guard squinted from the tower. Recognition dawned on his face, and he jumped for joy. "Pent! Hanar!" He reached down and grabbed a horn. Drawing it to his lips, he blew into it, the sound booming through the forest and unsettling the birds from the trees. "You've returned! Many of us, well, we had begun to lose hope, but to see you here, and with the children as well! Lyle will be so relieved. Please, come in!"

Monty made no mention of the strangers that Pent and Hanar had brought with them. *I'll have to remind him to be more diligent later. These guards can't let things slip, not anymore.*

Their group marched to the village square together. The horn had awakened the town, and many villagers were emerging from their homes, more people than Pent remembered living in Somerville. All around him, Pent saw tears streaking dirty, fatigued faces as children were reunited with parents, and cries of joy rang from one end of the village to the other. Everyone wept heavily at the sight. Even Pent couldn't help but get misty eyed, watching the culmination of their struggles reach an end.

There was a feminine squeal, and Pent turned just in time to catch Ellie as she jumped into his arms. "You're back, you did it!" He spun her around, savoring the feel of her body pressed against his own. "Don't listen to a soul here, I knew you would return. I knew it!" she shouted at the top of her lungs.

"What can I say?" Pent said, smiling earnestly. "I'm a Crusader, right? Legendary hero, adventurer, warrior, loved by everyone he meets, you know." He shrugged. "This kind of stuff comes easy to me."

"My, what a change from when you left Somerville," she said teasingly. "You seem to have found your confidence somewhere along the way."

"Fake it till you make it, girl."

"And some things don't change at all. You should write a book of all your absurd phrases." She hugged him tightly and laughed into his chest. She drew back when she felt the scar. "You're hurt." She ran her hand along the wound. "This was a deep cut, and so close to your heart. You could have been killed! What happened to that armor Cenk gave you?"

"It's nothing, El," Pent said, shifting in place nervously. "I'm fine, really. Hanar got the worst of it. You really need to check him out; he's been getting bad news after bad news." Hanar frowned and twisted away from them both.

"And what of Hanar?" They all turned at the voice of Chief Lyle. She was smiling ear to ear. "I thought I sent you both to find the children; you've come back with scores more people than I expected." She crossed the square and embraced Hanar and then Pent. "It's great to see you both again, and in one piece. Somerville's people have been near panic, but we've weathered the storm. Many here did not believe we would ever see you again." She smiled knowingly. "But I stand with Ellie there; don't consider me among their number."

Her smile faded when she saw Hanar's bandaged hands.

"It's all right, dear sister," he said, waving her off. "I'll meet with Ellie, and she'll be able to settle this small matter. And if not her, there are other means for me to heal this ailment. Just a minor wound, nothing to concern yourself with."

Pent nodded, wondering whether he was speaking more for Lyle's benefit or his own. "We've got a lot to talk about as is, including where to put all these newcomers." He pointed to Tanan, who approached with his arms crossed. "There's a village all the way to the west called Tofac. This is their chief's son." He patted Tanan on the shoulder. "Things are a bit out of whack in Tofac... Tanan and his people figured they would have better luck here."

Tanan bowed gracefully. Lyle smiled and nodded to him, along with the rest of the crowd. "Of course, I'll be needing to acquaint myself with all of you personally. My name is Lyle, and I am the leader of the village you find yourselves in. Somerville has been swelling as of late. Many people have come seeking shelter and safety from the wildness of the world. You may all find safe harbor here, as long as you bear my people no ill will."

Faldo had walked up to the group, and, after embracing Pent and Hanar, he began counting up the newcomers. "It seems I have a lot of work to do. Somerville will need to expand if we're to house all of these new people. It might be that this chasm alone won't be enough any longer."

The large group began to mingle, as newcomers met with

residents of Somerville. They all spoke of their hopes and dreams, and reveled in love, having been reunited with their children. Above all, they cheered to Pent and Hanar, who had brought new hope in dark times.

Eventually, people began to break away, the newcomers meeting with Lyle and Faldo to discuss where they would stay, while the families of Somerville returned to their homes, eager to begin healing the ills visited upon their children. Hanar left with Ellie to discuss his ruined hands, leaving Pent and a single man alone in the village square.

Pent's smile turned when he caught sight of the haggard farmer, who had fallen to his knees, his head hanging low. Marall's eyes were misty. "I've been searching in the crowd. Plenty of newcomers and familiar faces alike. The children, who had been missing all this time, they've all returned. But..." He raised his head slowly, not bothering to clear the tears from his eyes as he looked pleadingly to Pent.

"Marall, I'm so sorry."

He lowered his head again and wept in silence. "Y... you said to me—before—before you left..." He groaned. His miserable sounds made Pent's stomach shrivel up. "You made a promise—that you would return my son to me."

"I know I did. I know, man. So many things happened on this journey—horrible things. We've had to fight through madness all the way to Tofac—got ambushed a bunch of times—don't know how many blades I've had to my throat. We got thrown in one of those wooden stocks, straight out of a movie or something." He shook his head, knowing he wasn't getting his meaning across. "I don't know what to say. We were too late. I always meant to keep that promise to you," Pent gestured to the houses in Somerville, "I meant to keep it for everyone here. I'm just... I'm so sorry about Bart. I'm sorry, man."

Marall didn't stir from his spot. He shook as the tears continued to fall from his eyes. Pent rested a hand on his shoulder. "I'm sorry, man." He walked away, leaving the grieving father alone in the town square.

Pent's eyes were locked to the ground as he trudged away, just wanting to put distance between himself and Marall. *That... that was rough. Think I need to talk to El, I can't handle all this.* He was so snared by the misery that he did not notice the three people approaching him until he barreled into one of them.

"Ouch!" Walter said. He stumbled back and fell on his butt. "This was not quite the welcome I had in mind."

Pent let out a startled laugh as he recognized the man in the dirt. Quickly, he gave Walter his hand and helped pull the man to his feet. "Looks like you made it to Somerville."

Greil nodded, resting a hand on his belt. He opened his mouth to speak, but Aisa beat him to the punch. "Wasn't much of a journey, Greil found the way easy enough. Had we not crossed paths with you, we would have made our way here eventually."

Greil opened his mouth again, but this time Walter cut him off. "Not that we ain't grateful. We're beyond grateful. People here have been very accommodating." He tugged on his moustache, and then flicked his nose. "That lady doctor even set my nose straight."

There was a pause. Greil looked to his left and right before opening his mouth a third time. "Our thanks to you, and to Hanar. I had hoped to have a chance to thank him personally, but he ran off with the doctor."

"Yeah..." Pent started, not sure how much to share. "He's going through some stuff right now, but hopefully Ellie can help him out." The three of them looked much healthier than when they had first met. Walter's nose wasn't a bloody mess, and he had filled out some. Greil had already been filled out, but his hair was cleaned up and tied behind his head. And Aisa had lost her slouch; she was standing taller and more confidently than when she had pulled a knife on him.

"I'm happy you've all settled here." Pent said the words

automatically, almost as a formality, but as soon it was said he realized how true it was. *Between Bart and Hanar's hands, I've been wrapped up in everything we lost.* But that wasn't the whole story. "It's not the whole story..."

"Hm?" Aisa furrowed her brow. "What was that now? You're mumbling something."

"Nothing, never mind," Pent said. "I've got to go see Ellie myself. I'm sure we'll have plenty more time to speak now that you've made Somerville your home."

They nodded in unison and stepped aside to clear a path for Pent.

As he was nearing Ellie's home, Pent crossed paths with Hanar. The woodsman's hands were still bandaged. Pent spared them a glance, but Hanar just shrugged.

"So? What's the word?"

"I shall wait for Gordenthorpe's word," Hanar said. His voice had a dull edge to it. "I'll leave the celebration to you, my friend." He strolled past.

"Hanar, wait!" Pent called to him. But Hanar continued as if he hadn't heard. "We'll catch up later, we've still gotta deal with Catherine," Pent shouted. Hanar raised his arm without turning and continued on.

Pent crossed the threshold to Ellie's home and entered without knocking. He felt a weight on his shoulders lifted. The smell of freshly plucked and cut herbs teased his nostrils. The table was cluttered, and every counter space had a medical article on it. *She's been busy too, then.* He pulled a chair from the table, the legs scratching along the ground, and sat down on it. He looked up at Ellie, crossing his arms.

"Another audacious entrance from the Crusader," Ellie said, grinning. Her face turned red as she glanced at the table. "We've had a lot of newcomers, and I've been tending to their medical needs. I would have tidied up, had I known you were arriving."

"Don't even worry about it, El," Pent smiled. He stared at her, studying her rosy cheeks. "This is the best thing I've seen in weeks."

She grabbed a chair and dragged it next to his. "I've missed your flattery," she said, stifling a giggle. She grabbed his hands and laced her fingers with his, sitting in silence. They locked eyes, their faces drawing closer and closer together, until their lips met. When they parted, she smiled. "And I've missed that as well."

"Sorry to keep you waiting," he said, reaching over and starting to massage her shoulder. He frowned and pulled his hand away a moment later. "I hate killing this mood, but, how's Hanar doing?"

Her face turned sour. She leaned forward, pressed her elbow into the table, and rested against her palm. They sat in claustrophobic silence and considered each other sadly. "Oh Pent," she said finally. "I do not know if I should be soft or hard with you on this."

Pent's face paled, and beads of sweat formed on his forehead. "Just be real, honest. Whether it's hard or not, that's what I need to hear."

She nodded. "I've seen burns before, of course. It happens from time to time in daily life here in Somerville. And then there was the matter of the battle against Yozer. Your firebomb weapons were ingenious, but some of us fell prey to them as well." She looked away. "Oddly, I've never treated Cenk for a burn. With that fire always blazing in his hut, I would have expected to see him at least once."

"I bet it happens to him," Pent said with the ghost of a smile, "and he just ignores it. Doesn't want to walk away from his important work."

"I have herbs. I grind and press them until they become a paste. I use that on wounds incurred by flame, and with rest the wounds go away. But Hanar's wounds are unlike any I've seen. The flames that scarred him... they could not have been normal."

Pent nodded. *No normal flame then. That's what happens when we mess around with all this magic crap.*

"Wounds heal with time, or most do," she said at last. "I cannot speak to the wonders time will work, but my medicine will not help. As things stand, he can wield a bow, he can brandish a knife. But doing so will bring him pain, and I don't believe he'll be able to aim as true as he once did."

Pent hung his head. He had managed to walk away from the battle with the Scribes with little in terms of lasting scars. A line across his chest was a small price to pay for what they had gained. *But Hanar...* "And all these people, calling me a hero, a Crusader—needing me to step in for him to get his accolades." He scoffed. "Not that fame really helps him much. Damn. Between this and Bart..."

"Stop that," Ellie commanded. She sat up straight, staring into him with a piercing gaze. "Stop that now. You cannot speak of everything you've lost without thinking of everything you've won. There was loss, of course: Hanar's wounds, and the children who did not make it. But think of all the ones you've rescued. Think of all their families. Think of all the people who can rest easy now that the threat of the Scribes has been extinguished. You cannot make the bad your entire story; it is only a small piece. You're a hero to everyone here, Pent: to Somerville, to me, perhaps, even to the world."

Pent sighed and shuffled uncomfortably in his chair. "Maybe. But being a Crusader does nothing for Hanar, after all the times he saved my ass. Feels like I made out like a bandit, and he got left behind."

"So be there for him now," Ellie said softly. "You're his friend, you're closer to him than anyone I've ever known, even his sister. Stand by his side." Ellie rose to her feet and walked to her cabinets. She began to grind herbs in a bowl, whistling to herself. Pent stared after her.

She worked the herbs into a paste, folded it into a small parcel, and set it on the table. "For Hanar, when you see him next." She laid her hand over his. "Somerville has been lively in your absence, but it will calm again, I'm sure of it. For how long, I don't know, but seize these calm moments while they're here. Don't waste them wallowing in the misery of things you cannot change."

Pent patted her hand and slipped the ointment into his pocket. "Got it. Doctor's orders."

She giggled. "Glad to see you still know who's in charge." She stepped away from the table, her smile fading. "I'm sure you have others you need to speak to. Lyle or Faldo, or some of these newcomers you've helped usher in."

"I'll stay awhile, if you don't mind. In fact..." He rose to his feet and rummaged through one of Ellie's cabinets, withdrawing a hammer. "Been meaning to do this for a while," he said as he carried a chair into the bedroom and stepped on top of it. He pushed the loose roof beam upwards and began hammering it into place. Ellie was never going to get this done herself; she was too short for one, and too busy to bother anyone else with such a trifle. *But I promised I would take care of this when we had a calm moment.* Pent believed he was someone who kept his promises. *Best get started on this, while I've got the time.*

Days passed, and the cluttered village of Somerville began to fall into a new rhythm. Pent made his rounds as the days came and went, making sure that everyone was settling in. The village was more populous than it ever had been before. Even after Pent had returned with the children, bringing half of Tofac with him, newcomers continued to arrive. Lyle saw no reason to turn good-minded and weary travelers away. Most homes housed two families these days, but it wasn't a long-term solution. *Something has gotta give—gotta build new homes for all these folk.*

Pent braved Cenk's caustic hut to greet the diminutive blacksmith. None of the new population dared bunk with the man, as his home was unlivable to anyone who didn't love sucking in smoke. Pent couldn't help but wonder how Cenk managed it himself.

The blacksmith had lamented the loss of Pent's armor. "It came in clutch though," Pent said, trying to sooth the man's temper. "If I didn't have that plate, I wouldn't be standing here."

Cenk stared at him dubiously. The clang of his hammer on glowing metal filled the hut.

"I'm serious. I even went toe to toe with a minotaur. You know what that is?"

Cenk raised an eyebrow. "Nah."

"Like a huge bull monster. Big horns on him. He slammed into me," Pent pounded his chest "but I barely felt a thing with that plate."

Pent wasn't sure, but he thought he saw a smile pass over Cenk's lips. The man stopped pounding at the metal for a moment. "Hm. Work to do then."

"Meaning... you'll make a new set for me?"

Cenk gripped the rough blade he was working and plunged it into a bucket. Hot steam floated up through the top of the hut, sizzling in the air and searing Pent's skin. "Aye. New armor." Cenk pounded his chest with his free hand. "But better. Stronger."

Pent grinned. "Good to know our equipment is in such capable hands. I'll try not to lose it this time." He turned, gesturing to Cenk as he went, thankful to step out into the fresh air.

Later, Pent met with Chief Lyle and Faldo in one of the farms near the edge of the village. The stalks of corn ran to the edge of the cliffside. Pent ran his hand up the length of one, grabbing an ear and yanking it free. "Glad to see we've got plenty of food to go around."

Faldo crossed his broad arms. "Our farmers have been diligent, of course, with one notable exception." He rubbed a hand along his smooth jaw. "Not that anyone blames Marall; he's experienced something no parent would ever want."

Lyle cleared her throat. "Let's not dwell on that. You've done a great thing for us Pent, and we'll never forget that. Rescuing our children—they'll make stories about you someday, of that I'm sure."

"And Hanar," Pent added. "Don't forget to include him, if you're thinking about writing up a manuscript or something."

Lyle nodded. "Of course. Ha... have you seen Hanar recently?" She looked away, biting her lower lip. In the past few days she had been a model of leadership in the village. Standing tall, her shoulders straight, her long, red hair done in a braid—*Daley or Ellie's work probably*—her speech always confident, unwavering, practiced. But she looked vulnerable now. "Since his return, he's retreated to the forests to the south. He seemed wounded when I spoke to him last."

"Broken might be a better word." Faldo added. Lyle shot him a look that could have cut diamond. He flinched back, unfolding his arms involuntarily. "No disrespect meant. He's a hero, same as you Pent."

"He's a Crusader," Pent corrected. "I haven't seen him, no. I'm planning on going to visit him after this though; we've got some business we haven't finished, business I need his help with."

Lyle nodded solemnly. "Give him my warmest regards then, and if he would have it, invite him to spend some time in my home. My brother has always been a solitary man, but I fear it does him no good in this case."

"Solitary actions won't serve us moving forward," Faldo said. He reached into his battered tunic and withdrew a hand-drawn map. "I've made some changes, based on what you've shared."

Pent observed the map. It was more detailed than the old, with the rolling hills below Gilbrand Castle more clearly marked. Brighton and Tofac were added, as well as several small villages that Pent had never seen before. *Not just what I've shared then, but what everyone has.* Pent wondered about inaccuracies; the entire map was based on nothing but hearsay. *Is that how mapmakers always do it?* There was even a rough path to the northeast, and the city of Vinalhaven was shown.

The city stuck in his mind. He had still done nothing to find his way home—to his old home, his old world. He imagined the major city of this world would have more answers than Somerville could ever hope to. *Another day, when Hanar is up to travel again. Can't make it without him.*

There was an X marking a spot to the north of Gilbrand Castle. It was a unique symbol: the towns and villages were labeled by houses, the hills by half circles, and the trees by triangles. "What's this X supposed to be? Buried treasure? Shiver me timbers..." Lyle and Faldo stared at each other, an oblivious expression on both of their faces. "Never mind."

"Somerville has been my home as long as I have been alive," Faldo said. "With some pain, I've come to acknowledge it as a limited space."

Pent blinked, unsure he had understood. "What's he talking about?"

"There are too many people," Chief Lyle said. "More are coming each day. It hasn't been long since you've returned, but we don't know when or if they'll stop coming. They seem to see Somerville as a safe haven in these dark times."

"We've you to thank for that," Faldo said. "More than that sorcerer anyway."

"Who, Gordenthorpe?" Pent had been planning on visiting the man with Hanar. *I forgot, he said he was going to help out here.* "He didn't come then? That damned coward."

"No, no," Faldo said, waving his hands. "He came. He's a bizarre man, and I've no question about his power, but he's a skittish man. He would give aid, and then retreat back to the forests." He shook his head. "I don't think a soul outside of this village even knows of the man, but I've heard strangers speak your name as if they've known it their entire lives."

"Mine?"

"Pent, the Crusader," Lyle said. "Answer this, hero: we could build more homes, but then what? If we're to expand, we would be better served further west. This chasm has defended us in tough times, but now it strangles us."

"A whole new village?" Pent said. "You would leave Somerville behind?"

"It won't support us anymore," Lyle said. "I'll always love this place, and in my heart, it will always be home. But for as long as I've been here, it has been unchanging." She ran her hand up a stalk of corn. "The farmers have always farmed; the fishermen have always fished. Families of people, generations who have lived in this spot, have calmly let the years pass by. Some few have come and gone, true, but these are new times."

"New times, with new challenges," Faldo added.

"New challenges, which require us to devise new approaches. You are not so detached from all of this, Pent."

"Don't start blaming me for these new dark times now," Pent said. "I've had my fill of that for one lifetime."

"I don't speak of the past. I speak of the future," she said. "It was you—with your ingenuity, your ideas, and your bravery—that helped us defeat Yozer. And once again you have answered our prayers, rescuing the children from a horrible fate. We need you, Pent. I need you."

"I don't know the first thing about making a new village," Pent said uncomfortably.

Lyle shrugged. "It seems we are the same in that regard. But I would have you all the same. This is an undertaking, greater than I can meet myself." She walked to Pent and bowed her head slightly to him. "Please, I will beg you if I must. Join us. Promise me you will help build this new home for our people."

Building a new village, putting down roots for people who had become the closest friends he had ever known... *Before I came to this world, I wasn't doing anything. I was bagging groceries all day and spending my nights drowning my despair down at the bar. My wheels were spinning, but I wasn't going anywhere.* He could never in a thousand years have dreamt of this. In Cinraia, he was a hero, and now he was going to help build a village? *All that talk about my potential—is that what I'm meant to do?*

He scratched at the back of his neck, uncomfortable under Faldo's and Lyle's expectant stares. "All right, all right," he said, raising up his palms. "I promise I'll help you make this thing. I don't know what I can do besides help you cart things around. I'm pretty good at that by now." Pent looked down the ravine toward the towers marking the village entrance, then back at Lyle. "Whatever you need, I'm there, chief."

She was beaming. "That is a relief to hear. You've a value that you don't even understand, Pent. But these villagers understand it—and so do I."

Faldo grunted in affirmation. "If nothing else, you can keep an eye on that stiff newcomer, the one always wearing leather."

Pent paused for a moment, running through the newcomers in his head. "Who, Tanan?"

"Yes," Lyle said, casting a glance over her shoulder. "The one from Tofac. He seems well enough, but he always has a piece of advice or a new idea to toss into the pot, always has a need for my ear. Every time I turn around, he's there, acting as the unwanted sage."

"Since Riven betrayed us, I've found it hard to trust men such as him," Faldo said. "Those who let their ambition blind them; they'll walk us all over the edge if we let them."

"I don't think he means anything bad by it," Pent said. "I'm sure it was like that for him in Tofac, advising his father on how to run the village." Pent recalled the scathing remarks he had for his father when they had returned from the Scribes' caves. *He had a right to be upset, but to say those things of his own father?* "You're the boss, Chief Lyle. I'll keep an eye on him."

Pent brought a small pack with him on his excursion out of the village. He took Ellie's ointment for one, and his sword as well. *Just in case I run into any kind of trouble.* He could probably make his way to Gordenthorpe's hut alone—he had been through the forest enough times already—but without Hanar, he was not sure he could summon the sorcerer.

He had waved goodbye to the villagers as he left, ensuring them of his pressing business, and that he would return soon. Most cheered him as he walked past their homes, inviting him inside for food and blessing him for his courage.

Two faces looked starkly different from the rest. The first was Tanan. He stared at Pent, his eyes narrowing as he walked past. He said nothing, simply stared, and even after locking eyes with Pent, he would not break his gaze. Pent wondered what the man was thinking. *Maybe Lyle and Faldo are right. Definitely need to keep an eye on that one.*

The other was Marall. Pent put a large distance between them when he saw the farmer sitting in the dirt, with his head hung low. He was weeping on the ground, his hands covering his face. Pent passed him silently, rubbing at his forehead and picking up the pace as he walked on. Marall lifted his head for a moment, and, over his shoulder, Pent saw the wicked glare he sent his way. The farmer rose to his feet slowly, cursing under his breath as he watched Pent walk away.

Pent crossed the bridge to Somerville and climbed the path to the south. He spared a glance over the edge of the cliffside into the village. There was no path into the forest, but Pent thought back to the last time he had entered the southern woods with Hanar and Fen. He counted the steps. *I don't know, was it twenty feet from the path to Somerville? Or was it thirty?* He found a spot that felt right and pressed in through the brush.

Without Hanar to guide him, Pent found moving through the thick forest slow, difficult, and painful. Several times he was struck in the face by a tree branch. Thorns tore into his skin and clothes alike. Once, he caught his leg on a root that jutted out and fell hard into the dirt, tearing his green cloak as he did so.

He cursed as he slowly pulled himself up from the ground.

"Hopeless," he heard a voice call out from behind a tree. Hanar stepped out from the shadow of the woods, chuckling lightly to himself. "You're hopeless in the woods without me, my good friend. It seems the shoe is on the other foot!"

Pent laughed. "You know, you said that right, I just don't know if it applies to this situation." Pent took a good, long look at the man. His cloak was battered and torn all over, as was his tunic. His hair and beard were matted. Pent's eyes locked on Hanar's wrapped hands.

"So, no good news there?" Pent said as he pointed at the bandages.

"No news. I've been tending to myself, fishing where I can—healing in my own way."

"Healing in your own... You haven't spoken to Gordenthorpe about your hands?"

Hanar chuckled to himself, and Pent couldn't tell if it was in good humor or in pain. "It's—it's just a matter of time for them to heal. The pain will stop, I'm sure of it. I can feed myself fine with the fishing pole, and I've even caught some small game. I would wager you couldn't manage that yourself. Even with my lame hands, I've sprung on two of them!"

"Yeah, you're right about that," Pent said. He rested a hand on Hanar's shoulder. "But Gordenthorpe might be able to get you back to a hundred percent."

"But what if he cannot?" Hanar burst out. He looked as if he was on the verge of tears. "What if he says what everyone else has said until now? What if he has no answers either?" He reached into his pack and pulled out the Scribe's book. "And what of Catherine? What if he cannot save her? We might both be doomed, and it all rests on that man's word. I couldn't bear it Pent—I can't."

"You don't have to bear it alone, man." Pent gripped Hanar in his arms, hugging him tightly. "I'll always be here for you. I think it's owed. How many times have you saved my neck by now?"

Hanar sniffled. "More times than I would dare count."

Pent nodded. "Don't I know it. Come on, man, let's close this out. For better or worse, we owe it to Catherine at least."

CHAPTER FORTY-SIX

Pent and Hanar made their way to Gordenthorpe's hut. They moved wordlessly, both of them thinking of what the sorcerer would say. Hanar raised the magical key-stone and shouted the familiar words: "GORDENTHORPE! REVEAL YOURSELF!"

The hut faded into existence, and they let themselves in.

"Oh ho!" Gordenthorpe said, greeting them as they entered the hut. He waved them to chairs and danced whimsically around. "What a wonder to see you both again! I thought as much when the village's children stopped being charmed by the Scribes' magic. I take it you were successful."

Hanar raised his hands slowly. "Not completely, but the threat of the Scribes is over, for now. We walked away with our lives at least." He stuck his hands out for Gordenthorpe to see. "There are matters to discuss, but I was hoping you could take a look at these first."

"The work of the Scribes?" Gordenthorpe asked. He pulled his bifocals from the wall, then unwrapped the bandages in order to examine Hanar's wounds.

"In part their work, in part my own. We were pushed to the brink in that fight, and I acted swiftly."

"It was a bunch of close calls, back to back," Pent said. He leaned back in the chair. He was relaxed but felt guilty at the same time. Hanar had been by himself in the forest for a few days; Pent had hoped that time would help set them right, but with the bandages removed, they still looked deformed and warped.

"These wounds..." Gordenthorpe said cautiously, "These are no wounds I can treat on the spot. I will try, but these are grievous burns. It was no ordinary flame that caused them. I can only do so much to aid you. With time... with time, perhaps." He tugged at his thick, white beard. "I'm certain there is aid to be had, with more time—perhaps researching Karpas' texts. I was never well versed in the arts of healing. It's a difficult thing, mind you. But maybe someday."

Hanar looked sadly at the injury. "I had hoped for more of a solution. Whatever you can do, that's all I can ask for." He lowered his hands and slouched, his question answered. "But yes, we have other things to discuss. I will return later to see what you can do about my burns."

"Yes, the Scribes," Gordenthorpe said. "Horrid monsters, specters of a long-gone age. Their destruction is of great benefit to the world."

"We can tell you all about them," Pent said. "But first, you need to take care of something else." He glanced at Hanar. *All of that waiting and stressing over his hands, and that's all the old man could come up with?* He shook his head in frustration. It wasn't Gordenthorpe's fault, but all the same he wanted to throttle the sorcerer. *Hopefully he's got more in his bag of tricks for Catherine.*

Hanar brought out the book they had carried all the way from the Scribes' cave. He handed it to Gordenthorpe, who studied it closely. "The Scribes use all manner of magic that involves books," Hanar said. "As a sorcerer, you would probably have a better idea than us, in explaining how it works."

"I profess that I don't know much of their abilities," Gordenthorpe said absently, still staring at the tome. "Breaking their trance was simple enough, as there seems to be some overlap in the schools of magical thought there."

Pent leaned forward, staring at the book. "Well, we saw them create creatures with those books. They were using the blood of children, mixing it with their own. Somehow that allowed them to use the magic of the book." He leaned over and tapped on the cover. "They can draw things from the book, but they also trapped our friend in this book as well."

Gordenthorpe raised an eyebrow at that. He began flipping through the pages, searching in vain for a clue of how to work the magic. "I see. So, you believe he's still inside this tome?"

"She," Pent corrected. "And sure, why not? Where else would she be?" Pent raised his hands in frustration. "I don't know, man. I looked at a book in my world and ended up here. I picked up a book in their library with my home's name on it. I don't know a damn thing about this magic stuff. You're the expert."

"I suppose I am." He laid the book face up on his table. "Let me try what I can. Perhaps a simple sealing spell? If the root of magic began with the Scribes, then it stands to reason that all this would be is a crude seal..." He continued to mumble under his breath, pacing back and forth.

Pent and Hanar watched as he attempted a dozen different spells. After what seemed like ages, Gordenthorpe sat down with a grumpy huff, equal parts exasperated and exhausted.

"The power of the Scribes has diminished, but none of my abilities are having any effect." They all looked desperately at the book. Gordenthorpe tugged at his beard, his voice betrayed how fatigued he was. "There must be another angle to attack this from. What of the milk? Was it effective?"

"Yeah, yeah it worked," Pent said. "Against the Scribes' monsters anyway. We didn't get a chance to use it against the Scribes themselves."

"Oh?" Gordenthorpe said. "I don't have a glass of milk with me regardless. But if you did not use milk, what did you use?"

Hanar stared at his hands. "Fire. Flame was the other weakness."

"Ah hah! Of course!" Gordenthorpe looked very pleased with himself. "It's a wonder that I did not remember it at the time. My apologies. However you discovered that weakness, I'm sure it would have helped to know of it beforehand. The essence of life—fire."

"Sure, sure," Pent said. "But how is fire going to help us now? If Catherine is really trapped in that book, I'm not willing to risk us burning her to death."

Hanar mumbled something under his breath that Pent didn't hear. Gordenthorpe had wandered over to his wall and was scanning for something. He hopped up and down when he found what he was looking for.

"The Stone of Sienne." He held out a mundane-looking rock with circular markings all over it. A symbol of a sun stood out in the middle of the stone.

"What's that supposed to do?" Pent vaguely recalled him mentioning the Stone before, but he had never seen its use.

"Heat, enough to be the brother of the sun itself. Heat to scorch the cold hearts of the Vampires of Umbro Mountain. Master Karpas gave this to me many, many years ago. Just holding it again reminds me of our engagement with those dread monsters, the sacrifices of the old Crusaders..." He looked at Pent with misty eyes. "The hunter, Pay, you remind me of him Pent. He was a huge man—his strength frightened me—and he moved with a strange grace that a man of his size shouldn't have had." The old wizard shook his head, and then pointed the rock at the book. "Right, my apologies. This stone could disrupt the Vampires' magic; perhaps it can disrupt the cold magic of the Scribes as well."

The wizard flipped the book open and began to rub the stone over the pages. The edges began to smolder. Hanar and Pent both jumped forward to stop the wizard before the book went to ashes completely, but he waved them back.

The book was hot to the touch. Gordenthorpe abruptly dropped the stone and ran his fingers along the pages. Pent's eyes went wide as Gordenthorpe's hand first dipped into, and then was fully submerged in the book. He grunted, suddenly strained as he grappled with something in the pages. "Ah, I need assistance. Help me!"

Pent and Hanar ran behind the wizard and began tugging along with him. They pulled against otherworldly forces, struggling with the book, which now floated in the air. Pent let out a shout, his muscles bulging as his grip tightened. Hanar cursed under his breath, mumbling about the pain, but he wouldn't let up. They pulled together as one, falling backwards as they yanked a figure out of the book.

Catherine lay sprawled on the floor, her small sword still in her hand. She sprang to her feet at once. "W... where am I?"

Gordenthorpe smiled and tried to greet her, but she leveled the tip of her sword in his face. "Stay back!"

"Easy girl, easy," Pent said, putting himself between the two of them. "You have a real bad habit of talking with that sword instead of your mouth." She lowered her sword, but did not let it go, and looked at Pent as though unsure if he was real. "This guy just saved you. His name is Gordenthorpe."

The wizard had recoiled behind Pent and Hanar. He waved timidly from behind Pent's broad figure. "Hello there! I would appreciate it if you put away your weapon. I wouldn't want to force you to."

She studied the room for a moment, taking in Pent, Hanar, Gordenthorpe, and all the strange devices hung around the cramped space before sheathing the sword slowly. "What has happened? How have I come to be in this odd place? The last I recall, I was charging that tall monster in the field."

Pent and Hanar both sighed at once, and Pent offered her a chair. "There's much to tell," Hanar said. They shared their tale with Gordenthorpe and Catherine alike: the horrible hallucinations they suffered through in the cave; the battle with the Scribes themselves; the horrible wound that Pent had suffered after struggling against them; Hanar's impotent rage as their milk bottle was destroyed; and his ingenious improvisation.

"How could you remember milk, but not fire?" Hanar asked. "That was a piece of information that nearly cost us our lives!" He said it as a joke, but there was a hint of bitterness in his voice.

"Oh, ho," Gordenthorpe laughed. "My greatest apologies to you both again. Fire makes sense, good sense at that, but milk is so odd. It seemed notable when I was originally taught about the Scribes. I never believed I would actually need to use the information, otherwise I would have taken better stock of it."

They spoke of their trip back to Somerville. Pent paused for a moment to share with Catherine the story of their stop at Gilbrand Castle.

"When we first ran into you in the castle, the place was a dump." He looked at her with sympathy. "We cleaned it up a bit on our way back, so we could stay there. The smell... well, I don't think I really need to elaborate on that. When you're ready, I'd be willing to take you back there."

Catherine stared at him through wet eyes. She let out a singular sob, and the three men looked around uncomfortably. "After all I've said and done, after everything I've heard... You really are a kind person." She nodded towards Pent and then Hanar. "Thank you, thank you both."

"Don't mention it," Pent said, glad to have the tale telling done.

"It was a mercy we would be heartless to not grant you," Hanar added.

She looked away, clutching her tunic tightly. She bit her lip so hard Pent was sure she would draw blood. "I went into that cave, before the both of you. I... I had one of those nightmares as well." She closed her eyes. "I saw my mother, torn to ribbons by that Hubard bastard."

"Hubard?" Hanar repeated. "Why does that name sound familiar...?"

"And I saw you," Catherine said, pointing to Pent. "I saw you standing over my father. But you were taller, and more frightening—and your sword was bigger than a man. You towered over him; his body lost in the shadow you cast. You stared at him with your devil's eyes, and you cackled through the darkness, blood dripping from the edge of your blade."

Pent stared at her in silence.

"But the worst... the worst was a horrible landscape. It went on for a lifetime, a field of my greatest failures staring me in the face. I saw him, alive. I reached out to him, time and time again, but no matter how I tried, I was never able to save him.

"I must ask," her eyes became sharp, and her body tensed up, "what of my brother? What of Peter? And speak honestly." Her knuckles were white around the hilt of her sword. "Do not treat me as some doe girl; if he is dead, I must know it."

Pent shot a glance to Hanar. He nodded back. "We don't really know. I wish we did, we asked the kids, but they hadn't seen or heard of any young boy named Peter. They were all really close in their little prison, so if he had come through that way, they should have known." Pent shook his head. "We just don't know."

"Then my quest is not finished," she said resolutely. "I cannot stop, not until I find my brother."

Pent and Catherine left the hut shortly after that. Hanar intended to stay, to see what could be done to mend his hands, and Pent wasn't going to try and convince him otherwise. He studied the girl as they walked towards town. Catherine kept glancing to the left as they walked.

"Gilbrand Castle is off in that direction, correct?" She nodded forward. "West of Somerville. You're leading me the wrong way."

Pent looked off to the west. "You're in that much of a rush to go back to that castle? I wouldn't bank on it being safe. Monsters in the woods, and bandits poking their heads in and out?"

She narrowed her eyes at him. "I'm very familiar with the

dangers of this land. Don't believe for a moment that I need you to protect me. I must return to my home."

"I know how capable you are," Pent said. "That hallucination thing in the cave that you were talking about? I had one too, and it felt so real. There's this tiny voice inside my head that keeps telling me how I'm a horrible person for abandoning my family." He looked meaningfully at Catherine. "I made a choice one day, that I was gonna be something better, that I was gonna reach for the potential that everyone always said I had. So, I stepped into that library." He waved his hand around. "I didn't choose all of this, but in a way, maybe I did. That book took me someplace else, somewhere I can be someone better than I was.

"But that voice—that little voice—keeps saying that I just wanted to run away from my problems all along. And in the cave, that voice was so loud." He stopped and turned to face her. "I made a vow there, that I wouldn't abandon the people that I really cared about. Not as long as I'm alive."

She stared up at him. "Then you know I can't stop either. I won't abandon Peter."

"Of course," he said, "and I'm not asking you to. I'll help you find your brother, Catherine. I'll search until we find some answers. We'll find him, and a way for me to get home—and a way to help Hanar too. All I'm saying is, you don't need to cut out right now." He pointed ahead. "Come and stay in Somerville for a while. We'll regroup, lick our wounds, and then strike out to find him. You need to search, nothing wrong with that. But you need to live too. So, come live with us. The chief there has something brewing, a big plan for the future that she wants me to be a part of. And I'm thinking you can be a part of it too."

She stared at him for a long time. Eventually, her stoic face broke into a smile. "You know I don't need your charity, right?"

"I know you don't. I ran into your rabid ass out in the woods, remember? I'm not asking because you need it." He lowered himself to eye level with her. "I'm asking because you deserve a nicer life than living off berries and insects."

She sighed. "I haven't heard an offer so sound in a long time," Catherine said. "An offer I can't help but accept. Thank you for your kindness, Pent—for sharing your home with me."

Pent pondered the words as she said them. He ruffled her hair, earning himself a slap on the hand, then started walking again. Somerville opened up before them as they approached the chasm, and Pent couldn't help but smile. "Yeah. My home."

EPILOGUE

The Scribe ran and ran until it could not run any longer. It looked about in a panic. There was a horrible quiet in the air, a chilling quiet. It panted harshly through the slit that was its mouth.

All at once, it felt a sharp agony in its chest. The length of a knife ran straight through its body. It hissed, not unlike any weakened, wounded animal. It turned for a moment, catching a glimpse of its killer before it crumpled onto the ground.

Agme stood over his kill and chuckled to himself. He whispered something into the corpse's ear, and then lifted it with one hand. "Imagine my fortune!" he shouted to himself. "To find the cave, already aflame. And I didn't even need to use my bait!"

His happiness soured into frustration as he considered the amount of time he had spent planning his trap for the Scribes. *The boy,* he thought to himself as he rested a hand on the ensnaring gourd strapped along his waist. *I still have the boy, but what a waste of resources and planning.* The boy had been entranced by the Scribes' magics and had not been difficult to capture. *Not difficult, but still tiring using such exhausting spells.*

He shook off the feeling. "I suppose the boy will serve another purpose. Perhaps for experiments in the future. But with this," he clutched the body of the Scribe tightly, "with this, Master Yozer has come one more step closer to rising. My master will surely praise my efforts and success."

It had been months since he had set out from Castle Draemar. The hemite was easy enough to procure, but the Scribe, that was more difficult. *It was as the Master said: with the seals removed, they eventually revealed themselves.* He had traveled far in search of the Scribes, and he had nearly missed out on his goal.

It had been luck, in the end. Not his planning, not his skill, just dumb luck that had thrown the Scribe into his lap. He studied the horrific creature: the pale folds in the skin, the jagged ears. It matched the description in Master Yozer's texts; there was no doubt what this creature was. *And in my hands, it rests eternally, all based on luck.* Agme cursed under his breath.

He had abandoned his former master to become a disciple of Master Yozer, under the promise that he would learn great things from the man. And he had, so long as he served the Master, loyally and eternally. *And I've stepped into success based on luck.* Luck would not be enough moving forward. He would need to be craftier, more forceful. *I must not lurk in the shadows, not any longer.*

He considered Master Yozer's thoughts on the matter, letting his mind work while he hauled the corpse onto the back of his frightened horse. *Of course Master Yozer will praise me. Luck or not, I've managed to gather the Scribe and the hemite. Two of the three pieces to the puzzle are in our grasp.*

The thought gave rise to another, and Agme smiled. The Scribes had served their purpose well enough, and with one in hand, Master Yozer's return was surely coming. All that was left was the vessel of a Crusader. "Pent," Agme said to himself. He would be easy enough to find but finding him would not be enough. They would need to draw him out of the company of others, so he could be finished swiftly and quickly.

"Perhaps we will need a more.... human touch, moving forward." Agme laughed into the sky, kicking Horse harshly in the sides and galloping back to his master.

FROM THE AUTHOR

Thank you for reading my book!

Please subscribe to my newsletter, so you can get updates on future releases.

If you have any questions or comments, you can reach me at williamcaliwriting@gmail.com

Made in the USA
Columbia, SC
26 February 2020